Surviving the Summer

Yes, it was going to be a long, long summer all right. Mother blasting away in the newspaper, and Daddy slaving away at the dairy and spending his evenings getting weepy over Bach. Isn't it hard enough, she thought, to be the tallest girl in the eighth grade and be skinny and flat-chested and have stringy black hair and big boats for feet, without also having wacko parents?

The Sandy Bottom Orchestra

Garrison Keillor
and Jenny Lind Nilsson

HYPERION PAPERBACKS FOR CHILDREN

New York

A hardcover edition of *The Sandy Bottom Orchestra* is available
from Hyperion Books for Children.

First Edition
1 3 5 7 9 10 8 6 4 2

The artwork for this book is prepared using pen and ink

The text for this book is set in 12-point Adobe Garamond.

Library of Congress Cataloging-in-Publication Data
Keillor, Garrison.
The sandy bottom orchestra / Garrison Keillor
and Jenny Lind Nilsson.
p.   cm.
Summary: Fourteen-year-old Rachel comes to terms with her
eccentric family while taking refuge in her violin playing.
ISBN:0-7868-01 (trade)
ISBN 0-7868-1250-8 (paperback)
[1. Violin-Fiction. 2. Family life-Fiction.] I. Nilsson, Jenny Lind.
II. Title.
PZ7.K2519San
[Fic]-dc20   96-41404

CONTENTS

THE GREENS

*R*achel Green woke up on a shining May morning, her bedroom window wide open and white curtains wavering in the breeze, to the sweetness of lilacs and a Mozart symphony, squares of sunlight crinkled on the sheet. The Mozart came from the bathroom down the hall, where Daddy had his portable CD player cranked up, perched on the toilet tank, while he shaved. Mother said he was going to electrocute himself, the way he splashed water all over the place, but Mother didn't have a good grasp of electricity. Mother was downstairs in the kitchen; Rachel could hear her turning the pages of the newspaper. One right after the other. Mother was not one for dawdling.

Daddy hummed along with the Mozart clarinets in his soft baritone, and Rachel remembered her bad mood from last night, after Daddy said that no, he didn't think they would take a vacation trip this summer, thank you very much. And Mother laughed and said, "Can you imagine the three of us spending two weeks together in the car?"

"Yes," Rachel said. "I can. Other families do. Why not us?"

"We're not other families, and besides, Daddy has to run Dairy Days on the Fourth of July, remember? It's less than two months away. And I've got church services to play and I've got to stand guard and keep the mayor from turning that old Ramsey Building into a parking lot. If I leave town, the place'd be rubble in ten minutes."

"Couldn't we go to San Francisco? You said last year you wanted to go."

"We're going to Milwaukee to see Grandma and Grandpa in August. Maybe we'll spend a day in Chicago with them. San Francisco's too far, and the hotel rates are just exorbitant."

Daddy said, "Why should we pay good money to go be miserable someplace else when we can be perfectly miserable right here at home?"

Rachel gave him a dry look: *not funny*. "I wish you'd at least *consider* it instead of automatically saying no. If I have to sit around here all summer . . ." She shuddered at the thought.

And then Mother said something about developing one's Inner Resources, and the true test of a worthwhile person being her ability to keep herself busy and entertained without outside help. Developing Inner Resources. That was why they had no television set, because it created habits of passivity, et cetera et cetera, and so forth, blah blah, woof woof.

Rachel looked around her room. The bedspread and one of the pillows and a pile of clothes lay in a heap at the foot of the bed. The alarm clock said 7:32. The little maple bookcase was jammed tight with books and music, and more music was piled on a card table, along with Rachel's violin case. Books and folders and schoolwork lay strewn across her white wooden desk, and clumps of newspaper clippings—Mother was a habitual clipper of interesting newspaper articles. Rachel's jeans and a blue T-shirt hung on a chair, and the bureau top was crowded with hairbrushes, headbands, pencils, sample perfume bottles, and stuff. Whenever Mother walked in the room, she looked around and sighed. It was a mess all right, but there wasn't anything Rachel could throw out.

She stared up at the plaster bumps on the ceiling. A few more weeks of eighth grade and then a long summer vegetating in Sandy Bottom, Wisconsin (*Pop. 4,500, A City on the Grow*), with not a single thing to do. Of course, if you loved the smell of chlorine, you could go swimming at the Charles Shanks Memorial Municipal Pool and have boys gawk at your body, or you could go to the public library and peruse the encyclopedia—how about a long article about Sophocles? The South Pole? Soybeans? There was the youth recreation program, of course, but Rachel didn't play sports. Either you did or you didn't, and she didn't. She sort of wished she could, but the girls who played softball were so serious about the game and got furious with you if you dropped a fly ball, and if you ever got yourself into a game, you stood there worried sick that the ball might be hit toward you, and then if it was, you panicked and dropped it and everyone rolled their eyes and groaned and said, "How *could* you? It was right *to* you!" and turned away as if you had committed some deliberate destructive act.

Sometimes Rachel wished she had an older brother to teach her softball, but she was an only child. An odd term, *an only child*. Like *a single woman*. As if it were an unnatural state of existence.

The Wymans next door were driving to Wyoming in a rented motor home and camping for two weeks in the Grand Tetons. Carol Wyman had been Rachel's best friend since grade school. Carol was a sort of only child, too, now that her older brother, Mike, had enlisted in the Coast Guard. Rachel wished that Carol would invite her to come with them to the Grand Tetons and say how cool it would be, the four of them, cruising around, and Rachel would say, "Oh, I don't know. I'm pretty busy," and Carol would say, "*Please, please* come," and Rachel would say, "Oh, well. Okay." And off they'd go. But Carol hadn't invited her, and Rachel doubted that she would.

Carol seemed distant lately. Carol was *her* best friend, but Rachel wasn't sure if she was Carol's best friend. Sometimes it seemed that Carol had a lot of best friends and that Rachel had been demoted to Second B. F. or lower—to Lady-in-Waiting, or Assistant Friend. Carol was always busy—she had been the star forward on the Sandy Bottom Junior High School girls' soccer team that had gone to the state tournament and won second place against big tough teams from Milwaukee and Madison and Green Bay. Carol had starred in the school play, *The Diary of Anne Frank*—Rachel had been on the scenery crew—and now Carol was gearing up for a big summer as the star shortstop in the Minneota County junior girls' softball league. So what did Carol need a nerd like Rachel as a friend for anyway?

Rachel propped up the pillows and pulled the sheet up to her chin and pretended she was sick with liver cancer. A nurse looked down and smiled and whispered, "Your mother is here to see you," and Mother walked in and burst into tears—"Oh my darling Rachel, how can I make it up to you? All those years I neglected you! If only I could have those years back! We'd do wonderful things together! We'd go on vacation trips!"

The problem with the Greens taking vacations was that Mother and Daddy were so different, and on trips they made each other miserable. Daddy hated leaving home; he hated driving on freeways, he was terrified of flying, he was restless and twitchy in strange cities. Mother looked on a trip as a unique educational opportunity, and she studied for it in advance and gave you books about it with the important parts marked with yellow Post-Its and worked up a detailed itinerary and by George she made good and sure you *did your job and saw what you were there to see.* But all that poor Daddy cared to do was sit in a quiet hotel lobby, drink his coffee, read his newspaper, and wait for the vacation to end, when he could go home and do what he really wanted to do, which was to run the Sandy Bottom Dairy.

Daddy had been president of the dairy for three years, since Mr. Sorenson retired to Arizona, and he loved it. His employees got all happy when Daddy walked through the plant—he knew their names and the names of their kids, he had introduced employee profit sharing, he had improved their health benefits, he was the Good Boss, and he was smart. Mr. Sorenson had run the dairy his own way for forty years—he believed the business consisted of milk, cream, butter, ice cream in four flavors (vanilla, chocolate, strawberry, and butter pecan) and three kinds of cheese (Colby, cheddar, and Swiss), and when yogurt became popular, he harrumphed and said it was a fad and not to bother. When Daddy took over, the Sandy Bottom Dairy got into yogurt and frozen yogurt and added a new line of expensive ice cream called Bluebird with six new flavors including Aïda (fudge, cookie chips, and pistachio), and Ludwig van Blueberry, and Madame Butterfly Brickle, that sold like crazy—ninety-thousand gallons shipped last June alone and this year it could be a quarter million. Daddy got excited about this stuff. The dairy had built a gleaming new plant along the river, near the lumberyard, and hired twenty-seven new people to work there.

Daddy loved to take people on tours of the new place and show them the stainless-steel vats and how the ingredients got mixed in uniformly so there would be a cookie chip in every bite of Aïda without turning everything to mush. Why should he go suffer through two weeks slouching around San Francisco when he was perfectly happy at work?

Daddy was always thinking up new ideas, and three years before, he had decided the dairy would sponsor a big Fourth of July Dairy Days celebration and give away hot dogs and ice cream and there would be fireworks and a big concert. Last year it was the Chatfield Brass Band and this year he had hired the Dairyland Symphony Orchestra.

"Just imagine, classical music in old Sandy Bottom. Won't that be something?" said Daddy. When he wasn't at work, he loved to lie on the old red sofa in the tiny book-lined den with a glass of wine in his hand and listen to the Beethoven Symphony No. 6 or a Prokofiev violin concerto or Anna Moffo singing Mozart arias and let his mind drift far away. That was how Daddy preferred to travel.

Rachel rolled out of bed and stood and stretched and did her groaning exercises. What did it take to convince these people to *go* someplace? They had gone to Italy last summer. Mother's best friend from college, Phoebe Hanson, lived in Florence. She was an art historian, tall, with blond hair tied in a braid, cool and smart, unmarried, no kids, who lived in a sunny two-room apartment (a big kitchen with a couch, a teeny bedroom) across the Arno River from the center of the city and who treated Rachel like a grown-up and listened to her opinions and told her secrets. Rachel stayed with Phoebe while Mother and Daddy lived in a small hotel near the cathedral. Every morning, Phoebe and Rachel traipsed across the Ponte Vecchio, an ancient stone bridge lined with jewelry shops, and went to a café and drank coffee and made up stories about the people passing by. It was a game they called Novel. "She's a laundress and she's on her way to buy a lottery ticket and her son is gay and her teeth hurt," Phoebe would say about an old woman in a black shawl hurrying across the street, and Rachel would see a boy pedaling a bicycle, a knapsack on his back, and say, "He's failed his math test and is afraid to tell his father and he's supposed to see a movie with his girlfriend tonight and he's wondering how to get the money for the tickets." They could do this for hours.

Mother walked through museums looking at acres of art, and Daddy sat in the hotel lobby and read the London *Times* and waited until afternoon, when it was morning in Wisconsin and he could call his office and ask about Bluebird sales and gossip with Florence, his secretary. Phoebe and Rachel sat in the sidewalk café by the piazza and watched rivers of people flow by, Germans and French and Japanese and English and Americans—"He is a social studies teacher and she is a beautician and she's mad at him because he's mad at her for buying those pots yesterday, and they've got four more days here and they're going to spend it being mad and arguing about whose idea it was to come here anyway." Their waiter Rodolfo brought Rachel cups of coffee with *grande latte*—lots of milk—and she said, "Grazie, signore," and he complimented her on her accent. It was the most wonderful trip.

Over Rachel's dresser hung a picture of a little gang of angels painted by Ghirlandaio that she had brought home from Italy, in a gold frame. The angels looked eagerly to their right, as if someone outside the frame were bringing them ice-cream cones. On her desk stood a pair of silver candlesticks and long white candles that she sometimes lit at night and imagined she was back in the café, talking to Rodolfo.

Grazie della serata (GRAH-tsee-ah DAYL-ah say-RAH-tah). Thanks for the evening.

Il piacere è stato mio (Eel pee-ah-CHAY-reh EH STAH-toe MEE-oh). The pleasure was mine.

But the Italian trip wore Daddy out. He worried about pickpockets, food poisoning, being cheated by shopkeepers—and what if they missed the flight? And then, having rushed them to the airport in plenty of time and checked their luggage, he turned pale as he boarded the plane. Beads of sweat ran down his forehead and he stiffened as the plane ascended into the clouds. Daddy sat, silent, frozen, breathing rapidly, heart pounding, for nine hours over the Atlantic, and another two hours to Milwaukee, and every time the plane bounced a little or shook, or he heard a funny grinding noise from down below, he closed his eyes and clung to the armrests. When they finally touched down on Wisconsin soil, he looked like the ghost of Christmas Yet to Come.

"That's it for me," he said. "No more airplanes for a while. I'd rather die at home."

So there was not much hope of going to Italy again.

San Francisco was out. Nothing to look forward to—Carol would be busy all summer, and Rachel would be stuck at home with a couple of nutcases.

The bathroom door opened. "All yours!" called Daddy as he went downstairs. Rachel ducked in, brushed her teeth, took a fast shower using Mother's Natural Aloe shampoo, put on plain white cotton underpants. Once, when she had chosen fancy lacy ones in a shop in Milwaukee, Mother said it was ridiculous to pay extra for lace and made her put them back. She blow-dried her short black hair and wished it was thick and curly, more like Carol's. Her closet was stuffed with clothes, but there was something wrong with everything. Her pants were either too short or too long, her shirts were the wrong colors, or the ones she wanted to wear were in the laundry pile in the basement.

Finally she pulled on a pair of khaki pants and a dark blue T-shirt and trudged down the stairs.

Daddy was in the den drinking coffee, standing at the bookcase, listening to a Bach cello suite. "Good morning!" Rachel said, and Daddy looked at her, teary-eyed. Bach really got to him sometimes.

In the kitchen, Mother sat at the table, handsome and tall, her long black hair bursting out of its bun, her right foot tapping on the tile floor. She was wrapped in her old green plaid bathrobe, drinking coffee, writing furiously on a yellow legal pad, the Sandy Bottom *Register* spread out in front of her.

"Morning," said Rachel.

"Good morning, sunshine," Mother said. She didn't look up.

Rachel got out the yogurt and spooned a glop of it into a bowl and poured bran flakes over it.

"Look at this!" Mother said, stabbing the newspaper with her pencil. "Can you believe this? It says they're eliminating *Spanish* at the high school next year!"

"Well, if you never take trips anywhere, what does it matter if you learn a foreign language?" Rachel said.

Mother ignored her. "There used to be Latin and French and German *and* Spanish, and they cut it back to Spanish, and now they're cutting that too! This idiot mayor is trying to ram through a bond issue to spend a half million dollars on new curbs and gutters and they can't spend twenty-five thousand on a Spanish teacher. It's a horror show! They eviscerate the public library, they demolish what few beautiful buildings they have and make them into *parking lots*, for crying out loud, and now they go and dump the *only foreign language taught in school!* What's left? Are they going to close the school and just buy the kids laptops and plug them into the Internet?"

"What does eviscerate mean?"

"It means to rip the guts out of something."

"Oh."

Rachel crunched her bran flakes and glanced at Mother's legal pad. Sure enough, she was writing a letter, and it was addressed: "To the Editor." Oh boy, Rachel thought. Here we go again. One right after the other.

"I tell you," Mother said, "this mayor has consumed

too much red meat, and his brain is full of suet. That's his problem. He has an IQ that's right around room temperature, and if anybody dares to question his judgment, he goes bananas. He's nothing but a senile delinquent!"

Senile delinquent! Mother liked that phrase. She picked up her pencil and started scratching away again. It looked like she was already up to four pages.

Daddy wandered in from the den. He smelled of lime cologne. He bent down and kissed Rachel behind her ear. He kissed Mother and said, "Good morning, General." He poured himself a bowl of bran flakes and made such a face of disgust that Rachel laughed.

"What is it?" said Mother, not looking up. Daddy loved fried eggs and sausage and toast slathered with butter, but his cholesterol count was high, and Mother had put her foot down. No more fried food.

Rachel smiled at Daddy. "The bran flakes are excellent this morning," she said.

"Glad to hear it," Daddy said. "The ones we had yesterday tasted like sawdust."

"These are better, they're fortified," said Rachel.

"I am about ready to pack my bags and leave town," said Mother. She looked at both of them. "I mean it. I am so mad." She tapped a cigarette out of its pack and lit it. Today was the day Mother had said for two weeks she was going to start quitting smoking.

"We noticed," said Rachel.

Daddy chewed his bran flakes.

Mother pushed the legal pad aside. "Mayor Broadbutt

is absolutely hell-bent on tearing down the old Ramsey Building, and he won't listen to anybody who dares to think otherwise!"

"His name is Broadbent, honey. Mayor Eugene Broadbent."

"It's absolutely the last remaining architectural treasure in this town, and the man cannot *wait* while we try to figure out how to make it into an arts center—no! He's got to rip it down and give the world another parking lot! It's vandalism by men in suits! That's all it is!" Mother thumped her fist on the table and the bowls of bran flakes jumped.

Daddy sighed. He hated arguments. He couldn't bear it when people got mad at each other.

"You can't work miracles, sweetheart. The Ramsey Building is grand and everything but it's sat vacant for years, it's in rough shape. Plumbing is shot, and the electrical, and there's a lot of water damage. You start fixing up an old building like that, there's no telling how much it could cost. It's like pouring money down a drain. It's cheaper to replace it."

"That building can never *be* replaced!" said Mother. "It was built in 1895. Big sandstone carvings over the entrance, those terrazzo floors, the mural of French voyageurs and the Court d'Oreilles Indians in the lobby—" Mother shook her head sadly. "He can't wait to send people in with crowbars to rip it apart!"

"And I know you hate it when I say this," Daddy said, "but you'd do a lot better if you fought one battle at a time

13

instead of taking on everybody all at once." He smiled sweetly at Mother. She looked at him sternly.

"I am *not* going to sit back and let them kill off Spanish without making a peep," she said. She turned to Rachel. "I want you to play your violin piece today. I heard you practicing last night. You need to work it up a little faster and do more with it—put some fire into it."

Yes, it was going to be a long, long summer all right. Mother blasting away in the newspaper, and Daddy slaving away at the dairy and spending his evenings getting weepy over Bach. Isn't it hard enough, she thought, to be the tallest girl in the eighth grade and be skinny and flatchested and have stringy black hair and big boats for feet, without also having wacko parents? *Look at us.* Daddy works late and comes home and escapes into his CD collection and stands there waving a pencil at the speakers, and Mother camps at the kitchen table with a stack of her clippings, and writes big harangues at people. And when you sit down to eat a meal, she reaches over and grabs a clipping off the stack and reads it to you. Something about a scientific study showing that even smart people use only one percent of the brain's capability. Something about herbicides. Something about the health benefits of eating flax. In a normal home you sit down to a nice dinner and everyone is cheerful and the parents talk about normal friendly chirpy things, they don't give angry speeches about how dumb everybody is. A normal home has a big TV in the den, and a *little* piano in the living room with a wedding picture and an African violet on it, but Mother's

14

piano sat in the dining room like a petrified whale, and when she played Chopin or Beethoven or Brahms, the music boomed through the heating ducts, it shook the floors, it made the doors quiver on their hinges. Sometimes Rachel wanted to yell at her to please stop it.

Last fall, Daddy hired a new sales manager named Jerry Mason, who had moved to Sandy Bottom from Minneapolis, a big cheery man with a beard who liked to sing, so he wound up in the Community Choir, which Mother played piano for, so they became friends, and his daughter Valerie was Rachel's age. One day, Rachel invited her home after school. Valerie walked in, pretty and athletic and smart, and Mother said hello to her, and Valerie said, "Me and Rachel were captains of the math team today," and of course Mother couldn't let that go by. Oh no. "You mean, Rachel and *I* were captains of the math team," Mother said.

"Right," said Valerie. "Yes."

"*Me* is the objective," said Mother.

"I see," said Valerie.

"I hope you don't mind my correcting you," Mother said.

"No," said Valerie, but of course she minded: It made a person feel *dumb* to have her grammar corrected by somebody's mother. What was so terrible about saying "me and Rachel"? You knew what she meant. But Mother was strict about grammar. "Sloppiness is a weed," she said, "don't let it get a start." So Rachel led Valerie past the den to go upstairs and look at Rachel's scrapbook from Italy, and

15

Valerie glanced into the den and there was Daddy waving his arms and conducting the Berlin Philharmonic. Valerie stopped and stared at him. He grinned as he turned to the violin section and flung his arms out—and then he noticed the two of them standing in the hall. He wasn't the least bit embarrassed. He cried, "Listen to this! The last part of the adagio! Listen!"

Valerie turned to Rachel. She said, "I forgot. I have to be home now." She avoided Rachel after that. She thought the Greens were nuts, Rachel could tell. When Rachel said hi to her at school, she gave Rachel a pained smile and looked away.

Out of the corner kitchen window, Rachel saw, beyond the back of Mother's head as if emerging from her right ear, Angie Wyman in big pink plaid shorts and a green softball jersey, carrying a paper sack, a knife, and a pair of gloves, coming out to do battle with the dandelions. Now *there* was a normal family. Angie and Fred liked to snuggle on the couch eating big bowls of ice cream and watching their favorite TV shows. Mother said that TV turned people into vegetables. But when the Wymans watched, Rachel thought, they were like happy cats piled in a nest, purring, licking their spoons. Angie would pull you down and give you a hug and squeeze you and put your head on her shoulder—Angie was a major hugger—and during the commercial, she'd ask what you were up to, and if you said, "I'm working on a new piece on my violin," Angie would fall all over herself. "That's wonderful. You are the most talented person I know, Rachel."

Angie was astonished that a fourteen-year-old girl could play the violin. Mother wasn't astonished, not one tiny bit. She was watching you like a hawk, making sure you didn't slack off. Mother kept pushing you to improve yourself. If she caught you twiddling your thumbs, she would pull down *Wuthering Heights* from the shelf and say, "This is one of the great classics, you know. I read it when I was about your age."

Spending a whole summer with a mother who corrects everyone's grammar and a father who stands in the den conducting *La Bohéme*, in a town where nothing ever happens. You couldn't even sit and play Novel. And anyone who walked by, you'd know too well already.

ODD DUCK

After breakfast, Rachel loaded up her bookbag, kissed Daddy and Mother good-bye, and walked across the yard to the Wymans' big white house, and out came Carol with her blue backpack and they walked to school together down Prairie Avenue with its canopy of elm trees to Main Street and over the bridge across Sandy Bottom River and through downtown and past the park and the band shell to Sandy Bottom Junior High School. Carol was excited about summer coming. There was the trip to the Grand Tetons, of course, and she was looking forward to playing shortstop for the O'Connell Jewelers team and maybe going to the state tournament in September. "You ought to try out," she told Rachel. Oh sure, thought Rachel, and after that I should run for governor. When her gym class played softball, Rachel was always the last one chosen. Usually, they made her play in short center field, where the second baseman could cover for her.

"Wouldn't that be fun to be on a team together?" Carol said, and she put her arm around Rachel's shoulders. "Teammates!" she cried. "We're O'Connells and we're no fools! We got the brains and we got the jewels! We got the diamonds, we got the rubies! All you got is a pair of boobies!"

Rachel laughed.

"We made up cheers last night. That was the one that Valerie came up with," said Carol.

They got to school as the big orange buses full of kids from the country were pulling into the parking lot. Rachel was afraid of some of the farm boys. She had seen them grab a girl's bra strap in back and snap it hard, and then they'd all laugh. And even if you tried to act like it was nothing, you could feel your face turning bright red. Carol forged through the bus crowd, and Rachel followed her, up to the main entrance and through the old marble pillars and past the brass plate inside the front door, the Honor Roll of Those Who Gave Their Lives, and into the front hall packed with hundreds of kids. A lot of them said hi to Carol but not many noticed Rachel.

She said good-bye to Carol and went to her locker and put her backpack in it and took out her notebook and her English assignment.

On the inside of her locker door Rachel had taped a picture of Carol grinning, her pug nose crinkled, her sandy hair nice and tangly, and underneath Carol had written, "To Rachel, My best friend forever and a day. Love Carol." Please don't ever not be my best friend, Rachel thought. Even if I'm not good at sports, and my parents are weird, and we have a piano for a dining room table.

The bell rang and Mrs. Erickson stood at her desk and waited for her English class to settle down. She leaned against the desk, in her khaki skirt and her starched white blouse, her long legs crossed, her blond hair tied back in a French braid. There were no flies on Mrs. Erickson. She did not shush the last whispers of the two girls in the corner gossiping, and she did not glare at poor Lonnie Glenn, who lumbered in, breathless, a minute late, half a candy bar in his mouth; she did not show even a flash of impatience, but stood intelligent, perfectly composed, until the power of her dignity had brought them to silence. Then she uncrossed her legs and stood, hands clasped behind her back, and said, "Good morning, everyone. Today we begin our oral histories as told by an object in your home. The assignment was to imagine that you are some familiar thing in your home—a chair, a plate, a picture—and to tell your story."

Rachel sat in the front center desk, directly facing Mrs. Erickson's belt buckle, a large brass clasp with a mother-of-pearl inlay of a guitar. Did Mrs. Erickson play the guitar? She looked more like a harpist or cellist, Rachel thought. "Each of you has written seven hundred words for today, and since these are oral histories, I'd like to hear them read aloud," said Mrs. Erickson. "Sharon?"

Kathy Stickney sat behind Rachel. She leaned forward and whispered, "Was this for *today*?" as if it were all a big surprise to her. Kathy was none too bright, Rachel thought—anyone who would have Daryl Darwin for a boyfriend had to be working with less than a full deck. But she was Carol's cousin, so Rachel tried to be nice to her. Rachel scribbled a note: "700 words as told by an object in your house, it's not that hard!" and passed it back.

Sharon Tennesen was short and pudgy and serious. Her essay was entitled "The Tablecloth Talks," the Tennesens' lace tablecloth recalling memorable meals, but none of it sounded very interesting to Rachel, just a lot of Thanksgivings and Christmases, with turkey every time. Mother was an original when it came to holidays, you had to give her credit for that: Last year, Mother had paid a farmer to raise a goose for her and feed it corn and licorice whips. She had read about this in a book somewhere. On the day before Christmas Eve, Mother and Rachel drove out to get the goose. The farmer went around to the back of his house and they heard two loud accusing honks and a tremendous *whack,* and then a great gooseless silence. Rachel tried not to cry on the way home, but it was hard not to feel sorry for the poor goose, who had been alive and munching on corn a few minutes before and now lay plucked and cold, wrapped in brown paper in the trunk of the car. At home, Mother put him in a pan and stuffed him, and as he roasted in the oven, she sat and wrote a long letter to the Milwaukee paper about why their school-

21

voucher scheme would be the end of education *period,* and then she played through a few Chopin preludes, and later she served the goose stuffed with wild rice and chestnuts, and she and Daddy got in a big argument over whether their first date had been to see the Bach Mass in B minor or the *St. Matthew Passion.* Rachel couldn't taste the licorice in the goose but Mother claimed she could.

Rachel's essay was entitled "What the Piano Knew," and she sat and worried about it as Lonnie read his (his family, as seen by their Ford Explorer), and then Valerie and Julie and Barbara, three softball girls in a row. Valerie's was good, about a television set watching the family watching TV. Rachel thought that her piano essay might seem like bragging, because it was about Mother's grand piano, which was from Germany. Her face felt trembly and her heart pounded when Mrs. Erickson smiled at her and nodded, and she had to peel herself loose from her seat and take the four steps to the front and turn and feel all the kids' eyes locked on her. Oh God, if only the fire alarm would go off. Lonnie grinned at her, his hands behind his head. The softball girls smirked. Daryl tried to catch her eye so she would look and then he would pull a long invisible booger out of his nose. Rachel held the paper up high and launched into it.

What the Piano Knew

I am a piano, nine feet long, black, though not so shiny as I once was, but still grand, and people say I sound better than ever. Boesendorfer is my name, and it is written above my keyboard in gold script, stamped there when I was made, in Hamburg, Germany, in 1896, when there was a king in Germany, the Kaiser, and Einstein was a young man. I was carefully, lovingly made by craftsmen who were proud of their work. I was bought by Mr. Walter Weidman and given to his wife, who kept me in her house in Frankfurt until 1938, when the family fled from the Nazis and moved to Milwaukee. I was sent to America by steamship and arrived in Milwaukee on the train. In America, the Weidmans did not do well, unfortunately. Mr. Weidman died the following year, and Mrs. Weidman stopped playing music. After she died, I went to a cousin's house, where nobody cared for music very much, and I was only a piece of furniture, until 1970, when I was bought by a man named August Mueller, a wholesale butcher.

They laughed when she said "wholesale butcher" and her face turned red. But that's what Grandpa had done before he retired. It wasn't funny. Had she used the wrong term? Even Mrs. Erickson smiled a little. Rachel read faster—

August Mueller had a daughter named Ingrid who studied piano at the University, and he was worried because she had met a young man named Norman Green who was in love with her. Norman studied English and music history at the University. He played the violin a little bit but never had time to practice. Norman walked past the music building every morning on his way to class. The music pouring out of the open windows of the practice rooms made him feel happy. The sound of one piano in particular had attracted him. When the beautiful young pianist with the long dark hair gave her senior recital, he planted himself right in the front row and listened to her as she played Rachmaninoff and Chopin. August Mueller was proud of his daughter and did not want to see her give up music. He was afraid that Norman was not cultured enough for his daughter. He decided to give the young couple a piano so big and so wonderful that they would never be able to put music behind them. Whenever they turned around, there I would be.

I was hoisted into their first home, an apartment on the third floor of a building in downtown Madison, by a large crane. The apartment was tiny, and I occupied all of the living room and dining room. When Ingrid and Norman gave parties, their friends sat on the bed or in the bathtub, and she played Chopin and then Norman said, "Come on, Ingrid, it's a party!" and she played "Beautiful Brown Eyes" and "Red River Valley" and 'There Is a Tavern in the Town" and everyone sang. When they moved to Sandy Bottom with their baby daughter, I took my place in the dining room, and when I am played, I can be heard anywhere in the house. And I hear everything in this house. A piano keeps its secrets, of course, and doesn't go telling stories, though I have plenty to tell, some happy, some sad. No, a piano is here to give music, which can drive away so much sorrow. And when people have sadness or joy in their lives, it makes the music even better. I do sound better, the older I get, and the more I know.

The end.

Rachel's face ached when she finished, her ears rang, and she felt embarrassed. *Why* had she told so *much*? She took the four steps back to her desk and sat down. "That was very good, thank you," said Mrs. Erickson. "Todd?" A pair of big basketball shoes, untied, came clomping from the rear corner of the room. Todd Gustafson teetered forward like a big sad giraffe. He began reading, rapidly and under his breath, something about a toaster.

Rachel's face was hot. A bead of sweat ran down her forehead into her eye. She wished it were Saturday.

That was one abysmal low point of the day, and the other was Mr. Gilbert's history class. Mr. Gilbert coached football, and if you didn't play sports, you were nobody in his book. Usually, history class consisted of people taking turns reading newspaper articles aloud, and they'd wind up talking about spring training or the breakup of some Hollywood romance.

Today, Mr. Gilbert called on Rachel, and she read an article from the *New York Times* about the exiled Dalai Lama, who had given a speech at the U.N. in New York. A boy behind her said, "Dolly who? Dolly Parton?" and everyone laughed, including Mr. Gilbert.

The article was long, and halfway through, when she glanced up, she saw Carol smiling uncomfortably at her. When she finished, Mr. Gilbert said, "Huhnn, the *New York Times*. Pret-ty fancy. Anyone have something a little more *local*? Something we regular folks could relate to? Anybody following the Brewers this week?"

After class, Rachel walked to her locker with Carol. "Who is the Dalai Lama?" Carol asked.

Rachel said, "He's the spiritual leader of the Tibetan people, and he lives in exile in India because China took over Tibet and they're trying to destroy the Tibetan culture."

"Oh. Interesting," said Carol, looking off down the hall.

"What're you doing Friday night?" said Rachel. "Why don't you sleep over?"

"I don't think I can," Carol said. She smiled a sort of uneasy smile. "I made other plans. Sorry."

Rachel guessed she was going to a party with the softball crowd. "That's okay. No problem," said Rachel. She turned away.

On the way home, she could imagine a conversation, the mother of one of her classmates asking, "How did your English essay go?" and the classmate saying, "Okay. Rachel Green read such a dopey one, I couldn't believe it, it was all about how her family has this big fancy piano from Germany and her mother can play classical music and everything. Everybody thought it was so stuck-up. Why are they like that? They think they're better than everybody else! And then in history, she gets up and reads a story about Tibet. And we're all sitting there looking at each other and going, Like who cares?" and the mother saying, "Funny you should mention it. There's a letter to the editor in the paper today."

3

MOTHER AND THE ARTS CENTER

*C*arol had Drama Club after school, so Rachel walked home alone. She was going to practice her violin and write a letter to Phoebe in Italy and then fix supper—Mother had to be at church at six for a wedding rehearsal. She was playing the organ. Rachel stopped at Carol's dad's dime store to look at the stationery.

Wyman Five & Dime was a little brick storefront with a green awning and a display of birthday party decorations in one window and antique typewriters in the other. Fred Wyman stood behind the counter in his green plaid shirt and khaki pants, wrapping a gift package for Mrs. Sykes and curling the ribbons with a scissor blade. "Hi there, Rachel," he said. "How's school? They still teaching things there?"

"A few things," said Rachel. She said hi to Mrs. Sykes, who gave her a pained look. Mrs. Sykes was tall and thin and pale and looked pained most of the time. Mother said she looked as if someone had made her eat a bucket of raw clams at gunpoint.

Rachel went back to the stationery shelves. Fred had the usual goofy stuff with balloons and Garfield the cat and Snoopy and Schroeder at the piano, but also boxes of cream-colored or pin-striped or pale blue notepaper and envelopes with flowery linings. There was stationery imported from Italy, white, with a delicate filigree across the top. Too serious. There were pages the color of a blue winter sky adorned with bunches of blue violets. Rachel chose a box of that, and then she stepped to the glass case full of pens.

"Here's a nice one we got in today. Roller ball with a thin point," Mr. Wyman said. He reached in and pulled out a bright red pen, and she wrote with it on a scratch pad. *How do I love thee? Let me count the ways. 1, 2, 3, 4, 5.*

"How much?" she said.

"For you, a deal. Three bucks. My best offer. Take it or leave it."

"Okay, it's a deal." She fished a ten dollar bill out of her billfold. Half of her weekly allowance. Every Saturday, on the way home from her violin lesson in Oshkosh, Daddy would reach into his pocket and pull out a crisp twenty and give it to her and say, "Don't spend it all in one place."

Wyman's Five & Dime was across the street from the Ramsey Building, which was owned by Mayor Broadbent,

Mother's old adversary. He was a truck driver who had gotten tired of life on the road, Daddy said, and bought the Standard Oil station on the south side of town. He had bought the Ramsey Building ten years ago and, later, two buildings behind it, a tavern and a laundromat, and a vacant lot next to the Ramsey where the school parked its buses, and now he wanted to level everything, pave it, and build a 24-hour gas-station-grocery-video-rental-and-pizza complex called Broadway. Mother referred to it as Broadbutt Plaza. A place you could stop on the way home from school and get a slice of pizza seemed just fine to Rachel, but of course you wouldn't mention that to Mother.

The windows of the Ramsey Building were boarded up, and a rusty steel-mesh fence enclosed it, with signs saying KEEP OUT and WATCH FOR BROADWAY RETAIL DEVELOPMENT COMING SOON! Not if Mother could help it, it wasn't.

Fred Wyman gave Rachel her change and the pen and box of paper in a bag. "Your mother is one brave woman," he said. "Tell her I liked her letter about the mayor's little shopping complex."

Don't encourage her or she'll write six more just like it, thought Rachel.

She went home, and as she came up the driveway, she could hear Mother playing a Mozart sonata on the piano, and she stood by the side of the house and listened for a moment before going in. She could look through the screen door and see the reflection in the oven door of the dining room and Mother at the piano. How elegant she looked, her head moving slightly with the music, her back straight and her eyes closed. When the music stopped, Rachel went inside.

"Hi sweetie, how was school?"

"Good enough, I guess. Anything to eat? I'm starved."

"Well, there are some of those rice cakes and some apple juice, but we can't go in the kitchen yet. Mrs. Dortmeyer just washed the floor and it's still wet."

Mrs. Dortmeyer came and cleaned the house every other Thursday. She was a large middle-aged woman who made a lot of noise with the vacuum cleaner, and after she left, the house smelled of ammonia. She managed to rearrange the stacks of papers just enough so that Mother spent most of Friday looking for things.

Mother got her cigarettes out and lit one. She took a deep drag and let the smoke trickle out of her nose. "I have to start giving these up," she said. Then she took an even deeper drag. The thought of stopping smoking made her a little panicky. Rachel thought she should try hypnosis, though it was hard to imagine anyone being able to hypnotize Mother. Mother was not too good at deep relaxation.

"The wedding rehearsal should be over by seven," said Mother. "There's a recipe for gazpacho soup in *Light and Easy* if you want to make that for supper. Just don't put too much yogurt in it. And the lettuce at the store looked terrible so I got cabbage for coleslaw instead, but remember Daddy doesn't like the dressing too vinegary."

"Who's getting married?" said Rachel.

"I don't know. Somebody's daughter. Emerson or Anderson or something. She wanted a Bob Dylan song called 'Forever Young.' Told her I don't do torch songs."

"Well, it's her wedding," said Rachel. "Why can't she have what she wants?"

Mother squinted. Her hairy-eyeball look. "I'm a church organist, not a nightclub entertainer, dear."

"It's all music," said Rachel. Mother harrumphed.

Rachel went up to her room and took out her violin. She put the music stand in the middle of her bedroom where she could see herself in the full-length mirror that hung on the back of the door. She imagined herself on a stage, her Carnegie Hall debut, in front of a big audience, wearing a long flowing satin gown. She put her bow on the strings, looked in the mirror, got a serious artistic look on her face, and whipped into a piece called "Brindisi." It wasn't as difficult as it sounded. A few tricky places where the composer throws handfuls of notes at you all at once, but most of it flowed right along. She thought how pleased Mr. Amidore, her violin teacher, would be to hear her play it perfectly next Saturday. Then Mother knocked on the door.

"Don't go overboard," she said through the door. "You sound like you're playing for the tone deaf. And your D string is sharp."

"Yeah, okay," Rachel muttered through the door. Mother left, and Rachel stomped her foot and made a face at the closed door. She played the piece again, played it stiffly as if she were a coin-operated violin-playing machine, but Mother wasn't listening anymore.

She loosened the hair on her bow, laid the violin in its case, and tucked its satin cloth around it, and took out her new writing paper and pen and wrote, "Dear Phoebe."

Rachel had written to Phoebe often after the trip to Italy. She was a good person to write to. You could tell her anything and it wouldn't change the way she felt about you. You didn't have to be cheerful. You could write grumpy letters about the gorpy food at home, the geeky clothes Mother wanted you to wear, her long letters to the editor, the Chopin marathons that went on for *hours* and *hours* until you wanted to scream, as Daddy played Beethoven CDs at top volume while the lawn got a foot high and the dandelions bloomed and the railings rusted and the soup burned and the warped siding fell off the garage and the weeds choked out the tulips beside the dying lilacs, and everyone who drove by said, "Well, that's the Greens for you!" You could tell Phoebe this and she wouldn't tell you not to be that way.

Dear Phoebe,

It is warm and sunny out and the town smells like a big cow pie. The farmers have been fertilizing and our windows are open. I should be practicing but I felt nauceous. (Is that how it's spelled? I am too lazy to look it up.) Mother is on the warpath again—more letters. She's in a battle at church where the minister is trying to fire her as organist because she refuses to play the quiet churchy stuff, and now she's blasting the high school for dropping Spanish, and she is in a war with our mayor over an old building he wants to tear down so he can build a mini mall. Mother doesn't seem to realize that *I* have to live in this town too, and in fact *I* have to see these people more than *she* ever does. I mean, I go to school every day and people look at me like *Oh, there's Ingrid Green's daughter, look out.* She may be doing a lot of good but she is single-handedly ruining my life and Daddy is not much help. He just smiles and goes into his cave and turns up the Sibelius. Escape, that's his secret. Mother sees the world as populated by fools whom she has to run around and whack over the head and Daddy sees it as a Norman Rockwell painting, the flags flying, the bands playing. I'm the realist in the middle. Other than the fact that they are driving me nuts, everything is fine. There is going to be an orchestra playing at Dairy Days on July Fourth. My violin teacher, Mr. Amidore, said they were looking for violin players for their summer concerts, and he gave them my name! How are you and how is Italy? I want to go back immediately but first I need to learn Italian. Buon giorno!

Love,
Rachel

She sealed the envelope, addressed it, put two stamps on it, and set it on the hall table, in the big orange dish, for Daddy to mail. Then she put on a CD of Pinchas

Zukerman playing the Dvořák romances for violin and turned up the sound so she could hear it in the kitchen. She studied the gazpacho recipe and hauled out the ingredients. She cooked up a bag of frozen corn and chopped the cucumbers, avocados, and the garlic, and dumped them into tomato juice along with the corn and some lime juice and cumin and hot pepper and a dollop of yogurt and put it in the fridge to chill. Poor Daddy. Gazpacho wasn't exactly what he was hoping for. Gazpacho and coleslaw. Hardly a feast for a steak-and-potatoes man. Oh well, he could listen to Tchaikovsky afterward and let his sorrows bubble to the surface. The *Symphony Pathétique*. It was all about hoping for prime rib and finding gazpacho instead.

The phone rang. Angie, looking for Mother. "She's at church," said Rachel.

"Oh," said Angie. "Kind of dumb to call you up, right next door. If I lean out the window, I could wave to you. How are you? I was calling to see if you guys wanted to come over for supper. I got too big a ham for just the three of us, and I made this big rhubarb pie."

Rachel wanted to say yes, but she said, "No, I've already got supper in the oven. And we're kind of busy tonight." Lie, lie, lie. "But I'll tell Mother you called." All invitations were supposed to go through Mother. She was the social director. She was also Daddy's nutritionist, trying to limit his ham and rhubarb pie intake. And she was the smoker. The Wymans didn't smoke. So Mother had to weigh the pleasures of socializing against the misery of going for two hours without nicotine.

Once, when no one was home, Rachel had tried one of mother's cigarettes. It burned her throat and almost choked her and she had to lie down to make the room stop spinning. That was after two drags.

There was a camp in northern Wisconsin for people who wanted to quit smoking; one of Daddy's managers, Don Breckenridge, had gone there for two weeks, and bang, he was cured. Came back a new man. Looked good, felt great. He told Mother about it at the Dairy Christmas party. "Beautiful place, Ingrid, lots of sports and hiking and swimming, and you get thirty-two cigarettes the first day, and each day they reduce that by half. Day number seven you're clean. They teach you relaxation techniques. By about the tenth day, the urge is completely gone. I can't recommend it highly enough." Mother looked at him with suspicion, as if he were trying to sell her a load of aluminum siding. Don was in choir at Zion Methodist and his singing had improved a hundred percent after he quit smoking. "But of course I'm not a singer," Mother said. "I'm a musician."

Mother had been organist at Zion Methodist for a year and a half, hired after the old one, Mrs. Ferguson, fell on the ice and broke her hip. The ice was on the front steps of the church, and the church board was scared to death that Mrs. Ferguson would sue them for big money because the ice was their fault. The custodian, Mr. Slocum, had quit in a huff and the church board had failed to get someone else to shovel the walk and sand the steps, so when the old lady wrote to them from the hospital and said she hoped that they would hire that nice Mrs. Green as music director, they hired Mother in ten seconds flat, no questions asked. Mrs. Ferguson had heard Mother play Chopin programs at the Ladies Club luncheons and knew what a fine musician she was. Most of the choir members thought so too, and Wednesday night choir practice became louder and happier than in the old days, like a big singing party, and Mother gave them new music to sing—Anglican plainsong and Catholic hymns like Mozart's beautiful "Ave Verum" that had never been heard at Zion before—but some of the older people got their backs up. The music was too hard for them. And Mother was a tough coach. She worked you hard and made you do it over and over until it was good, and if you were singing flat, Mother looked straight at you and said, "You're flat." Some people thought that was rude. Some of the older singers had been singing flat for years; flat was fine with them; they didn't know how to do any different. They felt faint when they looked at the sheet music Mother handed out and saw strange hymns. "I can't sing that," they whispered to each other—and they were right, they couldn't.

One night in February, in the middle of choir practice, old Mrs. Granlund raised her hand and said, "Mrs. Green, pardon me for being forward, but I don't think that this music belongs in the Methodist Church. It may be nice in a concert hall with professionals, but it doesn't do anything for me. Either you're in the wrong place or I am." And she put on her coat and left. The mutiny began. The next week, five more of the older members boycotted practice, and Reverend Sykes called Mother in for a meeting.

He sat behind his desk, wearing his most mournful doggy expression, peering at her over his tortoiseshell reading glasses, his jowls aquiver, his chins hanging low.

"There have been a lot of complaints," he said. "I think we must discuss them."

"Good. Let's do that," said Mother. She said that the complainers were all people you'd expect to complain: the dead wood, the loungers, people who looked on choir as their private club, people who didn't care as much about music as they did about wearing a robe and sitting up front where people could see them.

Reverend Sykes drummed his fingers on the desk. "The church is here to welcome people, not make them feel inferior," he said.

"You can be as welcoming as you like, but the fact is some people can't sing worth beans," said Mother.

Reverend Sykes gave Mother a pained smile. "Let me put it more simply," he said. "Mrs. Granlund is not a person who I want to see leave this church and go over to the Lutherans."

Mother asked him if he was trying to get the old lady's money.

Reverend Sykes drew a deep breath. He said that if Mother cared to seek professional help with her communications skills, he could recommend someone. She declined.

In March, the church board met to discuss "the music

situation," and one of the board members, Mayor Broadbent, said that he, for one, found it difficult to keep his mind on spiritual things during Mother's organ preludes, and that he was troubled by the "rancor" and "ill-feeling" that Mother had caused in the choir.

Mayor Broadbent had been mad at Mother since she began her campaign to buy the Ramsey Building and turn it into the Sandy Bottom Arts Center; Mother and Jerry Mason had come up with a plan for a little historical museum and a studio for art classes and a small theater and an art gallery. Mayor Broadbent wanted his shopping center instead. The week after the *Register* printed a story about the arts-center plan, with quotes from Mother and Jerry about what an asset this would be and good for the economy and so forth, the paper published a letter from Mayor Broadbent in which he referred to the center as "a hare-brained scheme to get the taxpayers to fund a private playground for the three or four people in town who like to listen to screechy-scratchy music and look at pieces of junk that someone stuck on the wall and called art." He said that the Broadway complex would create jobs and help revitalize downtown. He said that he wished the "whiners, the naysayers, the oh-so-chic radical element who expect government to build their fantasy world" would go away and let the decent, hardworking people enjoy the wonderful town that Sandy Bottom is and would be even more so if the radical element would go away.

Now he leaned forward, smiled at Mother, and suggested that she meet regularly with members of the

Worship Committee so that they could approve, or disapprove, the music she planned to use in church.

"Seems reasonable to me, Mrs. Green," said Reverend Sykes.

"Be glad to," said Mother, "if you're willing to let me edit your sermons." She said it coolly, and Reverend Sykes blew his stack. He whipped off his glasses and leaned forward and hissed, "I am so grateful not to be married to you!" And Mother said, "Frankly, Jim, the thought never crossed my mind." You couldn't put one past Mother. What got his undies in a bunch, she told Daddy later, was that she liked to read a book in the organ loft during the sermon. Sykes was a ponderous preacher whose sermons flowed like a bucket of bricks, and it got his goat to look up and see Mother leaning back, chuckling at Jane Austen or working the Sunday crossword.

It was Fred Wyman who saved Mother's job. He stood up and said he thought that Mrs. Green was a valuable asset, and that a person of her ability was rare in Sandy Bottom. He said that there were complaints, yes, but there also were plenty of people who thought Mrs. Green was just what the doctor ordered. He got everyone to agree that they would try a little harder to get along, including Mother.

When Mother came home after the meeting, though, she was steaming. She fixed a pot of alfalfa tea, and she and Daddy argued about Sandy Bottom. It was an argument Rachel had heard many times.

Mother: "I am fed up with people who can't color outside the lines. I don't want to please those people. They need to be riled up a little. It's good for them."

Daddy: "But you try to take them on all at once, and you wind up getting depressed."

Daddy was right. When Mother was herself, she played Chopin so sweetly and elegantly, the music seemed to come from a salon in Warsaw, with chandeliers and pale ladies with long black curls and blue satin gowns and brave cavalry officers limping in from the balcony and dying poets coughing into handkerchiefs. And when she finished, she was cheerful and jokey and fun to be with. But when she got depressed, the piano sat untouched for days and Mother smoked cigarettes and got disgusted with herself and grumbled about how she was wasting her life.

Mother: "I'm telling you, Norman, thirteen years in this town is enough. I've had it. Cooped up in a little town full of small-minded people whose main value in life is *niceness*. They sit and watch the schools crumble and smile and say thank you."

Daddy: "It's a good place to raise children."

Mother: "Raise them to be what? I want us to go to concerts, see paintings in a museum, get Rachel into a youth orchestra—what are we doing sitting here in a mud puddle? When did we get to be so conservative?"

Daddy: "There's a sense of community here. You don't have that in a big city. All you have is arrogance."

Mother: "A herd of cows has a sense of community, Norman. My community is the worldwide community of people who love beautiful things and they don't live here.

41

Just people with little teeny minds and great big lawn mowers."

Daddy: "That's unfair, Ingrid. These are good people. You wait until the Fourth—when that orchestra plays in the band shell—you'll see people listening to Mozart who never heard him before and they'll be absolutely stunned!"

Mother: "Ha. Stunned for fifteen seconds and then they'll turn to their neighbor and say, 'So—how are those walleyes hittin'?'"

Daddy: "I give up."

That night, Rachel lay in bed and worried about what would happen if Mother managed to convince Daddy to move to a big city like Minneapolis or Milwaukee. She was an odd duck in Sandy Bottom, but she had Carol, and if they moved she'd be in a strange school full of kids who already had best friends and didn't need another one and she'd be an utter outcast. Please, God, she thought, make Mother behave herself and stop making people mad at her.

4

CAROL

*T*he next day was a tough day at school. In gym class, they played softball and Rachel got put at first base and people threw the ball *hard* at her and in the dirt and she couldn't catch it and the other team screeched and laughed and Rachel's team got mad at her. Mrs. Erickson handed back a book report with three mistakes circled in red— "immanent" should have been *imminent,* and it should have been *who's one of my favorite writers,* not "whose one of my favorite writers," and Rachel had written "a person who changes their mind," and Mrs. Erickson had circled "their" and written, "How many is one person?" At lunch, Carol sat with the softball girls laughing and talking, and Rachel sat alone in the corner and Lonnie passed her a note saying, "Would you go to a Move with me?" and she wrote *"NO"* and shoved it back at him and spilled orange juice on her book report, which she was supposed to return to Mrs. Erickson, corrected. A truly lousy day.

She passed Wyman Five & Dime on her way home and it was closed and the shade was pulled in the front door. Odd, she thought.

She came home and saw Fred in his garage, replacing a tire on a bicycle. "Taking the day off," he said. "Didn't have any customers this morning and thought I might as well come home and be useful."

Mother had left a note on the table:

> At church until 5. If Jerry calls, tell him I can meet any night next week except Wednesday. Rice and beans are on the counter. Can you make? Thanks! P.S. I hate to mention it but your room has been declared a disaster area and the president has approved emergency disaster relief. In other words: How much can I pay you to please clean it up? Love, Mother.

She put water on to boil for the rice and beans, and then she got out a pack of bratwurst from the freezer and pried two of them loose, one for her and one for Daddy. And then she went up to her room. It wasn't so messy. She scooped up some of the clothes scattered on the floor and tossed them in a pile to take down to the basement to put in the laundry, and then she lit the candles and got out her stationery and red pen and wrote to Phoebe.

> Mother is in one of her vegetarian moods again—more spiritual—and she has decided that

44

her smoking is a spiritual problem, so last night for supper it was gazpacho—what Daddy calls Third World food—and coleslaw with yogurt. Next week it will be something else. I am skinny enough as it is. When Daddy and I go to Oshkosh on Saturday for my lesson, we go to a restaurant and order steaks. Daddy calls it our Red Cross refugee lunch. But Mother is like one of those ferns that live on air. She is going strong, challenging everyone in town who isn't up to speed. On my way home I passed the mayor, Mr. Broadbent, who was getting out of his pickup truck and when he saw me, he got back in so he wouldn't have to say hello. After he wrote that letter about Mother being "the radical element," she wrote one about him being "one of those people who look on asphalt as a solution for everything." There was a lot more. When Carol came over the other day, she didn't get to say *one thing*—Mother was going on and on about historic preservation. And then Daddy went and dug out a copy of Thoreau and started reading it out loud—*while Mother kept talking about historic preservation*—as if it were the normal thing for two people to talk about two completely different things at the same time. We are now almost the weirdest family in this entire town. The prize will soon be ours. Soon we will surpass even the Dribbles.

The Dribbles lived in a dark green trailer in an open field north of the river, their property littered with rusty old refrigerators, LP gas tanks, and dead automobiles with weeds growing in the backseats. Perhaps, Rachel thought, the Dribbles had once been like the Greens, a little nutty but still respectable, and then a run of bad luck had pushed them over the edge. Perhaps it was not impossible that the Greens could wind up in a trailer in a vacant lot, sitting around a space heater eating kidney beans out of cans. What if Mother suddenly went crazy? Sometimes she seemed to be halfway there—those days when she sat staring out the window and could hardly get words out of her mouth. What if the great yogurt-and-fancy-ice-cream experiment failed and the dairy went out of business? Things could change in a big hurry. Ships could sink, airplanes could crash, and nice families could wind up out on the street. Grandpa Mueller had money, but Mother and Daddy were proud people. Maybe they'd refuse help.

That night Daddy announced that he had hired a wonderful young conductor to do the Fourth of July show, a fellow by the name of Cornish. Adam Cornish. He had guest-conducted a concert with the Oshkosh Symphony this past season. He was from Boston, twenty-five, a rising star in the music world. Daddy had spoken to him today; he was in New York, auditioning singers for an opera he was conducting in Colorado, but he had open dates this summer and would be happy to do four outdoor concerts with the Dairyland Symphony—Sandy Bottom, Menomonie, Oshkosh, and Eau Claire. A man named Robbins would hire the musicians, mostly from Milwaukee and Madison, with some local players—Daddy smiled at Rachel—and the dairy was paying for everything, and now they had a wonderful conductor.

"Don't be so sure," said Mother. "You missed that Adam Cornish concert in Oshkosh. I didn't. The man is a butcher. It was an all-Bach program. He has no ear, Norman. Plenty of hair but no ear."

"Is he the one you called Hair Ball?" said Rachel.

Daddy laughed uneasily. "Well, anyone can have a bad night. He's got a good résumé, comes highly recommended."

"By whom?" Mother said. "His beautician?"

Rachel laughed, but Daddy ignored it. "We had a good conversation on the phone. Adam is a young man who believes in taking classical music out to people who don't usually go to concerts. And he doesn't cost an arm and a leg. And he's open to suggestions."

"I've got one suggestion for him," said Mother. "He should put hair on his baton and become a house painter. He's got the right arm motions for it."

The next morning, as Rachel and Carol walked to school, Carol asked, "Do you still want to sleep over tonight?"

"Of course," Rachel said.

"Oh." Carol looked down at the sidewalk. She kicked a stone ahead of her.

"What's wrong?" Rachel asked.

"Nothing. You just seem like—I don't know. Like you're not that friendly anymore or something. Like you're kind of off in your own world. Which is fine. But I thought that if you didn't really want to sleep over, that I'd make other plans."

Rachel felt as if she had been slapped in the face. "Don't you want me to?" she said softly.

"Sure," Carol said. "Of course."

"Then I want to."

That was an odd conversation, she thought, listening to Mr. Gilbert drone on about the Civil War. She went over and over it in her head, sitting in Miss Mortenson's algebra class. Had Carol talked to Valerie last night and the two of them decided they *had* to have a sleepover tonight, and then Carol said, "Oh no! *Rachel's* supposed to sleep over tonight!" and Valerie said, "Oh, that's too bad," and Carol said, "Oh shoot!"—was that what happened? And then Valerie said, "She seems so strange lately, don't you think? Like she's so *moody*." And Carol said, "Yeah, I know." Was that the real story?

Carol was with Valerie all the time, it seemed. Rachel saw them leaving school together in their softball shorts and jerseys on their way to practice, hauling bags full of balls and bats, talking their heads off the way she and Carol used to talk.

Rachel thought of all those summers when she and Carol had hung out together back before Carol had gotten serious about softball, before Valerie Mason moved to town.

When Rachel was little, she'd come out on a nice summer morning in her overalls, and there on the sidewalk would be Carol, waiting patiently on her trike in her green corduroy pants and a Mickey Mouse T-shirt, watching at the Greens' back door for Rachel. She'd smile and say hi, and off they'd go, and if Rachel came out and Carol wasn't there, Rachel would dart through the hole in the lilac bushes and plump herself down on Carol's back steps and wait for her.

They made a house out of a washing-machine carton and raised their doll families in it, and they took the dolls on trips in Carol's coaster wagon. They played store, taking turns waiting on each other and selling each other clothing. "Try this on," Rachel would say, and Carol would take off her T-shirt and put on another one. "Oh, I think green looks so much better on you than red. Oh yes." "Do you really?" "Oh yes, I do. It brings out your skin tone more." And then they'd play office in the Greens' basement, with Daddy's papers and rubber stamps and stuff. They'd stamp "Canceled" or "Paid" or "Very Important—Open Immediately" on blank paper and sign their names and stamp the date and file the papers in wire baskets marked In and Out. And then they might go up to Daddy's den and attend a concert. Carol would be Miss Upshaw and Rachel would be Louise Monbouquette, two old friends from New York in their fancy dresses, wearing the latest perfumes. Rachel would put on a record of soprano arias, and they'd sit in two chairs facing the stereo speakers. Miss Upshaw always said how *wonderful* the singer was, and Miss Monbouquette said how very *dreadful* and *disgusting*. The game was that Carol was prim and nice, and Rachel said mean things about the soprano—she sang like a scalded cat, her vibrato sounded like an ambulance, she sang like she had beans up her nose—until she made Carol burst out laughing, and then they went and did something else. There was always something.

Even when they were ten and eleven and twelve and Carol had joined a softball team, she would come straight home after games and look for Rachel. The two of them would go biking, their lunches in saddlebags, and ride to the old mill site up the river from town, sitting by the ruins of the dam, the water pouring over the millrace and foaming and boiling up at the base. There they would eat their sandwiches and talk. Talk and talk and talk. They'd lie on their backs and look up at the sky, the summer clouds scudding through the boughs of the oak tree, and talk for hours. When she was with Carol, Rachel was full of things to say, and so was Carol, so it all came bubbling out. Angie said, "I never saw two people talk like you two," but that was how it was with friends. You inspired each other. Rachel and Carol talked about their most embarrassing moments, told deep dark secrets, talked about what you would do if you knew nobody would ever find out, about death and what would you do if this were the last day of your life, or if you were sent to live alone on a desert island and could take with you only *six things* aside from food and clothing, what would they be? And they talked endlessly about what they would be someday.

What will you be when you grow up? Every day, something different. That was the idea. Each day you made up a whole new story about your future. Yesterday, you had said you would become a Broadway dancer and live in New York and study and dance in *A Chorus Line* and be discovered by Hollywood, like Shirley MacLaine was, and go make a movie—not a musical but a serious dramatic film. But that was yesterday's idea, and today you'd become a heart surgeon instead and specialize in heart transplants for infants and go to Africa and do operations on poor children from remote villages who suffer from heart valve problems, but you would also be a great dancer and maybe Hollywood would discover you and offer you a part in a picture, and you'd tell them no, you couldn't come, you had to save lives.

But what had happened to them? Had they run out of things to say? Did all friendships peter out eventually and you had to dump those friends and go find new ones? Rachel hoped not. Mother and Phoebe had been friends for twenty-five years, since college. They could still find plenty to say to each other. On New Year's Eve, Mother had called Phoebe, and though it was four A.M. in Italy, they talked for hours and ran up a phone bill of $130. But Rachel and Carol seemed to be water over the dam. You go along, you're like Siamese twins, no matter where you are there's the other one, and then suddenly you look around, and where did she go?

There was a letter from Phoebe waiting on the kitchen counter when Rachel got home, postmarked *Firenze, Italia, May 9,* a response to a letter three letters ago when Rachel asked Phoebe if she, Rachel, could come live there if her parents got a divorce. She wrote it after Mother and

51

Daddy had one of their big arguments about Moving to the City vs. Living in Sandy Bottom.

Dear Rachel,

Thanks for your letter. Your parents aren't going to divorce each other, take my word for it. They're as different as day and night, but they love each other. They landed there in Sandy Bottom like frogs in a wheat field, but they made themselves a mud puddle, and they do pretty well. And they've managed to make a life that gives them a lot of pleasure every day. Look around and you'll see some very normal people who are terrifically depressed and too polite to say so. Your parents are doing very well.

Anyway, that's how I read them. So don't worry too much, okay? But you're always welcome here anyway. In fact, people often stop me in the street and ask when you're returning. Complete strangers, cabdrivers, waiters, the man in the post office. What shall I tell them?

Rachel slept over at Carol's that night, and everything was wonderful—they were like sisters again. They watched *My Fair Lady* and ate cheese popcorn until one-thirty in the morning and curled up in bed together and whispered.

"You look just like Audrey Hepburn," said Carol. "I swear you do."

Rachel stuck out her tongue. "Liar, liar, pants on fire."

"You do. You have her hair and her eyes."

Rachel looked at the ceiling. "What scares me is that

I'll grow up to be like my mother. I can't stand her. She's always in a fight with someone, and she can never leave you alone. She's always in your face. 'Have you done your homework? What are you reading? I didn't hear you practicing today,' all that. She's so selfish. My mother cannot *conceive* of the fact that other people—like me, for example—may have a view of the world that is different from hers! So tell me, honestly—on a scale from one to ten, how weird is my mother? A nine?"

"No. Maybe a six. A six or seven. But I still like her."

"You do?" Rachel rolled over on her side and looked at Carol.

"Your mother is really smart. I think she's cool."

"Just promise me if I ever go above four, you'll tell me. Will you?"

"You mean if you start writing long letters to the newspaper, I should tell you?"

"Yes," said Rachel. "Promise."

"Valerie's dad says your mother is the smartest person he knows."

Rachel looked up at the ceiling. The mention of Valerie gave her an ache inside. It was stupid but it did. She wished Valerie would move away. Someplace like Madagascar. Or else get sick. Nothing too bad, something like poison ivy. Maybe she could eat some and her innards would swell up and she'd go to the Mayo Clinic for a small-intestine transplant and come home and have to lie very still for six months.

"What's wrong?" said Carol.

"Nothing. I'm thinking about what you said."

They snuggled together, their heads touching, and Carol put her arm over Rachel and whispered, "You know something? Even if we both move away when we grow up and we hardly ever see each other, we will always be friends. I know that's true."

Rachel felt ashamed. "Don't tell anyone what I said about my mother," she whispered. Carol promised not to.

Downstairs, Angie and Fred had been quiet for a long time. Rachel lay listening to Carol fall asleep. Her lips parted and her breathing got slow and deep. Carol was normal; she could throw a softball straight, people liked her, she had pretty blond hair and she had breasts, and she wasn't a crazy insomniac like Rachel.

Sometimes it helped to imagine walking home from school, past Wyman's and Western Auto and Hilliard's Bakery with the garish birthday cake with giant green walleyes leaping up from the frosting, and the bank and the Bon Ton store and Downing's Paint & Wallpaper, and the Short Stop Bar and Harry's Shoes and the River View Café, and other times it helped to think of all of the states of the Union, starting with Washington, Idaho, Montana, North Dakota, Minnesota, Wisconsin, Michigan, right straight across the top, and remembering the capitals too: Olympia, Boise, Helena, Bismarck, St. Paul, Madison, Lansing—and after that, she could see how many times she could go through the alphabet with composers' names: Albinoni, Bach, Chopin, Debussy, Elgar, Franck, Grieg, Handel, Ives, Joplin, Khachaturian, Liszt—her record was three times, allowing five skips per round because there simply were no Q or X or Z composers worth knowing and not many I or J or K ones either.

Rachel eased out of bed, put on a bathrobe, and tiptoed into the hall. At the other end, behind their bedroom door, Fred and Angie snored in a regular duet, baritone and alto, rising and falling. Rachel tiptoed down the stairs, thick-carpeted, brown with flecks of gold, past walls lined with pictures of Carol and her brother when they were babies, and looked around the shadowy living room. Angie worked part-time at the library, but still, there weren't many books in the house, and the ones the Wymans had didn't look as if anyone read them. *The Family Encyclopedia of Western Civilization*, *One Thousand Beloved Poems*—that sort of thing.

In the bookshelf, Rachel found a drawer and opened it. There were letters inside. She took one out. *This is wrong,* she thought, *this is evil.* But she took it over to the window and read it, a letter from Angie to her sister Cheryl in Oregon dated May 24—the day before yesterday—written in Angie's plumpish handwriting.

Dear Cheryl,

I am sorry about you and Chuck having those problems, as sorry as I can be. You poor lamb. Just remember there are ups and downs in every marriage, and you have to do your best and get through the rough spots and enjoy the good times, and when you get mad, don't say things so flat that you can't take them back later. I know that sounds like Mom talking but it really is true. Fred's thinking of selling the dime store and trying to get work with the dairy here in town. It's been a terrible year so far at the store. For a while we were afraid we might have to sell the house and file for bankruptcy, but then Fred's family settled his mother's estate (after three years of wrangling!) and we got our share, and that saved our skins. Carol's growing up so fast you probably wouldn't recognize her. Fred keeps busy busy with his church work and I am going to put the garden in next week. We had too many tomatoes last year and not enough sweet corn, and I'm going to try to plant cilantro again. Someone said that horse manure might help.

The writing stopped there. Rachel slipped the letter back in the drawer. She had no idea the Wymans had money problems. Bankruptcy? Wasn't that what happened to people when they hadn't a dime and they had to sell off the silverware at auction and eat macaroni and cheese and lock the door against the sheriff? And yet Angie sounded so cheerful. "You have to get through the rough spots and enjoy the good times." Poor Fred and Angie. Maybe she should tell Daddy to hire Fred, but then what if they figured out that she had read the letter? She looked out the window, and there, like a ghost ship fifty feet away, was her own house, dark except for the glow of an upstairs hall light. If the Wymans moved away and new people moved in, she could imagine them standing there in the window looking over at the Greens' house and saying, "Boy, those people're special, aren't they? Don't have all their cornflakes in one box, if you ask me."

She felt ashamed of thinking a thought so mean and disloyal, but it was true. Rachel Wyman would be a nice person to be. To have a mother who hugged you and kissed you, not one who was always poking you to try harder, be better, rise to the heights, a mother who was trying to make you an even bigger oddball than she was. The Wymans were fun. Television and sports and artificially flavored foods were just fine with them. They had a good time in life even when times were tough.

She crept upstairs and crawled back in next to Carol, curled up, asleep, only her tousled hair showing above the blue-and-pink flowered quilt. She wondered about Carol and Valerie and what they talked about at lunch. Carol had offered to teach Rachel to play softball, but those softball girls didn't like her, she knew that. They saw her coming and they thought, Here comes the one with the mother. If she sat down with them in the cafeteria, the conversation died, as if a teacher had sat down. And now what if Carol was telling Valerie stuff about the Greens? Rachel couldn't bear to think of it. She snuggled close to Carol. Please don't like Valerie more than you like me, she thought. And then she closed her eyes. And then it was morning and Angie was in the hallway calling to them to come down for waffles.

MUSIC SCHOOL

*I*t was Saturday morning, Rachel's favorite day of the week—her day to go to Oshkosh. After breakfast, Rachel went home, and she and Daddy piled into the car and headed for Rachel's violin lesson at the Amidore School of Music, and after that there was string ensemble. Oshkosh was an hour away, time enough for Daddy to play her his favorite new CD, which today was the Poulenc *Suite Française*, a really glorious piece designed to put you in a good mood.

"Can I say something?" Rachel said, when the music ended. "Promise me that we aren't going to move away."

"Who said we were moving?"

"I know Mother wants to. But I can't go. If you want to go, you have to let me live with the Wymans. This is my home here." Rachel felt the tears coming to her eyes. "I have some rights, too. I'm a person. I'm not just a puppet."

Daddy put his hand on her knee and patted it. "It's my home, too," he said. "And it's your mother's home. Don't worry about it. Before you know it, we'll be standing in the front door waving good-bye as you head off to school."

"What school?" she said. "Reform school?"

"I meant college."

"You're not going to hang on to your favorite child?"

"I'm hanging on as tight as I can. But you're supposed to struggle and try to get away, aren't you?"

In Oshkosh, Daddy dropped her off at music school and walked off to find a *New York Times* and to drink coffee with real cream and heaping spoonfuls of sugar.

The Amidore School of Music was on the second and third floors over Rexall Drugs. Next to a window full of crutches and bedpans was a door marked MUSIC SCHOOL, and you opened it and went up a long flight of stairs, then opened a grimy battered old door and walked into a flood of music. There was a long hallway with little practice cubicles up and down both sides. At the far end was the waiting room for parents, and upstairs were the teaching studios and the orchestra room. The walls were thin, so you heard everything: scales and arpeggios, little kids whacking out études on pianos, clarinets honking, trumpets blaring, trombones growling, and violins and cellos sawing away. In the waiting room, when Rachel arrived, three mothers were talking and drinking coffee from a thermos, and one mother was knitting what looked like a hotpad. Somebody's dad was reading *Time*—he had headphones on, and a yellow cassette player clamped on his belt. The walls were green and blue plaster, faded, chipped, covered with big posters of Zukerman, Perlman, Garrick Ohlsson, Yo-Yo Ma, James Galway, Gil Shaham. A bulletin board in the corner was plastered with index cards offering used instruments for sale and brochures for summer music programs, such as Interlochen and Meadowmount and Tanglewood.

Rachel headed upstairs to the third floor. Mr. Amidore's studio was up there. A boy with a crew cut ran past her and smacked her arm with his trombone. "Whoa! Sorry!" he yelled, and went clattering past and down the stairs to the street. Saturday morning was the busy day at the Amidore Music School. Lessons went on full blast from eight in the morning until three in the afternoon. There were folding chairs up and down the hallway on the third floor filled with students who hadn't practiced all week were practicing like crazy before they went into their lessons. It was a madhouse. Mr. Amidore called it the Oshkosh Home for the Musically Youthful, or OH MY. Rachel loved it.

She took a seat against the wall, next to a solemn boy clutching a viola and two little girls who kept looking at each other and bursting into giggles. Rachel took out her violin and tuned it. The girls stopped giggling.

"Ooh, your violin is so pretty!" said one of them.

Rachel smiled at her. "Hi, Rex," she said to the solemn boy.

The boy said, "Hey, Rachel, how're you?" Rachel knew him from string ensemble. He was a good player. Not such a good sight reader, but he loved playing, and he played in tune, not like some.

"Rex," she said, "do you ever have this experience of looking at your parents and feeling a fear of heredity?"

That made him laugh. "Yeah," he said. "Every day. My mother's a hypochondriac and my dad is bald as a bowling ball. So I'm just waiting for the genes to kick in."

She put her violin under her chin and bowed a tricky little passage from "Brindisi"—*dah-deedle-dah-deedle-skritch*—played it twice, note-perfect, and set the violin on her lap. The little girls were now bursting with admiration.

"What is that *from*?" one of them whispered.

"It's a piece called 'Brindisi,'" said Rachel.

"Wow," said the other girl. She whispered to her friend. "Where are you from?" said one.

"Florence, Italy," said Rachel.

Rex laughed. "Florence who?" he said.

The little girls were impressed. They said it under their breaths: *Italy*. Rachel smiled. She loved music school. It was full of kids just like herself. They had all heard of Mahler and knew what a Mozart symphony sounded like, and they didn't think it was geeky to play an instrument and try to play it really well. Not just go through the motions but really dig in and work at it and get the reins on a violin or an oboe or a piano and make it sound the way you wanted it to.

Mr. Amidore appeared in the doorway, exhaling the last puff of a cigarette. He was short and pear-shaped, with a big black mustache and long hair tied back in a ponytail. He wore black trousers and a red emroidered vest over a white linen shirt. "Signorina Rachel, *buon giorno*," he said. He bowed deeply and kissed her hand, and followed her back to his studio. The room was sunny; big windows faced east, a view of treetops swaying in the breeze and two brick steeples with crosses on top. A picture of Paganini and a color photograph of the Pope. Bookcases full of music. She put her music on the music stand, and Mr. Amidore offered her a licorice drop out of a blue tin that said *Amoroso*. He asked about her mother and her father, and she asked about his mother, Rosa. "Not so good, not so good," he said sadly. "She's"—he tapped his head—"crazy—stays in bed all day. Up all night, baking, cooking—we live like gypsies. It wears me out. But that's life. Now let's hear you play."

Rachel played. When you did well, Mr. Amidore always got excited, and now, he walked vigorously around the room, hands behind his back, nodding his head in time with the music. By the end of the second page, he had tears in his eyes.

He said, "You are my genius, my favorite." He kissed both her hands this time. Rachel wondered if he told all his students that, but it didn't matter.

He stopped her in the middle of a fast part. "*Spiccato!*

That means *bounce* the bow! *Off* the string! *Faster!*"

She tried it again, this time the bow bounced but her hands wouldn't do what she wanted them to. The fingers of her left hand got tangled up.

"Okay! Now how about the right notes!" Mr. Amidore was shouting.

Again she played it. "Better! Go on!" he cried. Rachel was feeling nervous, but Mr. Amidore seemed pleased. She finished the piece. "Wonderful," he said. "You're getting it. Enough fireworks. I think what you need is a little Mozart, something spiritual, more refined." He went over to his music cabinet and pulled out a Mozart concerto.

"This is one of the gems of the repertoire. Take this and see what you can do with the first movement this week." He asked her to play an étude and then scales and arpeggios—G major, D minor, A major, A minor, C major. She ripped through the scales and did almost as well on the arpeggios. When the hour was up, Mr. Amidore looked sad. "It was so good to see you again. So good," he whispered. "Students like you—*ahhhh,* I should be paying you. It makes up for all the others." He nodded toward the door. "Some of them—*aiiieeeee.* Not a clue. All noise, no music. Anyway, *arrivederci,* Rachello." A kiss on the cheek, and out the door she went, walking on air.

She met Daddy at the café, and they had their Red Cross lunch before she went back to school for string ensemble. Daddy ordered a filet mignon, rare, with french fries. "Now that's what I call *food,*" he said when the waitress brought it. He sawed off a chunk of steak and chomped on it, and his face beamed. "Your mother looks on food as a grim necessity, something you have to do to maintain life. She's into low maintenance."

Rachel chewed her hamburger. "Do you think it's possible that maybe later in the summer if you're not too busy we could take a trip to Chicago?" she said. "There's this really awesome exhibit, at the Art Institute, of Scandinavian painters, I read about it in the Sunday paper," she said. "And we could have a movie marathon. Remember when we did that in Milwaukee once?" They had seen three movies in one day, and then Mother dropped out, exhausted, and Daddy and Rachel went to two more. A quintuple! *Howards End* (for Mother), *Dracula* (for Rachel), Charlie Chaplin in *The Gold Rush* (for Daddy), and finally the two of them took in *Hamlet* and a cheapo movie about a gang of tough girls called *Switchblade Blondes* that was so dumb the whole audience sat and howled. It was all car chases and gunshots and blondes chomping their gum and smoking and shoving other girls down the stairs and close-ups of those girls glowering at the blondes and the blondes laughing their coarse cruel laughs.

"It all depends," said Daddy. He was focused on his filet mignon.

"I think it would be really good for Mother to get out of town for a few days," said Rachel.

"We'll see," he said.

String ensemble met in the big room on the third floor at three o'clock, after lessons were over. There were fifteen students who Mr. Amidore thought were good enough for string ensemble, sitting in two curved rows, and they played Vivaldi and Bach and Corelli, and Rachel thought there was nothing better in the world than to make such elegant music. She liked to imagine it was the St. Paul Chamber Orchestra rehearsing, and that Pinchas Zukerman was about to walk in and play with them. She sat right up front on the first stand with Linda Maxwell, across from Scott Miller, the first cellist, and the best student in the school. Scott was sixteen. He was tall and thin and had beautiful dark eyes, and Rachel thought she had never known anyone so handsome. Everything about his face was perfect, and his hair was always perfect—thick, rich, black curls. Rachel liked to watch his hands as he played, the graceful way his fingers ran down the fingerboard, his bowing, his concentration. He was always nice to everyone, not snooty like some of them. Craig, for example, one of the violinists, made faces when someone played a bad note. Scott wasn't like that. His mother Nancy played the harpsichord with them sometimes. She wasn't as good as Mother, but everyone liked her. Two weeks ago, Scott had tapped his bow on the music stand and mouthed "Bravo" at Rachel after she and Linda played a duet together. Rachel looked down and blushed.

Today, Mr. Amidore played with them. He stood, his eyes closed, playing from memory, ending with the slow air from a Bach suite. He never stopped them during string ensemble to criticize their playing; it wasn't for instruction, but for pleasure. When it was over, he simply said, "Bravo! Thank you," bowed, and went back to his studio and closed the door.

Rachel was putting her violin away in the case when Scott walked over. "That was fun, especially the Bach," he said. "So what are you up to this summer?"

"Not much. Mr. Amidore recommended me for that summer orchestra, so maybe I'll do that. If they let me in."

He laughed. "*If!* Ha. Of course they will. You're good. I'm hoping to play in that, too. Do you know where they play?"

"Oh, mostly parks concerts. They're doing one in Sandy Bottom."

"*Really.* That's neat." He looked at her quizzically. "Do you live in Sandy Bottom?" She nodded.

"You're the only one from there, aren't you?" he said.

"Yes, I'm the town oddball," she said, and she crossed her eyes and opened her mouth slightly, her tongue lolling in the corner. He laughed.

"I hope we both get in—it'd be nice to be around someone I like."

Scott was closing his cello case. "By the way, why don't you give me your phone number? Maybe we could get together sometime over the summer."

He wrote her number down on the back of a piece of music. And with that, she felt her heart skitter, and she blushed and looked at her shoes, then turned and almost crashed into the wall, and floated down the stairs to the street.

Daddy sat in the car out front, the windows rolled down, the Metropolitan Opera blasting on the radio, a tenor and a soprano singing their hearts out.

"How was ensemble?" he shouted over the music.

"Beautiful!" she yelled.

He handed her a twenty dollar bill. "Don't spend it all in one place," he said.

When she got home, there was another letter from Phoebe.

"Dear Rachel," it said in great big bold handwriting.

Spring is a glorious time in Italy except that the smell of green grass makes me homesick for Wisconsin. At this moment I am sitting in "our" outdoor café, drinking cappuccino and watching Japanese women with big sunglasses shopping for shoes, and Italian men jabbering on their cellular phones, and boys your age flying by on mopeds. I'm still working at the photography gallery owned by that Swiss woman with the helmet hair, Gerthe. She goes for black-and-white pictures that represent the Anguish and Emptiness of modern life. I prefer the 17th century. More charming. Anyway, A & E sell pretty well. It looks like I may come to the U.S. this fall. Hope to get to see you. Don't worry about being weird; in a world of A & E, who wants to be normal? Bunches of love.

She went to her room and got out a pad of paper. "Dear Phoebe," she wrote.

Thanks for your letter. Today I think I fell in

love for the first time in my life. And his name is Scott.

> He likes me a lot,
> A handsome fellow
> Who plays the cello
> So prettily
> It's like Italy.

6

DADDY'S DEBUT

*I*t was eighty-three degrees, according to the "Time & Temp" sign on the bank. A scorcher for May. Rachel's head felt hot, and the asphalt was soft under her sneakers. She crossed Van Buren Street on her way home from school, trying to stay ahead of Carol, who was walking with Valerie. "Walk with us," said Carol, but Rachel turned away.

"I told my mother I'd come straight home and practice," she said.

"You have to practice *every* day?" Valerie asked.

"Yes," said Rachel.

"Really?" said Valerie. "That's weird. Mr. Olson said if we practiced three times a week that would be good enough. I guess violin is different." Valerie was one of fifteen flute players in the marching band, which, though Rachel never mentioned it to anyone, was truly terrible. You couldn't even make out the tune half the time, it was all wheezing and honking and squeaking. She walked faster, two tears poised in the corners of her eyes, and when she stopped for the red light at Main Street, in front of the Short Stop, the tears made the light into a red kaleidoscope. Then they came loose and rolled down along her nose. She wiped them away as Carol and Valerie came up alongside. Carol was laughing.

"Oh, that's funny," Carol said. "That is a riot. Tell Rachel what you said."

"You tell her," said Valerie, and she smirked at Rachel, as if to say, This is a private joke. You'd never get it.

Carol was laughing so hard she had stopped walking. "Oh never mind," she said. She wiped her eyes. "It's so dumb, she probably wouldn't think it's funny anyway. Because it's not." And then she started giggling again.

Rachel's face burned and her throat got tight. "I don't want to hear your stupid joke," Rachel said, and turned away so they wouldn't see the tears. "I forgot, I have to ask my dad something," and she headed up Division Street toward the big redbrick Sandy Bottom Dairy on Monroe Street, a block away.

"Come over to my house after you practice," called Carol.

"I don't think so," said Rachel, not turning around. She walked past the front windows of the dairy with the big pyramids of Bluebird ice-cream cartons and ducked into the alley next to Gray Trucking and there, by the garbage cans, she stopped. Maybe Carol would come running after her, wondering what was wrong, and put her arms around her, *Oh Rachel, I'm sorry, I'm sorry.* But no, Carol was with Valerie, and Rachel was alone. Then she let the tears loose. Big, hot, salty tears splashed down her face, and she looked down at the ground and let them fall in the dirt. You big bawling baby, crying because you're jealous, she thought, but it didn't help to get mad at herself, so she cried harder. It just hurt so much, that was all. To be so close to someone one day and the next she's like a total stranger. How could Carol be so chummy with Valerie, a person who hated *her,* Carol's best friend? It was so obvious that Valerie couldn't stand Rachel—how could Carol not see this? Unless Carol was afraid to be loyal to someone as nerdy as Rachel. Was that it? Here she was, a perfectly decent person who happened to pick up a violin once in a while and play it, which was odd, yes, but not a terminal social liability—or was it? Maybe people can only be friends with people they do stuff with—softball players are friends of softball players, and violinists can only be best friends with other violinists.

Rachel crept up the back stairs to Daddy's office, which looked out on the lot where Mr. Odegard kept his brand-new Fords. In the flower boxes on the landing, outside the office, Florence's tulips were up, bright green blades of leaves. Florence was Daddy's secretary, a big friendly lady from their church who used to be Rachel's baby-sitter. Rachel opened the door very quietly, slipped in, and eased

71

it shut—Florence's desk was twenty feet away, around the corner—and she ducked into the bathroom, washed her face, and blotted her eyes with cold water.

"Well, what have we here?" cried Florence, when Rachel appeared. "My goodness, come around here and let me have a look at you. You're looking more like your mother every day, and you know she's the most beautiful woman in town." Rachel came around the big oak desk piled up with black ring binders stuffed with papers and stood by Florence's old Underwood typewriter and smiled at her. Florence touched her cheek. "Your dad says you're becoming *quite* a violinist, so when are you going to bring your violin down here and give us a concert? Huh? I want to hear you."

"I will, soon," said Rachel. She tried to smile. Mother had told her to be extra nice to Florence, who had no children, who had been abandoned by the only man she loved. Fifteen years ago, Mother said, she had been engaged to marry a local man, an insurance man. The date of the wedding was set, and then one week before *(one week!)*, he wrote Florence a note saying he didn't love her and slipped it under her door and left for California, having broken her heart in pieces. "You're the age of the child she was hoping to have," Mother said. "I'm only telling you this so you'll understand if she gets gushy."

"I've got to get you over for dinner one of these days," said Florence. "Just you and me. Just the girls. We'll play cribbage and watch TV, what do you say?" She stood up and smoothed out her blue dress and looked at

Rachel as if she were studying a painting. "I like your hair short like that," she said. "It's a very sophisticated look."

Daddy was in the front office, standing at the Xerox machine, watching it pump out paper. He gave Rachel a quick kiss. "Give me a hand," he said. "I'm doing a mailing to get volunteers for the Fourth of July. Want to get it in the mail by tomorrow. I need some help folding."

Three hundred letters, beginning "Dear Friend, As we observe our nation's birthday this year with fireworks and hot dogs, we also plan to present the *FIRST* full professional orchestra concert in Sandy Bottom's history, the Dairyland Symphony conducted by the brilliant young Adam Cornish. Here's your chance to be part of this TRULY EXCITING event. . . ." She sat at the table with a stack of sheets and folded them by thirds and stuffed them into envelopes. Daddy was thrilled about the concert, but Rachel wasn't so sure. People who loved to eat cotton candy and ride a Ferris wheel and pay a dollar to throw a ring around a milk bottle and win a stuffed bear were not people who generally liked to sit still and listen to an orchestra.

This wasn't Oshkosh, after all. The Greens had season tickets to the Oshkosh Symphony and went to all six concerts a year, though on the way home, Mother usually grumbled about the conductor, his sluggish tempos, his sloppy phrasing, or else she thought the piano soloist played like a plumber. Mr. Amidore was the concertmaster; he tuned the orchestra and led the string section.

Rachel liked to watch him in his tuxedo, playing with his eyes closed, ignoring the conductor most of the time. And sometimes Mr. Amidore spotted her in the audience and gave her a big grin. In March, he had played a Bruch violin concerto when the guest violinist got sick, and he did a beautiful job—even Mother thought so—and when he came out for his second bow, he winked at Rachel and crossed his eyes and wiped the sweat off his brow. *Whew!* The Oshkosh crowd gave him a standing ovation. In Sandy Bottom, people might just wander off after the first movement and get a hot dog.

The door opened. It was Florence. "A Mr. Robbins is on the line," she said.

"Oh, that's the man who's hiring the players for the orchestra," said Daddy.

He picked up the phone. "Norman Green here, Mr. Robbins. How are you?" he said. After that, there was a long silence. Then a "Mmmmm." And a "Yes. I understand, but still—" A silence. "Well," Daddy said, "I guess we'll have to see what can be done. You're sure there's no chance of his doing just this one performance?" Another silence. "I see. But I really can't cancel this. We've already started cranking up our publicity. People here are getting excited about it. Lots of phone calls. I'll tell you what—can I get back to you first thing in the morning? Okay. Thanks. Bye, now."

Daddy put the receiver down and ran his fingers through his hair. He groaned.

"What happened?"

Daddy crumpled up a sheet of paper and leaned back in his chair and looked disgusted. "Mr. Cornish has jumped ship. He backed out yesterday. He's history. Got a better offer somewhere else, I guess. We're sunk. This guy Robbins tried to get a replacement, but it doesn't look good. Nobody's available. He wants to bag the whole thing."

Daddy wiped his eyes.

"This Cornish—he's young, he's in a hurry to get places and be somebody, and that kind of person can be ruthless. I suppose he wants to build his résumé and what good would it do him to have a nice review from the Sandy Bottom *Register*, huh?"

Daddy looked drained. Rachel came to his side and put her hand on his arm.

"That's not fair. How can he just up and quit like that?" she said.

"My fault. We made the deal over the phone, nobody signed anything, and I guess he figures there's no point in keeping your word to someone from a town this small, huh?" Daddy smacked his hand on the desk. "Well, by George, the man is not going to ruin our Fourth of July." Daddy jumped up.

He drew himself up to his full height, his head high, his chest out, and he adjusted his tie. "If that turkey thinks he's the only conductor in Wisconsin, I say, *Ha*. He thinks he's some kind of *genius* that he can cancel out on a whim, I say, *Go ahead, Mr. Big Shot. I'll conduct them myself!*"

He smiled as if he had just said something perfectly sensible and reasonable.

"You?" Rachel said.

"Yes, of course," he said. *"Conducted by Norman Green.* It has a ring to it, don't you think?"

So Rachel unstuffed the envelopes and threw away the sheets, and Daddy typed up a new letter and where it had said "conducted by the brilliant young Adam Cornish," it said "conducted by yours truly."

"But you've never conducted an orchestra before," she said.

"There's a first time for everything," he said. "There was a time when Leonard Bernstein had never conducted an orchestra. So he got up and conducted one. And then he had. What's the big mystery about it?"

"Daddy, you're not Leonard Bernstein."

"So? He wasn't Norman Green either. But I can read music. I know music. And what is a conductor? He's not a magician. The musicians can read music. They know how to play their instruments. I'll only sort of pull them together and get them going in the same direction. I can do that."

"Whatever you say," Rachel said. She thought, Waving your pencil at the speakers in the den is not the same thing.

Rachel said good-bye to Florence, and as she went down the stairs, Jerry Mason was coming up, and she had to stop and talk to him. He said he was looking forward to the Fourth of July. Rachel smiled at him and thought, Your daughter hates me. Why? By the time Rachel reached home, Mother had talked to Daddy on the phone and was chain-smoking, pacing the kitchen, furious, and supper was burning on the stove. Rachel turned off the heat and lifted the lid: rice and beans and ground beef. Mother was carnivorous again. Rachel spooned the blackened food into the garbage. Mother looked out the window, oblivious to supper.

"I *knew* something would go wrong! Why did your father ever get involved with that twerp? Of *course* the man's a liar. Never count on people with no talent. Now who is your father going to dig up for a conductor?"

She pulled out another cigarette and lit it off the one she had been smoking. "Darn that Mrs. Dortmeyer. She comes here and cleans, and I can't find the matches anywhere."

Mother went outside, the screen door slammed, and she paced across the driveway, fuming, her arms folded. Obviously Daddy hadn't told her who Hair Ball's replacement would be.

Rachel sat down at the table. Maybe Daddy was right. What's the big deal about conducting? If Hair Ball could do it, why not Daddy? The mail was lying there. Rachel sifted through it, looking for a letter from Phoebe. No letter from Italy, but there was a large brown envelope addressed to Mother from the Office of Admissions, Interlochen Center for the Arts in Interlochen, Michigan.

The envelope had been opened.

Rachel knew a little about Interlochen from the brochure hanging on the bulletin board at music school. Campers there lived in cabins in a pine woods and they all wore uniforms of corduroy knickers and light blue shirts.

She remembered a picture of a big orchestra of kids her age playing with a beautiful lake in the background. Rachel had a sudden scary thought: What if Mother had applied for a job to teach there, and had been accepted, and she and Daddy were getting a divorce? But it wasn't about that. It was about her. A man named Hans Bowron was writing that, yes, they did have an opening for a freshman violinist in the Academy, and an application would be due immediately, as classes would begin in mid-September. There was a scholarship application and a course catalog in the envelope and a letter about dormitory living.

The screen door squeaked, and Rachel stuffed the papers back in the envelope and pretended to be looking at a *Smithsonian* magazine.

Her face felt numb, like wood. The thought was so big she almost couldn't get her mind around it: *They were thinking of sending her away.* And not just for a few weeks in the summer. For a whole school year.

Mother opened up the freezer drawer. "We'll have to start over with dinner. We could thaw these chicken breasts, toss in some beans, and call it a cassoulet. Chop some onions for me, would you, please?"

"I thought you said vegetarian food was more spiritual," Rachel said.

"I did say that. And it is," replied Mother. "And if I'd been very, *very* spiritual, my dear, you would not exist. So—I say let's have chicken."

Rachel got the onions out of the lower cupboard and peeled them and sliced them on the bread board while

Mother defrosted the chicken breasts in the microwave and opened up a can of navy beans. "Now Daddy's going to worry himself sick over this." She paused at the sound of Rachel sniffling. "You're not crying, are you?"

Rachel was weeping from the onions, but underneath the onion tears were tears about Carol and about being a Green and about the long summer, which was quickly heading down the hill to disaster. And tears about her getting on a bus and going away to Interlochen to live among strangers. She looked at Mother's back as she stood at the stove and thought, Why are you doing this to me? Why do you want me out of here? Am I too much trouble? Or are you sending me away so I don't have to be here to watch your marriage break up?

She wiped the tears away on the back of her hand. I mean, look at it, she thought. A man and a woman who hardly have time to talk to each other, who have their heads buried in their own little worlds, who are constantly bickering—her trying to get him to lower his cholesterol and not work so hard, and him trying to get her to lay off the big campaigns and quit smoking, and now he's decided he's a conductor. When Mother finds out about that, she's going to hit the roof. And then she's going to go into one of her black moods. A disaster of a summer, and then what about the fall? If Mother and Daddy asked her to go away, of course she would say yes, so she'd go to Interlochen and start all over trying to make friends. And weeks would pass and nobody would talk to her. Not voluntarily. They'd all hang out with someone popular. That's how it works, there's one queen bee and there's all the drones. So one night she tiptoes down the hall to the queen bee's room and puts her ear to the door and hears the drones in there, gossiping and telling jokes and talking about how much they love this and hate that, and she knocks on the door, and a drone opens it and sees her, Rachel Green, and then everyone in the room is extremely quiet, just like the soft-ball girls in the lunchroom when she sits down by them. *Oh, hi,* they say. And then she realizes the terrible truth. Her weirdness is permanent, she carries it with her every-where. It is on her skin, in her hair, like skunk smell. It will follow her all the days of her life: No matter where she goes, people will look at her and their faces will drop. *Oh. Hi.*

Mother sliced the chicken into strips. She didn't say a word for a long time. Then she stopped and lit another cig-arette. "Grandpa called today. He sounds so old and feeble. He's depressed about losing his hearing. I'm worried about him. My mother is so wrapped up in her fantasy ailments, she wouldn't notice if he wandered off and never came back." She walked to the screen door and blew the smoke out through it. "I was thinking today that, when I was your age, my father found somebody to run his business for a year and he devoted one whole year to my brother and me. He took us for walks in the park, he took us to museums and concerts, and that summer he took us to France. It was the most beautiful summer. We traveled around and I remember we wound up in a small town in Brittany called Landevennec, and we ate lunch in a pretty garden, under an orange tree, and I started crying, and

Papa asked me why, and I said, 'Because we have to go home.'" She sighed. Rachel tried to think of something to say, but couldn't. "I don't know what I'll do when I lose my papa," said Mother, and she began to weep. She went upstairs. Rachel thought, Good, now Daddy can come home and put on a Sibelius symphony and we can all cry together.

Daddy came home at seven-thirty. "Sent out the fliers," he said to Rachel. "The bridge is burned. There's no turning back." He reached up into the high cupboard where he kept the liquor and got down a bottle of red wine and dusted it off. "Got this as a gift from Grandpa Mueller," he said, "and I've been saving it for a special occasion and what's more special than this?" He wound the corkscrew in and braced the bottle between his knees and pulled out the cork.

Mother appeared in the doorway.

"The light of my life, the mother of my child, the woman of my dreams!" said Daddy, holding out a glass of wine to her. They clinked their glasses together.

"I am so sorry about the conductor, Norman," she said.

"Don't be," he said. "It's no problem."

Rachel put the food on the table, chicken swimming in globs of navy beans and onions. The brown envelope from Interlochen was gone: Mother had sneaked it away. Daddy poured a taste of wine for Rachel, and the three of them clinked glasses.

"I am not going to lose the concert," Daddy said. "Most of the orchestra has been hired and it's too late to back out. So, Ingrid, I came to a decision. I'm going to conduct the orchestra myself." He set his glass down, *thunk,* and looked Mother straight in the eye.

"*You?*" she said.

"That's right. Me."

"You're joking, Norman," said Mother.

"I am not joking, Ingrid. I don't claim to be a great conductor but I can manage, and at this point there is no alternative."

"I believe you are serious, Norman," she said.

Rachel grinned at Daddy, and he grinned back.

"I'm sure it'll be good, Dad," she said. "I'm sure it'll be great."

"My debut," said Daddy. "And with my daughter there in the violin section."

"I don't know. They haven't called me yet," Rachel said. "Mr. Amidore only *recommended* me. I'm not hired yet."

Mother reached for a cigarette. "I thought *I* was supposed to be the loose screw in the family," she said. "All of a sudden I feel like the sane one."

After supper, Rachel practiced the Mozart concerto Mr. Amidore had given her. An hour flew by, and by nine-thirty she had memorized the first two pages. Maybe she would be the first student ever to learn an entire concerto in a week. Next Saturday she would amaze him by walking in and playing all three movements perfectly.

She put her violin away and put on a pink flannel night-gown, and went to the bathroom and brushed her teeth.

She looked at her face in the bathroom mirror. "Plain" was the word that came to mind. If only her hair were thicker, she could put it up the way Valerie did, or if it were curly maybe her nose wouldn't look so pointy. She scrubbed her face with a washcloth and slathered lotion on her cheeks. Angie said it was never too early to look after your skin. Mother said the cosmetics industry was the great rip-off of the century. She believed in soap and water, period.

The thought of leaving Sandy Bottom and living in a dormitory in northern Michigan made her feel spooky and scared. The thought of going all that way and then what if she turned out to be a big bust? A really *lousy* violinist. Good enough for a small town, but put her among kids with real talent, who worked hard, and she'd be like a fudge brownie among the crepes suzette. What then? Some nice man at Interlochen would call her to his office, and he'd ask her how she was and she'd say "Fine" and he'd say, "That's good," and then he'd say, "I was thinking, Rachel, that maybe you'd like to try creative writing instead." And another terrible truth would dawn. Not only was she weird, she was also not that good a musician. "You know," he'd say, "it's perfectly normal for a person to try one thing and then go on and try something else, and I think perhaps you ought to try creative writing."

Creative writing. That was where they stick people who can't play, can't dance, can't act, can't sing, and can't draw. Give them a pencil and paper and let them write poems that, no matter what they're like, people will say, "Oh. That's interesting."

"Unfortunately," he'd say, "we don't have any openings in creative writing now, so perhaps you should finish the year at Sandy Bottom, and we'll see if we can't get you in for next fall. Okay?" And he'd smile at her in that smooth professional way, and ease her out of his office, and she'd be back home, Mother and Daddy disappointed in her, Carol a complete stranger, and who would her friend be? Why, it'd be Florence. She'd go spend evenings with Florence, playing cribbage and watching TV and learning how to be a lonely, disappointed woman.

FINAL EXAMS

*F*inal exams were on Wednesday and Thursday. Daddy left early Wednesday morning for his monthly Chamber of Commerce breakfast; he was going to give a speech about business and the arts. Rachel heard him rehearsing it in the bathroom, an odd rumbling sound. He used the word "partnership" rather often. In the kitchen, Mother sat reading the *Register*—on the editorial page was her long letter replying to the high school superintendent's response to her original letter about the importance of teaching Spanish, and she was checking it for any omissions. Rachel sat and ate a toasted frozen waffle and stared at her algebra notebook.

"Do you have a test today?" said Mother.

"Two today, and two tomorrow," said Rachel. "I

thought I understood this stuff, but I don't get it at all. What happens if you add x to y to the third and then multiply it by negative seven n squared? It's absurd! Who cares?"

Rachel closed the notebook and stuffed it in her backpack.

Mother laughed. "I suppose math teaches you to follow the rules, but then life is no good unless you break some of the rules, so I don't know what to tell you. I guess you need to know the rules before you can break them. Anyway, you'll do fine."

Mother said she had a meeting with the Historical Society in the afternoon and wouldn't be home until suppertime. "We're getting people lined up behind this arts center," she said. "Everybody but old Broadbutt."

"You mean Broadbent," said Rachel.

"Whatever," Mother went on.

"He still wants to build his neon asphalt monstrosity. What we're afraid of is that he might bring in bulldozers late one night and knock down the Ramsey Building, so Jerry is organizing a round-the-clock watch, and if we see a demolition crew moving in, we'll sound the alarm and everybody'll go down and surround the building with cars and if need be, chain ourselves to the fence."

"Good luck," said Rachel on her way out the door. "Just don't lie down in the middle of the street, okay? As a favor to me."

"I promise to be good," Mother said.

Rachel didn't look around for Carol when she left the

house that morning. She walked straight to school. You could tell it was final-exam day; the first-floor hallway was quieter than usual, no whooping and clowning around, and there were students leaning against their lockers, thumbing through books, cramming, trying to suck the information off the page by magnetic force and carry it into the classroom and dump it on the test form. Mrs. Erickson's final exam was not so hard: There was a take-home question about *Giants in the Earth,* and there was a classroom question about a poem by Emily Dickinson. "Please take the entire hour to think about this poem and write an essay setting forth your personal view of it—not your 'appreciation' of it as a poem but your own thoughts about what the poem says." A wide-open question, and you were supposed to walk through it and keep going, but Rachel heard whispering behind her—"What does this *mean*? What are you supposed to *do*?" Rachel just put her head down and wrote. That was the point. You were supposed to take the bit between your teeth and run.

> Success is counted sweetest
> By those who ne'er succeed.
> To comprehend a nectar
> Requires sorest need.
>
> Not one of all the purple host
> Who took the flag to-day
> Can tell the definition,
> So clear, of victory,

As he defeated, dying,
On whose forbidden ear
The distant strains of triumph
Burst, agonized and clear.

She started writing. "The poet says that a person has to lose something in order to know its value: For example, I know about friendship because I know about loneliness. The person who has many friends is afraid she may lose them and so maybe she will do anything to keep them. For example, change her own personality and views to be more like her friends. So she will never truly know the thing she craves and is so afraid of losing."

Emily Dickinson wrote about birds and snakes and sunsets as if they contained everything worth knowing; she looked out the window of her father's house in Amherst and saw the entire universe in an acre of orchard and meadow; and Emily Dickinson truly knew about friendship because she was so much alone. Small things were important to her. A little thank-you note was worth writing in exactly the right way, and a letter to a friend was, to her, as important as any poem. She didn't sit down and slap it together. Rachel wrote about that, how a person needed to look at the world and see what is there and not what *ought* to be there according to what you were taught or what you are *afraid* might *not* be there if you don't believe as you ought to. She wrote about her own backyard and about Carol and about seeing people as they are, not as part of your own schemes, but as beautiful beings in their own right. She wrote page after page, pretty good stuff. Mrs. Erickson said, "Time's up," and Rachel stopped writing, but she still had plenty to say. A good test.

A torrential rainstorm came pouring down as school let out. Eighty kids stood in the school entrance under the big stone arch, watching the rain descend in sheets. It fell so hard, the houses across the street were obscured and the streetlights came on. The boys yelled, the girls stood in clusters trying not to notice them, so the boys yelled louder. Every few minutes, a boy would dash out to the street and then come tearing back in, drenched, and everyone laughed at him. Rachel couldn't understand why someone would be so stupid. She stood with Carol and Valerie and the Wilson twins, Megan and Sara.

"So do you think your mom would come and pick us up?" Valerie asked Carol.

"Uh-uh. She's working at the library."

The twins said their mom was at work, too, and their dad was in Madison for the day.

They all looked at Rachel.

Valerie said, "Your mom doesn't drive, does she?"

Megan said, "What do you think? She rides a broom?"

They all laughed, and Rachel looked away. "I'd call her, but she's at a meeting."

"I guess that leaves *my* mom," said Valerie. "Who's got a quarter?" Rachel gave her a quarter and Valerie went off to the pay phone next to the principal's office.

When Mrs. Mason arrived, the rain had let up somewhat. The girls scrunched into the backseat—the front seat was filled with flowers for Mrs. Mason's flower-arranging class. Rachel sat in the middle, her feet on the transmission hump, her elbows close to her sides. Valerie's mother drove fast, and when she turned a corner, they fell over in a heap.

"Wasn't Matthew *funny* in social studies today? I thought I'd *die*!" said Valerie. She had a crush on Matthew Johnson.

"I couldn't believe the things he *said*!" said one of the twins. The four of them laughed, but Rachel was in a different social studies class.

"What? What was so funny?" she asked.

"Oh it's just Matthew," said Carol. "He sits in the back making all these *comments,* and we're sitting back there practically *dying*. Donaldson has his back to us, writing on the board, and Matthew is, like, sitting there humming in this tiny high voice and we're sitting there choking to death."

"Oh," said Rachel.

Mrs. Mason looked in the rearview mirror and smiled, and they went through a stop sign, narrowly missing a blue van that blasted its horn—she didn't even blink. "Oh, Val, I picked up the pizza crusts for your party. I got six. I hope that's enough.

"Thanks, Mom." Valerie turned to Megan. "You guys are bringing your CDs, right?"

"Yeah. What time?"

"Six, six-thirty.

Rachel felt sick. The windows were closed and the side windows were fogged up; there didn't seem to be any oxygen left to breathe. She sat stiffly, between Valerie and Megan, trying not to touch them, thinking to herself, *Please don't throw up now. Don't vomit. Not now. Wait.*

"So did you invite Matthew?" Sara asked. There was laughter.

"Maybe he'll just show up." said Sara. "Tell him it's a pajama party—he'll be there."

"No, tell him it's a *lingerie* party," said Megan. Valerie reached in front of Rachel and punched Megan in the shoulder.

Mrs. Mason was studying Rachel in the mirror. When Rachel caught her eye in the mirror, Mrs. Mason managed to smile. "So I imagine you keep pretty busy with your music, huh, Rachel?"

"Yes, I guess so," said Rachel. The car pulled up between the Green and Wyman houses. Carol got out, then Rachel. Carol stopped, as if to say something, but Rachel walked up the driveway and into the house. It was empty. She put her books on the table, and just as she did, the phone rang. It was Carol.

"I called to say I'm sorry," she said.

"Oh, it's all right," said Rachel.

"I really am sorry. The reason you weren't invited was because it's a team party—the softball team—but it was mean to talk about it in front of you. I'm sorry."

"Oh, that didn't bother me," Rachel said coolly. "I don't care."

"Well, anyway, I'm sorry about it," said Carol.

"I don't care if I'm invited to parties or not. I got over

that a long time ago. I couldn't care less," said Rachel. Thinking to herself, You lie like a rug.

"Well, you got sort of quiet so I thought maybe your feelings were hurt," said Carol.

"*Ha!*" said Rachel. "Not me. I've got skin like an old turtle."

"Rachel, is something wrong?"

"No, not at all. Why?"

"Because you get so quiet sometimes. You just disappear. I don't know. You can be sitting there, and then it's like you're not there anymore. I wish I knew what you were thinking about."

"I think about a lot of things," said Rachel. "I just don't have anybody to talk to about them, that's all."

It was a bad thing to say. Carol was hurt. She could tell by the way Carol said, "Oh. Sorry." Rachel wished she could take the words back, but there was no way to. Maybe it was the truth. It hung there between them.

"What can't you talk to me about?" said Carol.

"Lots of things."

"Like what?"

"It's not important."

"No, tell me."

"If I could tell you about them, I would, but I can't, so why talk about it?"

Rachel went up to her room, feeling miserable about Carol. It was nice of Carol to call, she thought, but it would have been nicer if Carol had said something in the car. But maybe those softball girls were Carol's true friends, so what was the point of worrying about it?

She opened her bookbag and got out Mrs. Erickson's take-home question—they had read *Giants in the Earth* and the assignment was to write about the hero and heroine, Per and Beret Hansa, poor immigrants who had left Norway and come to the barren plains of South Dakota: Could the story have happened in a different way?

The book was depressing: Per, the farmer, died in a snowstorm trying to find the Lutheran minister to come and give communion to Per's friend Hans Olsa who was sick—Rachel thought that Per and Beret deserved a little happiness after all they had gone through. So she wrote a new version, in which Per skied into the storm and ran smack into the doctor who was also on skis, trying to reach them, and the doctor gave the sick man a new serum that cured him, and spring came, and when the snow melted, Beret and Per found traces of gold in their cellar where the frost had heaved up the floor, and when he dug down into the rich black dirt, Per found a number of rather valuable nuggets—about six thousand dollars' worth, to be exact, which was a pile of money back then, enough to enable the Hansas to move to Minneapolis and for their son Peder Victorious to study the violin.

Thursday morning Daddy got all sentimental about it being the last day of school. The end of eighth grade. "This fall, you'll be a freshman," he said. "Hard to believe. I remember taking you to your first day of kindergarten. I walked in the front door with you, and there were several weeping children there, being comforted by their mothers, and you looked up at me and said, 'I think you're supposed to go now.' And you marched down the hall and into Mrs. Shaver's room and never looked back."

"And then *you* burst into tears," said Mother.

"I did," said Daddy. "Of course I did."

Mr. Gilbert's history exam was so easy that Rachel finished in ten minutes. Multiple choice: *The Civil War began in 1861 and ended in 186___—(a) 2 (b) 9 (c) 5 (d) 4.* With Mr. Gilbert, *c* was the correct answer about seventy-five percent of the time; he was a man of regular habits. He sat behind his desk, feet up, clipping his fingernails and reading the Milwaukee paper and sneaking salted peanuts out of a big bag he kept in his top drawer. Rachel cruised through the test. *Which of the following were not Northern generals in the Civil War? (a) George McClellan (b) Ambrose Burnside (c) Dwight D. Eisenhower (d) George Custer.* They just got sillier and sillier. Poor Gilbert must have written the test late last night. She imagined him coming home from playing eighteen holes of golf, stowing his clubs in the closet, putting a frozen pork dinner in the microwave, sliding a Three Stooges movie in the VCR, eating dinner on the couch, falling asleep, waking up at three A.M. the TV screen all snowy, static blaring, and him suddenly thinking, Oh no! Gotta write the exam!

She finished it and put it over to the side of her desk and took out her algebra book and opened it to the chapter on complex fractions, her weak suit, and pored over the first problem, and then she felt the great shadow of Mr. Gilbert over her.

"You're not allowed to look up the answers!" he barked.

She looked up and blinked. "I'm finished," she said.

"That's against the rules. I'm surprised at you." He snatched the test off her desk and ripped it into strips and tossed them down at her.

"This is an algebra book," she said. There was a flurry of whispering behind her.

"I don't care what kind of book it is," he said. "You're not allowed to look in *any* book until you turn in your test. Did you turn in your test? No, you did not. So you get an F."

"But this is *algebra*." Her voice was weak and trembly.

"I'm not arguing with you," he said. "There's such a thing as rules, you know. You don't go browsing around in a book with your test paper sitting there. I don't know what book that is. For all I know, that could be your history book." He wheeled away and took his seat behind his desk and resumed reading his newspaper.

It was so stupid. The test was no test at all, there was no *need* to cheat, and all he had to do was look at the book and he could see it was an algebra book. She picked up the pieces of her test and stood up and walked to the side of his desk. Her heart pounded, she told herself *Don't cry, don't you dare cry,* and she said, "Mr. Gilbert?"

He lowered the newspaper and looked at her coldly.

"Mr. Gilbert, this is not fair. I finished the test and I was studying algebra. I would like my test to be graded."

She drew a deep breath.

He put the newspaper down. "I'll tell you what, Miss Green," he said. "Why don't you take this down to the principal's office?" He reached for a pad of paper and scribbled a note and folded it. "Here," he said. "Go see Mr. Foster." He handed her the note and then he reached for the shreds of test. "I'll take that," he said.

"No," she said. "I want him to see this."

She marched down the empty hallway of lockers and down the gloomy green stairwell, and into the office where Miss Nelson, the receptionist, peered at her wearily through rhinestone-studded glasses and nodded toward the waiting area. Rachel sat. She waited for a half hour, watching Miss Nelson, the skinniest woman she had ever seen, as she banged away at her typewriter, her big plastic bracelets clattering, her brown permed hair bouncing, and every few bangs, she pushed her glasses up on her nose.

Finally, Mr. Foster came in, clutching an armload of papers and folders. He was a short worried-faced man with wiry black curly hair thinning on top and black horn-rim glasses and almost no chin. He listened as Rachel told her side of the story, and then Mr. Gilbert came in, all huffy, and said he thought he saw Rachel looking in the algebra book and changing the answers on her quiz—"her algebra book or whatever book it was, I don't know, it could have been her history book," he said. What a big fat liar he was, she thought. He *knew* it was her algebra book and he *knew* he hadn't seen her change any answers.

"I did *not* change answers," she said, and she gave Mr. Foster the shredded test, and he pieced it together and examined it. "Looks fine to me," he said. "I don't see any erasures or revisions here." He looked at Mr. Gilbert: "I think what we have here is a misunderstanding."

"No misunderstanding on my part," said Mr. Gilbert.

The upshot was that, though all the answers were correct, she would get a B on the test, which would still give her an A in the course. Mr. Gilbert rolled his eyes and marked it B, and Mr. Foster wrote Rachel a late slip to get her into algebra class, which was almost over by then, so she had to stay after school to take her algebra test, which was not that hard, it turned out. The building was deserted when she cleaned out her locker. The end of the school year. What a day. "Good-bye, old locker," she said. "Don't get too lonely without me." She closed the door with a loud *k-chank*. "Good-bye, school. I may not be back, you know." Her footsteps echoed in the hall, like a scene in a movie: the heroine, moving on.

When Rachel got home Mrs. Dortmeyer was down on her hands and knees scrubbing the kitchen floor. She turned and said, "Hi, Rachel. Long time no see." Rachel set her bookbag down on the kitchen table. Mother's stuff was strewn across it. A drawing of the arts center and some letters and clippings about education.

The phone rang; she didn't want to answer it. Then Mrs. Dortmeyer picked it up. "Green house," she said. That struck Rachel as funny. The thought of a big glass house with rows of potted petunias and the Greens

97

tromping around in rubber boots, their thumbs over the ends of hoses, making a fine spray.

"Phone is for you, Rachel," said Mrs. Dortmeyer.

"Could you take a message?" Rachel said, but Mrs. Dortmeyer had gone back to scrubbing, and the telephone lay there on the counter. Rachel wiped her eyes and blew her nose on a paper napkin. She picked up the phone and said hello. It was Daddy. "Congratulations," he said. "How'd you do? Straight A's again?"

"It was fine," she said. She didn't tell about Mr. Gilbert. Daddy would only get upset.

When she hung up the phone, Mrs. Dortmeyer had sat down at the table, a cup of coffee in hand. She put a heaping teaspoon of sugar in it, stirred, and said, "Say, you people ever go up to that Moon Shadow Café, up there near Lake City? Boy, it's good. Get a nice steak dinner, have a few beers. They got dancing in the back. It's fixed up real nice out there, new carpet and everything. And on Friday nights—ladies special from seven to ten—two drinks for one. I bet your parents would love it. They ever go up there?"

"No, they pretty much just stay home." Rachel couldn't imagine Mother and Daddy going to a roadhouse for a steak and drinks.

"They'd love it," Mrs. Dortmeyer said. She put her coffee cup in the sink and got down on her hands and knees and started in on the kitchen floor.

Rachel wished she would hurry up and leave. It was good to have a conscientious cleaning lady, but it took her hours to get done and she was such a presence in the house, lumbering from room to room, running the vacuum, looking at their stuff, seeing their lives laid out in front of her. She knew everything in Rachel's room, saw all of Mother's papers, she picked up Daddy's CDs and put them back on the shelves all out of order. She saw their dirty clothes. Once she put a red shirt in the washer with some white things and Daddy wound up with pink underwear. "I can't run around in pink underwear," he said. Mother laughed and said, "You can too. Unless you can find me another cleaning lady."

Mrs. Dortmeyer finished scrubbing the floor and picked up the pail of water and dumped it down the drain. The acrid smell of the cleaner drifted across the room. "Okay. Guess that about does it for today."

Mother came home five minutes after Mrs. Dortmeyer left. She put her canvas bag stuffed with papers on the piano bench, walked into the kitchen, lit a cigarette, and looked around. "What is that woman using for cleaner? The place smells like a toxic waste site," she said. "What she's dumping down the drains is probably enough to give the whole town pancreatic cancer. I buy baking soda in bulk to clean with and then she comes here with gallons of poison. I just can't win with that woman."

She wished Mother would ask, "How did your exams go today?" so she could tell her about standing up to Mr. Gilbert, but Mother was off in her own world as usual.

That night Mother burned the dinner again. She was playing Rachmaninoff while the kitchen filled with smoke; she claimed she couldn't smell anything except Mrs.

Dortmeyer's ammonia, so it wasn't her fault. The smoke alarm screamed, Rachel yanked the oven open, and Daddy waved wet towels, and they ate what was salvageable, the windows wide open. It was a quiet supper. Mother was still fuming about Mrs. Dortmeyer and Daddy talked a little about an interesting problem in yogurt packaging, and nobody said a word about the Fourth of July.

After supper, Mother parked her typewriter on the kitchen table and sat for a while staring out at the backyard, the weeds green and lush in the flower beds, and then she sat up straight, put a sheet of paper in the typewriter, and started pounding away. The table shook, the words marched across the page like an army of angry ants.

"Who are you writing to?" Rachel said.

"What?"

"I said, who are you writing to?"

"You mean to *whom* am I writing? I am writing to Mr. Broadbent, telling him that he and his ilk do not control this town and that someday he will walk through the front door of the Sandy Bottom Arts Center and he will be grateful that I persevered and that he did not."

Rachel went up to her room. Clearly, Mother was in a state of hypergraphia; after the missive to Mayor Broadbent, she would probably pound out another to the *Register* and one to Reverend Sykes.

Daddy was camped in the den. He'd play two minutes of Beethoven and then suddenly that stopped and a song by Schubert started, and halfway through that he switched to a Prokofiev symphony.

Rachel stood in front of her mirror with a hairbrush, trying to decide if her hair looked better parted on the side, when Mother yelled up the stairs, "Telephone. For you!"

Rachel ran into her parents bedroom and picked up the extension.

"Rachel Green?" A man's voice.

"Yes, that's me."

"This is John Robbins calling from Milwaukee. I got your name from Rudy Amidore. Would you be available to play four concerts with the Dairyland Symphony Orchestra this summer?"

He told her the dates, Oshkosh, Eau Claire, Menomonie—and the first one was Sandy Bottom on July Fourth.

"Yes," said Rachel. "I think I'll be free on those days."

"Good. Then I'll send you a contract and the schedule. We can pay musicians' union scale, which is $75 per concert, $300 for the series, and we'll deduct $75 from that to pay for your union membership, so it'd be $225, which you'd get half of on July fifteenth, the remainder on the thirtieth."

"That sounds fine to me," she said. "Thanks."

Rachel hung up the phone. Her heart was pounding. She ran downstairs two steps at a time.

"Hey! Guess what! They called! I'm hired! I'm playing in the orchestra!"

Daddy jumped up from his chair in the den and hugged her. "I was wondering when you'd start supporting your parents. Now I can quit the dairy and go to conducting school!" Mother hugged her and said, "Bravo, sweetheart! This calls for a celebration—let's have ice cream!"

Rachel felt absolutely gorgeously wonderful—for about two minutes—and then, just when it seemed *so* incredibly wonderful—her first music job!—she imagined Daddy up on the podium, lurching around, his arms waving like a windmill, and the orchestra going off in all directions, and everyone in Sandy Bottom watching, gawking, as the orchestra crashes through a Mozart concerto and Daddy shouting and dogs howling and Mother standing up and yelling, "That's not how it's supposed to sound!" Finally the music stops with a big *ker-thunk-splat*, and everyone laughs their heads off, and Rachel moves to Milwaukee and changes her name to Ramona Gray. Please, she thought, have mercy on us, God. It's bad enough to be oddballs. Don't let us make fools of ourselves on top of it.

 *8*

THE BAD LESSON

*R*achel woke up. It was still dark out, dark in her bedroom except for the thin light under the door from the hallway. There were voices. She sat up in bed and listened hard. It was Daddy moaning in the bathroom. "I feel like I'm going to die," he said. "Or worse." She looked at the clock: it was three A.M.

"It's only something you ate," said Mother.

"I don't know what it was, but . . ." Daddy's voice trailed off into a deep groan. Then the bathroom door closed and she heard water running and more groaning. She opened her door and looked into the hallway. Mother stood at the other end in her long white nightgown, her hair cascading down her back. "What's the matter with him?" said Rachel. "Should I call someone?"

"No. He's sick to his stomach, that's all. You don't feel sick, do you?" Rachel shook her head. "Good. Neither do I. Must've been something he found on his own. Anyway, nothing to do but let him throw up, so you go back to bed."

In the morning, Daddy stayed in bed. Mother brought him a tray with toast and tea, and he said the sight of it made him gag. Rachel knocked on the door and heard a faint "Yes?" and went in and Daddy peered out from under the covers, his eyes bloodshot, his hair mussed, looking glum and pitiful. She stood over him and stroked his hair. "I learned a new term from Mother. *Driving the porcelain bus*. Did you ever hear that before?"

"It's not funny," he said.

"I'm not saying it's funny," she said. "But Mother told me all of these different phrases that mean puke. Like *hitting the cookie tin*. Or *talking to Ralph on the big white phone*."

"I don't want to know them," he said. But he looked up at her and smiled. "Someday, when your mother is feeling under the weather, I'll tell you about the first time she drank beer. A very colorful story."

"Are you feeling better?" said Rachel.

"I feel like I'm ready to go into the nursing home," he said. "But I'll be okay."

He was too weak to drive her to Oshkosh for her violin lesson, so after breakfast, Mother got dressed up in black slacks and a turquoise blouse and backed the car out of the garage. Rachel noticed Mother had left her pack of cigarettes sitting on the kitchen counter. She called out a cheerful good-bye to Daddy upstairs and heard his faint reply.

Mother was a good driver, but she didn't believe in poking along and enjoying the scenery: Mother drove to *get there* and she drove fast and when she came to an open stretch, she liked to fly. As she drove through town, she pulled from under the seat a small black box like a radio and plugged it into the cigarette lighter. "What's that?" said Rachel. "Never mind," said Mother. "Is it a radar detector?" "Never mind," said Mother. "It *is* a radar detector, isn't it?"

"It is," said Mother. "And I'm not interested in discussing it with you."

"I'm just surprised, that's all. When did you get it?"

Mother set the box on the dashboard and pressed a switch on top of it and a red light glowed and it beeped a shrill beep. "Tuesday," she said.

"Aren't they illegal?" said Rachel.

"Technically, yes," said Mother.

"Technically illegal? What does that mean?" Rachel was enjoying this conversation already. It was wonderful to find something that Mother did *not* want to talk about. "I mean, either it's legal or it's illegal. Right?"

They were leaving the Sandy Bottom town limits now, and a long straight section of road lay ahead, between great green expanses of corn and soybeans, and Mother accelerated.

"Darling," she said, "there are small towns in

Wisconsin that like to earn money by hiding a patrolman in the weeds where the speed limit goes from fifty-five to thirty, who picks off motorists like he was shooting pigeons in the park.

"This little box is simply an armored vest for pigeons, that's all."

They came up behind a big Buick driven by a tiny old man, his head barely visible above the driver's seat, cruising at forty-five, and Mother zoomed around him without slowing down. She was going almost seventy. She passed a tractor pulling a manure spreader, and an old green pickup truck with a bumper sticker that said GET A FEELING FOR FUR: SLAM A DOOR ON YOUR FINGERS. It was driven by a man with a long ponytail who waved as they passed.

"Bet he's from the old hippie commune over by Sunrise," said Mother. "Nice people, but I never understood that commune business. All these smart people who didn't know a thing about farming or carpentry trying to raise organic crops in poor soil while they lived in shacks without heat or hot water. Most of them got mad at each other after a while and broke up and had nothing whatsoever to show for it. But they were idealists. You have to give them credit for that."

"Speaking of idealists—" said Rachel. Mother groaned. "Don't you think," said Rachel, "that if you disagree with a law, you ought to change it? Not ignore it?"

"Darling child," said Mother, "the speed limits in Wisconsin are like the educational system, aimed at the lowest common denominator. They're speeds for geezers.

Any person with normal reflexes and some driving experience can safely drive *well* over the speed limit."

"So it's all right if I do too when I start driving?"

Mother sighed. She took her foot off the gas and the speedometer dropped to seventy, sixty-five, sixty. "Let's talk about something else," she said.

Rachel wanted to ask about Interlochen, but she didn't want to sound *hurt* or accusing and get Mother all defensive and worried, so they talked about Mozart instead, their favorite pieces of his. "That 'Ave Verum'—I tell you, my choir opens their mouths and sings the *Ave* and I just fall apart," said Mother. "Even though some of them are flat. I get tears in my eyes." They arrived in Oshkosh twenty minutes early and Mother parked in front of the music school and went to the front desk and wrote out a check for the next two lessons. "I'll be back in an hour or so," she said. "And later I want to hear the string en-semble."

Rachel waited for Mr. Amidore in the hallway, and when she took out her violin, in walked Scott Miller with his cello, grinning at her.

"Hi, Scott. You got a new cello, didn't you?" she said. "Wow. It's beautiful. Is it a lot better than your old one?"

"*I* think so," he said. He held it up to the light so she could get a better look. He plucked the strings. "No one knows exactly who made it, but it's nineteenth-century Italian, and it has a really big warm sound. It practically plays itself."

Then he looked up and down the hall and leaned

forward and said, "I heard you got hired for that summer orchestra. Is that right?" Rachel nodded. He said, "So did I."

"You *did*?" she cried, and then immediately blushed. "I mean, of course you did. You should. You're good. That's great. I can't wait till it starts."

He said, "It'll be interesting to play with all those characters. I heard there's an old guy in the cello section with fish on his breath who hums as he plays. He dyes his hair black but it looks purple under the lights. He likes to smoke little black cigars and sneak sips of port out of a hip flask. And he calls everyone sweetheart. Unless you're under forty. Then he calls you kid.

"They're all from Milwaukee, I guess. Or Madison. I suppose they'll think we're just a couple of yokels from the sticks," said Scott.

"Who cares?" said Rachel. "If they don't like it, it's their problem, not ours." As soon as she said it, she thought: Look out. Mother Alert. You're sounding just like her.

"Just kidding," he said. He drifted away. She hoped she hadn't hurt his feelings. Sometimes, she slipped and got too Mother-like, too blunt, like Mother telling a soprano in choir "You're flat," instead of saying, as some people would, "I'm sorry, maybe it's me, but I wonder if it might not be a good idea for some of us to check our pitch on that note to make sure that we're hitting the note absolutely right in the middle and not on the edge, okay?" That's how some people would say it. Mother said "You're flat" because you were flat, no doubt about it. Flat is flat. But if the soprano felt hurt, if the abruptness of it felt hostile to her, then you ought to be diplomatic, shouldn't you?

Rachel waited for Mr. Amidore to finish his ten o'clock lesson. She held her violin like a guitar and plucked out "Old MacDonald Had a Farm" in octaves. Scott Miller was so sweet and friendly—how amazing that he'd be in the summer orchestra with her! Why would he be worried that someone might think he was a hick, though? So maybe someone *would*—so what? All that mattered was how you played. That was the great thing about music—you could always tell a good player from a bad one, no doubt about it—in two minutes, you could tell who could play and who was faking it—and if you played well, then it didn't matter if your hair stuck straight up and your ears straight out, you were a *musician*.

At eleven o'clock, the door popped open, and a boy with a mop of blond hair came out with his head bowed and his violin case hanging limply from his left hand. He sniffled as he got his jacket down from the coat hook. "See you next week, Josh," said Mr. Amidore. He looked at Rachel, his mouth firm, his eyes narrowed. "Come in, Rachel." He turned. The boy looked at Mr. Amidore, disappearing into his studio, and wrinkled up his face and stuck out his tongue.

"Big fat pig," he muttered.

Once in a while, Mr. Amidore got in a bad mood. He crabbed at you for how you held the violin, and even if you played pretty well he didn't bother to say so, and if you made mistakes he practically chewed your leg off. This appeared to be one of his bad days.

Rachel had been excited about surprising him with her mastery of the Mozart concerto, but now she had her doubts. She took her place by the window, a patch of sunshine at her feet, and Mr. Amidore plunked out the A on the piano and she tuned her violin. He paced back and forth, clearing his throat, and blew his nose. He did not inquire about her parents. He seemed to have other things on his mind.

He had her play a few scales and said, "Okay, enough of that, let's hear what you did with the Mozart. I hope you did better than Josh and that Vivaldi. The kid doesn't practice a lick and then he comes in here and butchers it, absolutely walks all over it, wastes your time, and then you try to teach him and he goes to pieces—oh well, let's hear it."

She smiled at him sweetly. "Mr. Amidore, I just want to thank you for recommending me for the orchestra. They called me to play those concerts this summer, and I am so happy! Thank you."

"Good," he said. "You're welcome. The Mozart now— let's hear it."

Rachel put the music on the music stand but didn't open the page. She figured Mr. Amidore would be impresssed that she had already memorized the first movement. She raised her bow and began to play and right away he stopped her. "What is this? John Philip Sousa? Start again."

She put her bow on the string and played the phrase softer.

"No! More sound!"

She played it louder. She went on. Out of the corner of her eye, she could see him shaking his head, but she kept going. And then suddenly she stopped. Her mind was a blank. What came next? Where was she? She tried to start again and again her mind went blank and her fingers froze.

"What's the matter with you? Play!" Mr. Amidore strode over to the music stand. "Aha! Why do you have the music closed? You don't know this piece! Again from the top!" He opened the music to the first page and jabbed at the first bar with his finger.

Rachel wished he would lower his voice a little and not stand two feet behind her. She could hear him sighing, and his cologne was too strong. She started again and made it through the first phrase, and then he grabbed her right wrist, and the bow screeched on the strings. "Good grief, why do you hold the bow like that? Have *I* ever told you to grab hold of it like that? Like a hawk clutching a dead rat? I think not! Look at how stiff your fingers are, and your right shoulder is all hunched up—you look like a witch! This is impossible—you can't play like this! A dying *mosquito* gets more sound than that! Look. Do like this."

Mr. Amidore picked up his bow and showed her. It looked exactly like what she had been doing, she thought.

"Okay, start again, only this time *read the music*. You can't memorize something you don't even know how to play."

Rachel played again. Mr. Amidore threw up his hands. "Look at you! The bow just skates around, you may as well

111

play with a piece of wet spaghetti, and you'll never get a decent spiccato like that. Spiccato! Know what that means? It means the bow *bounces* on the strings! You don't glue the bow to the strings! Let it bounce!" He sighed and turned away, and she put her bow up and played again, and this time he let her get to the end of the movement. And then he sat down on the sofa next to a pile of music and sighed.

"Have you ever heard this piece? You must have, but you play it like Brahms. This is *Mozart*. Light, elegant, youthful, innocent—this is not some big brooding romantic concerto where you're allowed some shlipping and shliding around. And what's with the great big cat vibrato?"

Tears of humiliation welled up in Rachel's eyes, but she blinked them back in.

Mr. Amidore looked at her mournfully. "Am I being too hard on you? I'm sorry, but playing the violin is not easy. You have to be willing to work. It's a *privilege* to be a musician, and it takes skill and finesse and style and intelligence! It is not like riding a bike—you can train a chimpanzee to do that. If you don't want to work hard, then it's much better to just quit now—hang it up, cash it in. Don't waste your time or mine."

Rachel's throat felt tight and achy. She didn't say a word.

Was this the same Mr. Amidore who loved her and helped her and told her how well she was doing? Maybe she had no talent, and couldn't play spiccato and her vibrato was ugly and she was wasting his time and she ought to learn how to play softball instead and talk to boys and be popular.

Mr. Amidore had to say it twice before she heard him. "Play just a scale very slowly—this time without that claw holding on to the bow." She tried, but her hand shook, and now the bow felt completely foreign to her. It wasn't a violin bow anymore, it was a hockey stick, a branch off a tree, a club, that she was being forced to hold in the most awkward way imaginable.

As she played, he kept saying, "Relax, loosen up those fingers!"

But her fingers felt weak and slippery with sweat, and then the bow dropped right out of her hand and fell on the floor. Without a word, he picked it up and handed it back to her.

It was a long, long hour. Rachel put her violin away without a word. She thought, Now I don't even know how to hold a bow! They'll have to send me back to Suzuki with the four-year-olds and learn to play "Twinkle, Twinkle, Little Star" and "Go Tell Aunt Rhody"!

As she closed the door, Mr. Amidore said, "I"m sorry if I was hard on you, forgive me." And the door shut and the tears came gushing out. Luckily for her, the hallway was deserted. She ran straight to the bathroom and into one of the stalls and latched the door and stood and cried. And then she heard snuffling from the stall next to hers.

"What's wrong?" she said.

A trembly girl's voice said, "I played really bad for my lesson and now they won't let me be in the summer recital and my mom is going to be mad!"

"What do you play?" asked Rachel.

"Clarinet."

"What's your name?"

"Melanie."

Rachel picked up her violin and walked out of the stall and set the violin on a ledge and washed her hands. Then she put cold water on a paper towel and held it over her eyes. "Come out and wash your face, Melanie. You'll feel better." she said. The girl crept out of the stall and stood at the sink next to Rachel's and ran the cold water and leaned down and splashed water on her face.

"The reason you played bad, Melanie, is that you're getting better so fast that it's hard to keep up with yourself."

The girl looked up at her, tears in her blue eyes, her blond bangs hanging damply on her forehead. "Really?" she said.

"Of course," Rachel said. "If you stay at the same level week after week, you'll always sound okay. It's when you're learning a lot of new stuff that you goof up. Mistakes are a sign that you're doing better."

Rachel wasn't sure if there was much truth to it or not, but it seemed to make Melanie feel better. She smiled and said, "I've heard you play in the string group. You're really good."

"Thank you," said Rachel. "But when I was your age, I could hardly play at all. Heck, when you start out on the violin, the sounds you make are so terrible, everybody has to stuff cotton in their ears. You practice for an hour and you come downstairs and everybody's hiding in the base-ment."

Melanie laughed. Rachel gave her a comb and she combed her bangs and they went out the door together. Mother was waiting in the hall. She smiled at Melanie, and when the little girl walked on, Mother whispered to Rachel, "I need a cigarette. Mr. Amidore smokes, doesn't he?"

"Yes, he does, but I can't ask him. I didn't have a very good lesson today."

"Oh," said Mother.

String ensemble was fun. They played through an arrangement of Dvořák bagatelles, and Scott and Rachel sat opposite each other, and when she looked up at him, he was looking at her, and he smiled. Mr. Amidore played too. He sat next to Rachel and there were no lectures about how to hold the bow or what the music was supposed to sound like: They simply played it through from beginning to end, and after the first piece, they looked around, all of them, and smiled at each other, and Mr. Amidore turned to the violins and said, "Bravo!"

Mr. Amidore looked up and saw Mother and said, "Mrs. Green! There's a piano part, you know!" And Mother walked right up and sat at the big Steinway and opened the music—she wasn't shy—and Mr. Amidore said, "Okay, from the top!" and he gave a big upbeat with his head and they launched into the second piece, a sad sweet tune that made Rachel think of October and the smoke from piles of dead leaves burning and everyone standing around in the chill and watching the sparks fly up to the stars. It sounded so lovely, she wished it would go on and on.

It ended and Mr. Amidore turned the page and sat quietly. Rachel thought maybe he would say something about Dvořák and how it should be played or tell Mike the bass player that he had been rushing a little bit, but Mr. Amidore seemed content simply to play with them. He raised his bow again and leaned forward and away they went into a waltz.

"I didn't know there were so many ups and downs in music," Rachel said to Mother on the way home. "I mean, one day you think you're playing great, and the next day it's garbage." Mother murmured something. "It'd be nice to get to where you sort of level out," said Rachel.

The car was speeding down the road past acres of bare dirt fields. It was a sod farm, and they'd just shaved off a few acres of sod and brought in fresh dirt to plant a new crop. Then, around the curve, the ruins of a gas station and a stretch of birches and pines. The radar detector sat on the dashboard, the red light glowed.

"Can I ask you something?" she said to Mother.

"*May* I ask you something," said Mother. "What is it?"

"Are you and Daddy happy? I mean, are you glad you married each other?"

"Of course we are!" Mother glanced at her.

"Well, then is it some problem with me?"

"Is *what* a problem?"

Rachel was quiet for a while. She wanted to say it right. Finally, she said, "I know it's wrong to look at mail that isn't addressed to you, but the other day I saw that envelope from Interlochen, and it was open and it didn't look like a personal letter, so I looked, and I saw the application for the Academy and I'm wondering why you want me to go there."

The car swerved a little over the middle line. "Rachel, darling! It has nothing to do with you being a problem. Or Daddy and me. It's a school for kids in the arts, it's as simple as that. I thought we should consider it. Talk about it, think about it, and make a choice. That's all. You thought we were trying to get rid of you? Honey—" Mother reached over and touched Rachel's hand. "You're the dearest person who ever was!"

"So tell me about this school," said Rachel. "And don't drive so fast." She turned off the radar detector and it made a sad little dying beep.

Mother talked about why she was angry at the Sandy Bottom school district. They were cutting corners left and right, cutting music instruction and art and Spanish and Latin and calculus and trigonometry, and when you did that, it was like selling off the two-thirds of the Grand Canyon that most tourists never set foot in, and making it the Okay Canyon, the Medium Canyon.

"The school just feels dead to me," said Mother. "All those troubled kids and bored kids and overworked teachers and some truly lousy teachers—but I'm glad to put up a fight and sometimes I even win one. But now we're getting into a battle I can't win, darling. And that's over computers.

117

"Everybody's in love with computers. Especially the school board. Computers are cheap, cheap, cheap, compared to hiring a teacher. So you plant a kid in front of a screen, hook him up to the Internet, throw a bunch of educational programming at him, he's quiet for hours, he's busy, and everybody's happy. Except it doesn't really teach. All it produces are these little test-takers and score-makers. There's nothing here." Mother tapped her heart. "No soul.

"I think you deserve better. A school where you can be yourself, be a musician, and not worry about anyone thinking you're a creep just because you have a fiddle under your chin."

The road ran alongside the river now, and Sandy Bottom was just ahead, the water tower high over the trees and the Zion Methodist steeple, the dome of the Catholic church, and the water tank atop the dairy. A man stood fishing in the river, a boy beside him, and a dog, and a little ways beyond them, where the river widened above the old dam, a boy swung out over the water clinging to a long rope and at the end of the long arc he flew free, hanging briefly in the air, his arms and legs spread, white, naked, and dropped into the river with a big cannonball splash. And then Mother slowed down, past the truck garden where she often went to buy fresh produce, corn and tomatoes and asparagus especially, and then the boulevard trees began, the lawns, the little stucco and frame bungalows of their hometown.

"What's wrong with studying with Mr. Amidore?" said Rachel. "Don't you think he's good?"

"Of course I do. But going to Oshkosh once a week isn't enough. And I see how happy you are in string ensemble, and I wish you could be happy like that every day and not just on Saturdays."

"I *like* Sandy Bottom, though," said Rachel.

"Good," said Mother. "So do I, sometimes."

But the moment Rachel said she liked Sandy Bottom, she thought: Do you really? Or are you simply afraid to let go of it? Emily Dickinson didn't live all her life in Amherst: She lived in Washington for a while too, and saw Boston and Philadelphia, and got around. So when she came back to Amherst, she knew it better for having been away from it.

"Of course, the decision is yours," said Mother. "Daddy and I would *never* send you away if you didn't want to go. And of course we'd visit you up there—it's not that far. Anyway, it's just something to consider. I didn't want to bring it up until after the Fourth, when things calm down around here."

Rachel felt better. They rode down Main Street, past the park and band shell, and turned onto Prairie Avenue. "I love you," she said.

Mother looked over and smiled her beautiful smile. "I love you, too."

Mother pulled into the driveway, and Daddy was at the back door, in his bathrobe, looking ill. "How's the patient?" said Mother.

"There is a dead chipmunk in the washer," said Daddy. "Would you mind dealing with it?"

So Mother got a pair of tongs and a garbage bag and went downstairs to retrieve the chipmunk. Daddy did not have the stomach for such things. He went to the den and closed the door and out came Tchaikovsky's *Serenade for Strings*, the big hymnlike opening. Rachel went upstairs and took out the Mozart concerto, but she was tired and it was hard to concentrate, and nothing seemed to work. Her fingers felt like old rubber bands, and the hard parts seemed much more difficult; she played the fast skittery run up to a high A, played it over and over and over, missing it every time. Then she went on to a simple passage, slow and melodic, but that didn't sound right either. It felt dull and lifeless.

She stopped and put the violin away without bothering to wipe the rosin off the strings. Once, when he was in a good mood, Mr. Amidore had told her, "If, after a half hour, things aren't working, take a break. Don't beat yourself over the head with it." She went downstairs. Mother was in the kitchen, smoking a cigarette.

"Not a good way to die, in a washer," she said. "He ate holes in Daddy's shirt, but there's not much nourishment in a shirt."

"Yucchhh," said Rachel. "Where'd you put him?"

"Put him in a hole by where the roses used to be."

Rachel phoned Carol. Angie answered. She said Carol was over at Valerie's.

"Do you have Valerie's number or should I find it for you?" asked Angie.

"Oh, no, I have it," said Rachel.

"Haven't seen much of you lately. How are you doing?"

"I'm fine, thanks."

Rachel went back up to her room, pulled out a sheet of the blue paper with violets at the top, and wrote, "Dear Phoebe," and sat chewing on the end of the pen, listening to the wind in the trees. Far away, a lawn mower buzzed back and forth, and a television audience laughed at something.

"We had a dead chipmunk in the washer today, one more adventure in the saga of the Green family," she wrote, and then she crumpled that sheet and threw it away and got a fresh one.

> Dear Phoebe,
>
> A peaceful day in Sandy Bottom. Something has changed in my life, and I'm not sure what it is but it's good. If you had asked me yesterday, I'd have said this is not going to be one of the better summers, but today it looks wonderful. Mother is busy and Daddy too now that he has decided to become Leonard Bernstein. Did I tell you? The conductor who was supposed to conduct the Fourth of July concert bagged out, and Daddy has volunteered himself to be the replacement. Luckily, Daddy is in charge of everything so he doesn't have to go in front of a committee and be interviewed as to his conducting ability. All he has to do is pick up a stick and wave it. *And* (it gets better), guess who will be sitting in the violin section of that orchestra, her little bow in the air,

looking for his downbeat? Yes. *Moi*. The Midori of the Midwest. (Though this morning I couldn't play a scale to save my life. I was holding the bow like a plumber holds a plunger, playing Mozart like it was ground sirloin.) But Scott talked to me, the boy I told you about, Mr. Cello, and he's playing in the same orchestra! Nice, huh? I am sort of crazy about him. I wish he'd put his arm around me or kiss me. (How do you get them to do that?) But that's not what changed my mind about summer. I've been moaning and mooning and grumping and groaning for weeks about my best friend, Carol, because we're not best friends anymore, and today I think I stopped doing that. We're not mad at each other or anything, we just aren't great pals anymore, and I've decided to stop being sad about it and wait for something else to happen. Hope I'm not being a pest, writing you all these letters, and remember: No Reply Necessary. Hope you're having fun selling Anxiety & Emptiness.

Lots of love,
Rachel

P.S. Can you picture me going away to a boarding school? Not one of those mean places you read about in English novels, but one where they have a lot of music.

9

THE GARDEN

Daddy stayed in bed Sunday morning, and Mother took him a pot of peppermint tea, a toasted bagel (plain, no butter), and a sliced peach. "He's okay," she told Rachel. "It's just nerves. By tomorrow he'll be Old Iron Pants. Nothing will faze him. This is exactly what happened when he was trying to decide about going a half million in debt to start up the yogurt operation. Remember? He came home, he threw up, he lay in bed pale as a ghost for two days, and then he marched down there and he was Mr. Executive, the Captain at the Helm of his Ship."

"You mean he's nervous about the Fourth?"

"Precisely."

Mother was in her organist dress, a loose brown shift, her soft-soled organ shoes in a plastic bag. You needed soft shoes to feel your way around the pedals, but the right kind of sole to grip them—your stocking feet might slide—and as loud as Mother played sometimes, she didn't care to make a mistake. It would make Mayor Broadbent much too happy to hear her blast out a clinker.

"Maybe I'll go to church with you," said Rachel.

"Then hurry," said Mother. Rachel jumped up, put her breakfast dishes in the sink, and ran to her room and got out of her jeans and T-shirt and into a blue cotton dress with little white flowers. She slipped on a pair of brown sandals, brushed her hair, yelled "Bye!" to Daddy, and dashed down the stairs and out the door as Mother was getting into the car.

The windows were open in the sanctuary, and a pleasant breeze wafted through, smelling of old oak pews and dusty cushions. High above the altar was a beautiful round rose-colored window and along the sides were high, narrow stained-glass windows depicting the miracles of Jesus—healing the sick and the blind, casting out demons, raising Lazarus from the dead, feeding the multitudes with the loaves and the fish, turning the water to wine at the wedding in Cana, and walking on the stormy waves of the Sea of Galilee as his panicky apostles grabbed at him from the boat. Rachel sat in the front row of the choir loft, her chin on the rail, and looked down at the people filing into the pews. Nobody sat up front. A few people sat in the fifth and sixth rows, and more around the middle, and a few in back. She counted fifteen people. She could see Mayor Broadbent's bald head and his wife dozing next to him. Mr. Foster, the junior high school principal, sat across the aisle from them. Reverend Sykes sat in a big thronelike chair behind the pulpit. All of Mother's adversaries were right there in one place, listening to her play a quiet chorale prelude by Bach.

She and Mother were alone in the loft—the choir took the summer off—and during the opening hymn, "How Firm a Foundation," she could barely hear a sound from the people below. Mother played at a good brisk tempo, no dragging, pausing a beat between lines for the congregation to take a breath. When Mother was a hotshot pianist at the University, soloing with the Milwaukee Symphony and everything, probably she never dreamed that someday she'd be plowing through hymns for a bunch of sleepy Methodists, but here she was, and Phoebe was right— Mother had made the best of it.

Reverend Sykes stepped up to the pulpit, and from this angle, he looked even sadder and saggier than usual. His hair was thinning on top, and he had combed it carefully forward to try to cover the bare places. His black satin gown rustled as he reached into it for his sermon and then adjusted the microphone, which made a loud raspy sound. He flinched, and then he began. "Dearly beloved," he said. "In these times of rapid change in which we find ourselves . . ." and his voice went into a murmury drone, like distant mooing.

He must be hot in that gown, Rachel thought, with his suit coat and his white shirt buttoned up and his tie, and he must be miserable, having to read this boring sermon.

And then go home with his sad wife and eat pot roast and potatoes. And talk about what? What did the minister and his wife discuss over dinner? Did they talk about the Greens? Those terrible Greens?

Well, so what if they did? Rachel thought. Let them. I don't mind being their entertainment, if that's all they have for entertainment.

And then she thought: That's something Mother said once, and now I've thought it as my own thought. I'm even more like her than I imagined.

Mother sat next to Rachel, reading a book of stories by John Cheever, slumped down slightly so the minister couldn't see. His voice droned on. It wasn't the voice of anyone who was trying to say something, it was more like a cello playing a very repetitive set of variations in one key, over and over. Reverend Sykes wasn't speaking so much as he was simply pulsating. And then suddenly he was done. Mother put down her book, slipped onto the organ bench, and began to play "I Love to Tell the Story."

Rachel called Carol as soon as they got home from church, but Angie said she had already left for softball practice. "Didn't you hear?" Angie cried. "She was chosen for the all-state girls' touring team. It's quite an honor. They play all over the state, you know. So we're postponing our vacation trip to August. What are you up to?" asked Angie. "You guys going anywhere this summer?"

"Probably not. Maybe go visit my grandparents in Milwaukee. But I got hired to play in an orchestra this summer. Did I tell you that?"

"Oh my gosh. Is that right!" Angie seemed pleased and astonished, so Rachel told her everything, how much she'd earn and how she'd go off to Menomonie and Eau Claire and Oshkosh for those concerts, and how her debut as an orchestra violinist would be right here in Sandy Bottom on July Fourth.

"Well! We're going to be right there in the front row cheering our heads off," said Angie. "Where will you be sitting? What will you wear? A formal?"

Rachel explained that only singers wear fancy clothes; orchestra players dress in black. And she, as a new player, would probably sit in the very back of the violin section.

"Will we be able to hear you?" asked Angie.

Rachel said she sincerely hoped not. "It's only if I make a horrible mistake that you'd hear me. Otherwise, you'll hear the whole orchestra together. Which is what we want you to hear."

Angie said she thought that Carol would be working at the ice-cream stand at the park on the Fourth, and she and Fred would be there, in their lawn chairs, waving flags.

Rachel got out her violin and practiced Mozart for a while. It was getting better. Then she played scales, slowly at first, then faster and faster. Time for an étude. That was boring. Two whole pages of spiccato and her bow felt heavy. Maybe she'd reached her peak. Maybe she was as good as she'd ever get. She put her violin in the case, sat on the edge of her bed, and leaned her elbows on the windowsill and looked out at the treetops and thought, I want him to put his arms around me and hold me close to him and kiss me on the lips for a long time. I want him to whisper to me that he is in love with me. I want him to say it first, and then I'll say it.

A movement in the bushes over at the Wymans' caught her eye. It was Angie, picking raspberries. She was into red today, red shorts, a red-striped shirt. Someone needed to tell her about fashion, Rachel thought—that large women shouldn't wear such bright colors. But who was she to talk about stylishness? The Greens' backyard was becoming more of a jungle every day. Grapevines had overgrown the old forsythia bushes and spread up into a spruce tree and the big oak. The oak was the only magnificent thing in the yard. Under its mighty limbs was a chaos of plants struggling to survive, the ranks of old irises and daylilies overrun by thistles, the old lawn eaten away by quackgrass and dandelions, the remains of a rock garden gone to weeds, and the evil grapevines now reaching their cancerous tendrils up to the oak tree itself, hoping to bring magnificence down into decay.

Rachel thought, Now there's something I could do today. Get a pair of shears and yank down the grapevines, and clean out the flower beds.

To make a pretty garden out of this wild tangle of growth—wouldn't that be the Italian thing to do? When you walked around Florence, you passed walls with iron gates and looked in and saw little green paradise places with gurgling fountains and flowers and flowering vines, in the shade of a majestic tree—she could make an Italian garden right here.

The garage was as big a mess as the backyard. The shears were in a box full of spiderwebs, and they were dusty and rusty. They would hardly snip at all. She didn't know how to clean them, or sharpen them. So she went through the lilacs, and there was Angie. "Hi, Rachel!" she cried. She gave Rachel a hug. Every time you saw Angie, it was like a big reunion. "I am so excited about your concert!"

"Me too."

"Can you believe Carol's team has practice on a Sunday? Boy, this new coach of theirs. He really works them. How's your folks? We've got to get you all over here for a barbecue one of these days."

"Let's do that. Angie, I was wondering, do you have a pair of shears I can borrow to cut down a grapevine?"

Why, of course. Angie had just the thing. She gave Rachel a handful of raspberries, and they went through the back door of the Wyman garage—a model garage, swept, clean, bright, tools on hooks, tools in rows—and Angie got down a shiny new pair of shears, a fork for digging up weeds, and a smaller pair of shears. And a pair of gloves. "Be sure to wear these so you don't get blisters," said Angie.

"Thanks," said Rachel. "Thanks an awful lot."

Rachel went back through the lilacs. She cut down every grapevine growing up the trunk of the oak tree and pulled them down out of the branches. Some of them were twenty feet long and had big leaves on the ends. Then she went to work trying to save the forsythia. That seemed to be a losing battle. The forsythia was only a bunch of dead stalks propping up a mass of grapevine. So she left it and

129

moved on to the rock garden, using the fork to pry up the big dandelion and thistle roots.

There was a flat place beside the rock garden, she saw, where she could lay some of those old concrete sidewalk squares that were leaning against the back of the garage. She could make a terrace out of them and put a table and chairs there. The oak tree would shade it at noon. She could pile up some rocks and hide a garden hose inside the pile, and there's the fountain. The water would trickle down the rocks and into the rock garden and water the poor old flowers who were trying to hang on there in the parched dirt in the midst of the jungle. Cool. Sit there in the afternoon, the fountain burbling and gurgling, the flowers blooming, and your friends would pass by and see you and call out, "Oh, hello, Rachel!" and you'd wave them into the yard, and they'd sit down at your table and say how *lovely* this garden was, and those *irises,* how splendid, and the begonias, and you'd pour them a lemonade and they'd say, "Why, thank you." That is what gracious living is. You make a beautiful place and people will want to be there with you.

Rachel spent the rest of the afternoon in the backyard. Mother came out to smoke on the back steps. "What are you doing out here?" she said. "I didn't know you were into horticulture. You must take after your grandmother."

"I want to make an Italian garden with a table and a fountain and flowers," said Rachel, kneeling by the weed patch that had been an iris bed. Only a few irises remained, blue ones.

"You can wreck your hands doing that," said Mother.

It was fun to dig around and pull up weeds, and by the end of the afternoon she was surprised at the progress she had made. A little planting, a little fountain-building, and one lawn mowing, and this'd be a garden fit for the Medicis. Wake up one morning and look out the window and there'd be an olive-skinned man in a gondolier's cap and striped shirt and pantaloons and shoes with curved toes, playing a mandolin and serenading her with a song about moonlight and orchards and young women with dark hair and their violins.

> Dear Phoebe,
>
> It's Sunday. I went to church with Mother, and today I am gardening. Two major changes (for me) in one day. This is my new philosophy. Everything changes, no matter how hard you try to keep things the same, so don't be afraid of change or be sad about what has changed, but try to live in the present. I learned this from reading Emily Dickinson, I think. Anyway. Church was sleepy, but the garden will be very grand! In the fall, I may go to Interlochen. It could be good, I think. It'd be lonely at first, but then it can be lonely here too. And boring. What Florence was to the Renaissance, that's what Sandy Bottom is to boredom. Sort of the center, in other words. People could come here to study boredom. Anthropologists could observe the people of Sandy Bottom and write books about the effects of tedium on boring

people. Would you like me to say more about this or am I boring you? Hello? Phoebe? Wake up.

So here is my plan. I go to Interlochen and study violin (and academic things) and play in the orchestra there, and see how I like it and how they like me. If it works out, fine, and if it doesn't, I run away, sell my violin, fly to Italy, change my name to Raquel Verde, and become a nightclub pianist. You know how much Italians love American music like *West Side Story* and Gershwin and that stuff? Well, I'd do that. I'd wear a black dress with a red gardenia in my hair. Raquel Verde the Jazz Queen. Playing nightly till 3 A.M. in the Café Molto. Big crowds. Men in blue suits throwing millions of lira at me, crying, "Hey baby, play that again!" Café packed with people. Then I'd buy the café. You'd be the manager. We earn way lots of money. And then we sell the café for way more money. Then we come out with the Raquel Verde line of fashions: the shoes, the black dresses, the perfume, and I do a promotional tour of America for Raquel Verde perfume, and I'm in Chicago and I have a free day and I tell the driver, "Oh, Marcello, drive me out to Sandy Bottom, it's about five hours north of here," and I fall asleep in the backseat and wake up and we're parked on Main Street and I get out and walk around and say "Ciao, baby" to everyone I see. They all ask for my autograph. *Raquel Verde,* I write on their paper. I spritz my perfume on them, and I wave good-bye and never come back again. But that's only if things don't work out at Interlochen. I'll try that first. Then the nightclub.

When Rachel came down for supper, Mother said, "Would you like to play some duets before dinner?" Mother stood, beaming, in her bright blue tunic and black slacks, her hair was tied back, she had put on lipstick, and from the kitchen came the aroma of homemade spaghetti sauce.

"Sure. I'll go get my violin," said Rachel.

Ever so often, Mother would surprise you with a sudden transformation from Frazzled Agitator to Glamorous Artiste. She'd go along for days complaining about the Broadbents of the world and how the public library is turning into a video store, she'd bang out letters and petitions, and moan about having wasted her life in a town of people who can't tell the difference between music and what you hear while you're waiting for the dentist, and she'd go *on* about this, and just when you were ready to throw a book at her, she suddenly appeared, lovely, affectionate, the Grand Dame, the Lady of the House, and fixed elegant meals and spoke sweetly to her husband and daughter. Another Mother entirely.

Rachel got out her violin and Mother sat at the piano. "I've been thinking of moving this piano down into the basement," she said, smiling. "Or keeping it at church, in the choir room. Wouldn't it be nice not to have to eat in the kitchen all the time?"

Rachel laughed. "I don't even *think* of this as a dining room," she said. "It's a piano room."

"I miss having dinner parties," said Mother. "Maybe we should buy a bigger house."

"Where? In Milwaukee?"

Mother looked surprised. "No, of course not. There's a house up near the high school. That big brick place that Dr. Mathews used to have."

The old Mathews house sat on a hill, it had white pillars and a circular drive and a big yard with hedges. "Why would you need a bigger place if I'm going away to school?" said Rachel.

"Oh. Are you thinking about that?" Mother said sweetly.

They played through two Handel sonatas, a piece by Corelli, and then Mother pulled out a couple of romantic things, "Midnight Carnivale" and "L'Amore." "Haven't played these in ages," she said. The pieces were so gushy, Rachel almost laughed out loud—it was music you might hear in a tea restaurant for old ladies with blue hair. "It's terrible and I love it," Mother cried during one big drippy glissando. "I love this stuff!"

Rachel and Mother and Daddy sat down at the kitchen table and ate the spaghetti with Mother's tomato garlic sauce and a cucumber-onion salad on the side and hot French bread. Daddy was all recovered from his stomach ailment, he said. He had taken a shower and shaved and put on a white shirt and that, he said, was what finally cured him.

"A clean white shirt has a tonic effect on a man," he

said. "A lot of men lie sick in hospital beds who, if they would only put on a white shirt and a tie, would feel ten times better. There's a lot of psychology in sickness, you know. You go lie in bed on a nice summer day in your pajamas and of course you're going to feel lousy."

It was a nice supper. They talked about normal things, no big harangues. Daddy said that when he was at the University, he worked as a dishwasher at an Italian restaurant. "When you finished the dishes, you started in on the pots, which had sat on the stove all day, and at the bottom of them was a black crust a half-inch thick that you had to take a chisel to. It took three hours to do the pots, and the restaurant didn't close until two A.M., so it was six before I was done. And my first class was at eight. I tell you, it was a long time before I could face a plate of spaghetti."

"I'm getting tired of this kitchen," said Mother. "It seems like I spend all my time in here. Why don't we add on a wing with a music room and a guest bedroom?"

"I don't want to put music off in some wing," said Daddy. "I want it right in the middle of everything. It was wonderful listening to you two play. You ought to play together more often."

"She sounds wonderful, doesn't she?" said Mother.

"Stunning. Both of you," said Daddy.

"Maybe we should talk about Interlochen," said Mother.

Daddy didn't hear her, or pretended not to. "Who wants ice cream?" he said.

COMMENCEMENT

*T*he next morning, Rachel came downstairs with her gym bag and a towel, and Mother looked surprised.

"Swimming class," said Rachel. Mother looked even more surprised.

"I signed up for it at school," said Rachel. "I can't swim, you know."

"Oh," said Mother.

"Didn't you know that?"

"I never stopped to think about it," said Mother. She looked taken aback. As well she might.

Rachel thought, What sort of mother would let her child get to be fourteen and not be a swimmer?

"You signed up for this yourself?" said Mother.

"Yes, of course," said Rachel.

The class was at ten A.M., with a man named Janks, and when she got to the pool, the changing room was full of girls from the nine A.M. class peeling off their swimsuits and dashing into the cold showers and the beginners class, the one Rachel was in, the Minnows, a bunch of seven- and eight-year-olds, undressing and pulling their swimsuits on. Rachel hated being naked in public, but she undressed, and then there was shouting outside—she grabbed up her clothes and held them in front of her—and suddenly a gang of boys appeared at the girls' room door and slung a small slender boy through it so that he slid on the wet concrete and fell and skidded into the room. He was naked. He bumped into the wall and jumped up and dashed back out.

Rachel put on her suit, a black one-piece, and trudged out to the pool. Mr. Janks was there, a tall man with a pot belly and a silver whistle on a lanyard around his neck. "Okay," he said. "In the pool and let's see you swim."

Rachel couldn't. "I can't," she said. He shook his head. "The only way to do it is to do it," he said.

So she climbed gingerly into the pool and tried to float herself toward the far end, kicking her feet. Mr. Janks walked along the side. "Come on," he said. "You can do it." She couldn't do it. "Sure you can do it," he said. She clutched onto the side of the pool, chlorine burning in her eyes. "Sure you can do it," he said.

"Don't be afraid to put your face in the water!"

She closed her eyes, pinched her nose, ducked into the water, jumped up.

"See? keep working on that," he said, and strode off to bully someone else.

"I'd love to teach you to play violin," she muttered under her breath. Stick a violin in his hand, a bow in the other, and say, "You can do it! It's not hard! What's wrong with you?" Then she pushed off from the side of the pool, her face in the water, kicking, thrashing her arms.

The next evening, and the next, and the evening after that, when they were through with dinner Daddy made a beeline for the den and sat listening to music over and over, figuring out what the orchestra should play on the Fourth. "We'll do 'The Star-Spangled Banner' first, with a tenor soloist, and I think 'The 1812 Overture' would go over darn well, and where Tchaikovsky indicates cannon, we could have an American Legion rifle squad. Or maybe cannon. Isn't there a bunch of Civil War buffs who dress up in uniforms and fire cannons at the county fair? Remind me to ask at work about that. But we should have some Mozart too. How about a piano concerto?"

Mother sighed. "Norman. A piano concerto! Where are you going to dig up a pianist?"

"No problem. They're a dime a dozen." He winked at Rachel.

"Whatever you do, choose something easy," said Mother. "The '1812' is no stroll around the park, believe me. Have you looked at the score? Remember you've only got two rehearsals, and this isn't exactly the Boston Symphony, either. Don't choose *The Rite of Spring*, for crying out loud."

So he marched into the den, and a minute later as Rachel washed and Mother dried the dishes, they heard Mahler's Symphony No. 4 blasting out. "What do you think!" he yelled. "Think we can handle it?"

"Norman, you've got to be kidding!" Mother shouted back.

"He's only kidding," said Rachel.

"Sometimes I'm not sure." Mother put down her dish towel and reached for her cigarettes. Then she checked her Smoke Tally sheet on the wall beside the refrigerator: It was her latest scheme, a strict regimen of tobacco, and she had already smoked fifteen today, so she was allowed only two more. Rachel knew Mother was deliberating whether to spend one now and have the other at bedtime—but then what if she couldn't sleep and wanted another? She fished out a cigarette and looked at the tally sheet. The system wasn't simple: Mother had worked out a credit arrangement whereby she could *borrow* a cigarette from tomorrow's allotment and carry the deficit for days. At the moment, she was in hock to the Smoke Bank for about thirty-six cigarettes.

Mother put the cigarette back in the pack and plopped down in the armchair at the end of the table and looked at Rachel and sighed.

"Do you think he's really going to have a pianist on the program?" she said.

Rachel smiled. "Sure. I think it'd be great. Why not?"

Mother frowned. "You could get one who couldn't play, that's why not." She looked at the cigarette pack and pushed it away. "It worries me that he's got so much invested in this concert and if he hires the wrong person, he could blow the whole thing."

"Maybe you ought to volunteer," said Rachel.

"Ha!" Mother shook her head and laughed. "Just what I need. I haven't played a piano concerto in fifteen years."

"You play everything else though. You play in church every Sunday, and you play for weddings, and you played for the Historical Society last year."

"That's different."

"But you could do it," Rachel said.

"Of course I could do it," Mother said. "The question is, why would I want to? Who needs the aggravation?"

And then it dawned on Rachel. How sweet! Mother wanted Daddy to *ask* her to be in his concert! She was like a teenager waiting to get invited to the dance. Rachel knew Mother and it was pure Mother to want something badly and then scoff at the very idea. She'd mention an art exhibit in Chicago she'd like to see, and then when you suggested that she go, she would say, "Pffffffff. Go to Chicago? Drive down there into that craziness and spend a fortune on a hotel room? Why would I want to do that?" When a visit to Chicago was the fondest desire of her heart.

Rachel slipped in behind the chair, and Mother leaned her head forward, and Rachel put her hands on either side of Mother's neck and started kneading the muscles with her thumbs. "You're a wonderful pianist," she said softly. "You would do beautifully. And Daddy would love to have you do it. He's afraid to ask you, because he thinks you'll say no. You ought to go in there and tell him that you're going to do it and that's that."

Mother groaned. "Oh, it's too much," she said. "I've got church to worry about and—" Her voice trailed off as Rachel's thumbs found the tight muscle and pressed in hard. Mother groaned again. Rachel twanged the muscle gently back and forth. Mother moaned.

Four days passed with no sight of Carol. Rachel called and left a message on the Wyman machine, but Carol didn't call back. Rachel practiced her violin three hours a day. She wanted to sound good in the orchestra. She worked on the garden: The work went slower now, digging weeds, planting plants. She rode her bike to the old dam and sat under a tree and read a biography of Emily Dickinson she had found at the library. It was sad, somehow, to think that Emily probably had never sat next to a man and kissed him on the lips, with her arms around him. She thought about Scott and wished he would call her. He'd had her telephone number for two weeks now. She wondered about the boys at Interlochen: Would they be sweet to be with and talk to? Boys at Sandy Bottom seemed mostly alike: tall, loud, eating vast amounts of food and eating it loudly, dropping garbage around them, doing loud goofy things, shoving each other, whispering dirty jokes and whinnying, and then when they were with a girl, they got all silent and looked at the ground and suffered. Rachel thought that going out with one of them must be like dating a goat.

Mother said that her stop-smoking plan, the tally system, was working, and that she was paying back her debt to the Smoke Bank. One day, at noon, Rachel counted only three butts in the ashtray. "Congratulations," she said.

"Don't forget you're playing at high school commencement later on today," said Mother. Rachel groaned. Why had she said she'd do that? What if Scott called?

A postcard from Phoebe arrived in the mail.

> Dear Rachel,
>
> I miss you too! Sorry if my handwriting is shaky, but I'm on a train. I took a boat ride in a canal in Venice the way you're supposed to, and it smelled like raw sewage, and when I got out of the boat some creep followed me all the way back to the hotel. So much for romance.
>
> Love,
> Phoebe

Rachel practiced in the afternoon, until suddenly she heard Mother shouting. She ran to the stairs. "It's four o'clock!" Mother said. "Commencement is at five! I think maybe you're supposed to be there now!"

Rachel put on a dress and Mother gave her a ride to the football field. Crowds of parents were streaming along the sidewalk and through the jam-packed parking lot to the bleachers. She hurried across the grass to where the band was sitting, beside the platform erected in the middle of the field. It was the marching band, in uniform, all brass and reeds and drums, with a tiny contingent of strings

142

added for the occasion. The band director, Mr. Tibbs, rushed over and said, "Where were you? Rehearsal was an hour ago!" She smiled and said she was sorry and sat down with the other strings and looked at the music.

It was all easy stuff. Two marches, a hymn, big open chords, nothing tricky. Her stand partner, a skinny girl with blond hair, leaned over and whispered, "He hates violins." Rachel shrugged. She hadn't known there were other kids at Sandy Bottom who played violin. The school didn't have an orchestra, only a marching band. None of these kids went to Mr. Amidore's music school for lessons. And then Mr. Tibbs rapped on his music stand and gave a big count and a downbeat, and the band struck up Elgar's "Pomp and Circumstance" and Rachel could understand why he hated violins. These violins were pretty sour. The blond girl sawed away, completely out of tune, and the boy next to her sounded even worse, but behind them, six trombones blatted and blared and covered up everything the strings did so it wasn't a problem. As a joke, Rachel began playing "Pop Goes the Weasel" until the blond girl looked at her in panic and then Rachel went back to Elgar.

The graduating class came lumbering past the band in their blue robes and mortarboards with golden tassels, and then Mr. Tibbs waved the Elgar to a close and held up two fingers and counted off, "Three! Four!" and the band played "America the Beautiful."

The sky had been cloudy when Rachel came, but now the clouds had drifted east and the sun beat down, and she felt a little sleepy.

There were some speeches about facing challenges and life being a blank page we must fill, and it isn't how much you get but how much you can give, and then they sang the school hymn, "Sandy Bottom, we salute you, Alma Mater of our youth," which made Rachel laugh out loud. She imagined a fat woman named Alma who had sat naked on the sand and stood up and everyone stood at attention and saluted her huge white sandy bottom. Rachel started giggling and couldn't stop. Mr. Tibbs glared at her, but she still couldn't stop, and then the boy next to the blond girl started giggling. The blond girl looked at Rachel as if she were sick. "It's not funny," she whispered.

"How do you know?" said Rachel.

When Rachel came home, Mother was camped at the table, proofreading a letter to the newspaper.

"Listen to this," Mother said. "This is in response to that dorky column by the school superintendent about the school needing to be more sensitive to the ever-changing needs of its constituency. Boy, what a dope."

She started reading:

"Mr. Brock's argument for dropping Spanish because 'students these days demand a curriculum relevant to their perceived needs and career goals' is convincing until you stop and think about it. School is not a democracy. We don't ask children whether they'd rather learn to read or eat ice cream. We know they are immature, as we once were, and we make certain choices for them, just as our parents and teachers did for us. A good education opens up children's minds to needs and goals they may not have perceived before. The education Mr. Brock seems to prefer is one that locks them up in the narrowest path a child can imagine."

Mother read on as Rachel got a carton of ice cream out of the freezer, gouged a couple giant scoops out of it and put them in a dish, and poured fudge sauce over. One advantage of going to Interlochen would be that Mother probably wouldn't be writing letters to the school newspaper fussing about the curriculum.

That evening after dinner, Daddy sat in his favorite old wingback chair, his feet up on a hassock, listening to the Mozart C-major Piano Concerto, the famous one that was used as a theme in a movie. He reached over and turned down the volume. "I think they'd like this, don't you?" he said. "Jerry Mason says there's a kid up in Green Bay who plays this pretty well, and I could get him for a couple hundred dollars—don't you think people would like that? He's thirteen, he's supposed to be good."

Rachel sat on the hassock beside his legs. "You know who you ought to get? Mother. Mother could play that better than anybody."

Daddy rolled his eyes and shook his head. "If I asked her, she'd laugh in my face. Your mother has her hands full trying to get the school shaped up and save the Ramsey Building from the law of gravity and goodness knows what else. And in the midst of it all, she's trying to quit cigarettes. It's all she can do. I don't want to throw something else at her."

"She'd be great," said Rachel.

"She *is* great. I grant you that. But it's out of the question. Besides, this kid is supposed to be good. Think of all those kids who'll come and look up and see *someone their own age* sit down and play a Mozart concerto. They'll be astounded. It'll be great. Suddenly they see that something they didn't think was possible *is possible*. It'll be magic."

"No kid can possibly play that concerto like Mother can. Why not ask her? See what she says."

"She'll only say no."

"What do you have to lose?"

"Well, that's another story," said Daddy.

Rachel looked him in the eye. "What do you mean?"

Daddy leaned forward and put his hand on her shoulder. "I mean," he said, lowering his voice, "that people would be *happy* to see some shiny smiley thirteen-year-old kid from Green Bay get up and play Mozart, and if your mother got up there, frankly, they'd be praying for her to plunk a bad note and fall off the bench."

"Mother wouldn't play a bad note," said Rachel.

"I don't know," said Daddy, and he leaned back and turned up the volume. That was his way of ending a conversation. Crank up the music.

"Dear Phoebe," Rachel wrote.

Nothing much to report, same old thing. Gardening, practicing, hanging out. Mother is down to a handful of cigarettes a day from her usual gazillion and she is blasting away at the school again, and Daddy is holed up in his den getting together the music for the Fourth of July. There's going to be a piano concerto, but Daddy won't ask Mother to play because he thinks she'd say no, though I know she'd love to do it. And so it goes. Scott has yet to call me. How's your love life?

She liked to toss in that question on the odd chance that someday Phoebe might answer it. Rachel was curious. She knew about marriage from Mother and Daddy, but what was it like to be single and pretty like Phoebe? Did men come swooping at you at dances and send notes to your table at sidewalk cafés asking if they could buy you an espresso? She imagined Phoebe going to the grocery store and standing by the frozen pizza section and a man kneeling and taking her hand and pressing it to his lips. "Mio babbino," he'd cry, his long black hair slicked back, his eyelashes wet from tears, kneeling in the Florentine supermarket as people brushed past him, muttering, swerving their grocery carts. Did men get wild about you and come veering into your life like a car skidding on ice, and if so, how did you know what to do about it and whether to say "Oh, maybe" or "Yes!" or "Get lost"?

She wanted to know. What does it feel like when a man is close to you and holds you in his arms? Is that nice? It must be, since so many women do it. But is it really? How do you know what to do? Do you hold your lips apart when you kiss? What do you say afterward?

A. *That was nice.*

B. *That was great. I'm overjoyed. Really.*

C. Would you like to borrow my lip balm?
D. Oh. Is it eight o'clock already? Got to run.

"I've decided on the program," Daddy said over breakfast. "'Star-Spangled Banner,' the Mendelssohn *Italian Symphony*, and the kid from Green Bay will play the slow movement of the Mozart. He won a competition in Milwaukee last fall playing some Liszt thing, so this shouldn't be that hard. And we'll wrap it up with the '1812.'"

Mother had poured herself a big bowl of bran flakes and yogurt and was eating with the *Register* spread out in front of her.

"Who is he? And why only the slow movement?" she asked.

"Drew is his name. Drew Johnson. Apparently he's quite a talent. And the slow movement is the easy one, and besides, we want to keep the concert down to an hour."

"The slow movement is not the easy one, believe me, Norman. Just because there are fewer notes doesn't make it easy."

Daddy let that pass. "How about the *Italian Symphony*?"

Mother laughed. "Put it out of your mind. That's what I think."

"But I know the work," said Daddy. "I've heard it a hundred times. I could practically hum it to you."

"So? Get up and hum it then. Norman, conducting isn't like listening to a recording."

148

"I'm aware of that," he said.

"With conducting, there's always the possibility that you wave your baton and nothing whatsoever happens because they haven't the faintest idea what you want."

"Yes, of course," he said.

Mother snatched a cigarette out of the pack and lit it. "Norman," she said, "it's sweet of you to do this, and very noble, but you're operating way over your head, and if you don't let me help you, you're crazy."

Daddy stood up and put his dishes in the sink. He put the milk in the fridge, the sugar in the cupboard. He adjusted his tie. Rachel wished he'd just come out and say it, for goodness sake: "Would you please play the concert? I don't want the boy. I want you." But he didn't. He smiled at Mother and said, "Guess what? Zion Methodist Men's Club is going to have a booth at the Fourth of July. A two-thousand gallon tank, with your pal Reverend Sykes sitting above it on a chair. Dunk the Pastor."

"You mean," said Rachel, "that we get to see Reverend Sykes sitting on a chair over a tank of water and people throwing balls at a target, trying to dunk him?"

"Exactly," said Daddy. "If only he had been a better preacher, he would've offended more people and it'd raise enough money to buy a new organ."

"Very funny," said Mother.

"Don't worry about a thing, General. It's going to be a terrific cultural event. I will bring no shame upon you. Either one of you." He kissed Mother on the forehead. He kissed Rachel. "Bye, gorgeous," he said.

The phone rang. It was Grandma. When Mother heard Rachel say "Hi, Grandma," she waved her hand and silently mouthed the words "I'm not home," so Rachel talked to Grandma for a while.

Rachel felt guilty that she hadn't written to Grandma or called her. Grandma and Grandpa Green died when Rachel was very small, both of them, within a year of each other. Grandma and Grandpa Mueller spent the winters in St. Petersburg, Florida, at a seniors' condo complex along the oceanfront, where they went for walks every day and ate lunch at the seniors' dining hall and Grandpa played bridge in the afternoon and napped while Grandma went to her book club and her folk-dance club and her pottery class. They always flew back to Milwaukee in the spring, but this year Grandpa told Mother they were getting too old to migrate and maybe they would put the Milwaukee house up for sale.

It was a wonderful old brick manse on the north side of Milwaukee, with a veranda curved around front and a walled garden behind. You walked through two leaded-glass doors into a front hall where a stairway curved around and up to the second floor. One door led to the library, one to the long dark living room with the fireplace, and one straight ahead led to the kitchen. It was a house of quiet, high-ceilinged rooms with large curtained windows and mysterious closets and paintings of sailing ships and golden meadows and shining temples and gypsy campfires and noblemen with long capes and tasseled swords, their wolfhounds at their side. The grandfather clock ticktocked in the front hall, Grandma yelled on the phone upstairs, Grandpa snoozed in the library. And there was the steady murmur of Grandma's television. She kept it turned on all day, not wanting to miss anything.

"How is Grandpa?" said Rachel.

"I don't know. He's downstairs," said Grandma. She said her knees were bothering her and she was having trouble with her eyes and she asked Rachel if she was getting enough protein. "A glass of orange juice every morning," said Grandma, "and it's nonsense what they say about milk, you need a big glass every day."

"Are you over your cold?" Rachel asked.

Grandma paused. "I may have to go to the Mayo Clinic in Rochester."

"Why? What's the matter?"

Grandma sighed. "This doctor I have, I don't think he knows what he's talking about. They try to keep you out of hospitals these days so when you tell them what you feel like, they always pooh-pooh it and say, Oh, that's just old age. Well, I'm tired of getting the runaround. I think I ought to go to Mayo and get a complete checkup." All her life, Grandma had been fascinated by disease and had been, for the most part, in disgustingly good health.

"Tell your mother to call me when she gets in," said Grandma. "Good-bye."

"She wants you to call her," Rachel said, after she hung up.

"When I quit smoking, I will," said Mother, reaching for her cigarettes. "One problem at a time."

151

11

JUNE

*C*arol and Valerie appeared on the front page of the *Register* the second week of June, a big photo of them in their softball uniforms, grinning, bats on their shoulders, under the headline "Local Girls Tapped for All-Star Nine." They would go to River Falls for three days of practice and then tour around the Midwest for ten days, playing exhibition games. They were the youngest girls chosen for the team, the story said, but they would be in the starting lineup, at shortstop and first base.

Rachel phoned Carol that morning. "She's still in bed," said Angie, "but let me wake her, it's time she got up anyway." It was ten o'clock. Carol came to the phone, sleepy, and Rachel congratulated her. "The picture of you looks really good," she said. "Both of you."

152

"Oh. Good," said Carol. She said she was tired and her back hurt. A girl had crashed into her, sliding into second base, and now it hurt to bend over and tie her shoes.

"When do you leave for this all-star tour?"

"Tomorrow," said Carol.

"Do you want to sleep over tonight?"

Carol said she couldn't. Her team, O'Connell's Jewelry, was playing in Oshkosh tonight, one of those late games. Ten P.M.

"Have a great time," said Rachel.

"Thanks, you too," Carol said.

Rachel almost said "I'll miss you," but she wasn't sure it was true.

The next two weeks flew by in a flash. Rachel worked in the yard, she wrote to Phoebe, she went to the pool and actually sort of learned to swim, she futzed around the house, she practiced violin, she took her last lesson with Mr. Amidore, who was tired and quiet and said he was looking forward to his summer vacation, and she visited Florence and learned to play cribbage. June twenty-ninth was circled in red on Rachel's calendar—the day of the first orchestra rehearsal—and it seemed like a tiny distant point on the horizon . . . and then it was two days away. And then one.

Mother's stop-smoking program had faltered in June. The campaign for the arts center heated up. There was another exchange of letters between her and Mayor Broadbent, in which the mayor said that if there were such a big need for an arts center in town, then why hadn't someone built one a long time ago? And when Mother sat down to the typewriter to respond, she reached for a cigarette.

"I can't write without smoking," she said. "It's like a tripod: the typewriter, the coffee cup, the ashtray. Remove one leg and you fall over."

"Maybe you could give up writing for a while," said Rachel.

"Ha! And give that old idiot the satisfaction?"

Rachel said she was sure that a person *could* write without smoking, that there was no logical connection between the two, and that the habit of smoking at the typewriter could be broken, like any other habit.

"Don't lecture me," said Mother. "I'm the mother. I'm supposed to be the lecturer. You're the daughter. You're supposed to be the sympathizer. The supporter."

"Ha!" said Rachel.

Rachel cooked dinner almost every night. It was fun. She rode her bike to the truck garden outside town and picked up fresh peppers and carrots and tomatoes and whipped up big bowls of pasta—penne or linguini or ziti—with fresh vegetables and a little oil and pepper and garlic and shavings of parmesan cheese. She made chicken with fresh sage, and she made thick hamburgers, rare, with raw onion, on kaiser rolls—Daddy took one look and was in hamburger heaven. Mother was tied up with the arts center, talking to a lawyer and an architect, lobbying the town council to form a planning commission, writing

154

fund-raising letters. Mrs. Ferguson, the old organist, donated $25,000, and Reverend Sykes had a fit. He had been courting the old lady, hoping for a gift to the church building fund, and he wrote a letter to the town council declaring his opposition to the arts center as "a drain on the town's limited resources."

Mother had softened toward him. She had decided his wife was suffering from depression, and maybe he was depressed too, and you shouldn't fight with sick people. Mother invited Mrs. Sykes to lunch, and she declined, saying that she was allergic to everything, and that she and her husband could eat only potato soup, boiled chicken, and tapioca pudding. Mother invited her to come have potato soup, and she declined: She needed to stay close to a phone because her mother in Tucson was ailing.

Rachel learned the sidestroke and the backstroke, all in one week, and then Mr. Janks said it was time to learn diving. It seemed unnatural to Rachel, jumping headfirst into the water, but Mr. Janks acted like it was something a person did every day: stand at the edge of the pool in a wet suit, hugging yourself, shivering, waiting for the terrible moment when you had to walk to the end of the board and jump. He waggled around in his swim trunks with his great big hairy feet. "C'mon, Ray. Don't be afraid!" he yelled.

My name is not Ray, Rachel thought. It's Rachel. And I am not an amphibious person by nature, so don't push me.

"Tuck your head, extend your arms, bend your knees

and aim for your spot, Ray. C'mon, let's go!" And Rachel closed her eyes, took a deep breath, jumped, and felt the water slap her hard. Water came up her nose, and she thrashed her arms, and when her head came up out of the water, she gasped and sneezed, and Mr. Janks yelled, "Good!" and the other kids laughed. Then she had to work on the crawl, with Mr. Janks walking along the edge, yelling, "Keep your head down! You're not breathing right! Turn your head left to breathe, then facedown in the water and exhale! Come on! It's not that hard!"

Every night, Daddy played a different recording of the Mendelssohn Symphony No. 4, following along in the score, marking the music. "What a wonderful town this is!" he cried one night at supper. "I ask you: Where else in this country could a forty-eight-year-old man get the opportunity to conduct a symphony orchestra for the first time in his life? Isn't that something!"

"It doesn't have much to do with this town," said Mother. "It has more to do with a certain jerk canceling out at the last minute. And it has something to do with being naive, but never mind me. I'm only the realist."

Rachel finally conquered the weeds in the backyard and laid the concrete slabs to make the terrace under the oak tree, and Mother saw an ad in the *Register* for a cast-iron table with a glass top and two chairs and bought them. The antique store on Main Street had a fountain for sale, an old bronze thing with cherubs and a dolphin spout, and the owner, a man named Wells, brought it over in his truck and set it up by the rock garden, and dug a shallow trench for the electrical cord for the pump. He filled the fountain with water, and the pump drew the water out of the basin and sprayed it up from the dolphin's mouth and it dripped down to the basin. "Now you're in business," he said.

Rachel sat in her garden, wearing dark glasses, reading books.

She read *A Tale of Two Cities,* which Mother had given her, and a murder mystery from Angie, who had a boxful in the garage. It was called *The Blonde in Room 436* and it had a private eye named Pete Murphy who burst into room 436, his pistol drawn, and yelled, "Okay, wise guys, put down the peashooters and put your pinkies up where I can see 'em, otherwise I'm gonna blow some holes in ya and use ya for a soup strainer!" and the Contrero gang threw down their guns and the blonde, whose name was Rosie, ran into Pete's arms and cried, "You sure are a sight for sore eyes, ya big lug!"

When Carol came back from the tour, Rachel rode her bike over to River Park to watch O'Connell's play a team from Menomonie. She sat in the top row of the bleachers, but Carol spotted her and waved and Rachel waved back. Carol's team wore bright red shirts, blue shorts, red socks, and red caps. Carol was a good shortstop—Rachel could see that right away. She looked loose and limber at her position, slapping her fist in her glove, her knees bent, bouncing on her toes, and when a ball was hit to her, she charged it, scooped it up, and threw *hard* to first. Once, a high, high, *high* pop fly was hit and right away Carol was running to her right, toward the fence. She flipped her visor down and yelled, "I got it! I got it! I got it!"—and she *did* have it. She caught the ball as she bounced off the fence, and she threw the ball back to the pitcher *hard* and ran back to shortstop, one finger up in the air—one out— and yelled, "C'mon, guys! C'mon, Becky! Big pitch! Big pitch! Here we go!"

It looked like great fun, the team running off the field at the end, slapping each other on the back, the shouting, the cheering, but Rachel remembered how it had been in her gym class, the pain of it, the embarrassment of people not looking at you, not talking, after you'd made a dumb mistake.

Every morning, Rachel came home from swimming and looked through the pile of mail on the hall table, the circulars and bills and pleas for money from charities and the copies of *Time* and *Clavier* and *Strad* and *The New York Review of Books,* and looked for a letter from Phoebe, and finally one day there was one: a tissue-thin blue envelope with her name in Phoebe's elegant fountain-pen script and Leonardo da Vinci's picture on the stamp and the postmark *Firenze, Italia.*

Rachel opened the envelope.

Dear Rachel,

I've been writing a guidebook called *Standing Still in Rome.* The idea is that you sit down someplace and look around and the guidebook tells what you're looking at. What do you think? Yours, Phoebe.

It wasn't much of a letter. Maybe Phoebe was getting tired of her and this terse note was her way of saying, "Give it a rest, kid. Write to someone else for a change." So she wrote a letter to Scott.

Dearest Scott,

You are the most talented musician I know, and when I hear you play the cello I know you have a beautiful soul. I have thought about you every day, which must mean that I am quite in love with you. But because I am, there is something you must know. I may go away to Interlochen in September. My heart aches at the thought of not looking into your eyes in string ensemble every Saturday afternoon, but the time has come for me to leave my old life and go on to something new. I will be in a place where I can play music with people every day. (But of course no one could ever replace you.) So, my darling, this is my farewell. I will see you at the concerts this summer, but it would be too painful to say this out loud. Just know that I love you and I will not forget you.

She looked at it momentarily and then tore it into strips and stuffed them in the wastebasket. Too dumb. It was what she wanted to say but it sounded dopey to say it.

One night, Mother got a call from Fred Wyman, who said that Reverend Sykes was leaving at the end of September. He was going to leave the ministry and move to Minneapolis and take some courses and get a license to

159

sell real estate. "Poor man," said Mother. "But all in all, I think the Gospel of Jesus Christ will be better off for him not preaching it." The next day, she launched into a house-cleaning campaign, and filled up six big boxes with books and clothes for the Zion rummage sale. "Clutter can cause illness," Mother said. "I read that somewhere." Mother came barging into Rachel's room to see if Rachel had some clothes to donate.

"I hate it when you walk in like that," said Rachel.

"I knocked," said Mother.

"And then you opened the door before I could say 'Come in.'"

"Didn't you want me to come in?"

Mother could be so dense sometimes. "That's not the point," said Rachel. "This is my room. You're supposed to ask. And then you're supposed to wait for an answer."

"Sorry." So then Mother felt bad. She went outside and smoked a couple cigarettes, standing looking at the fountain. Rachel called out the window, "You can sit at the table if you like."

"That's all right," said Mother. "I'm fine."

Rachel emptied half of her closet and put the clothes in green plastic garbage bags for the rummage sale. Then she looked at them and got in a weepy mood. She was nostalgic about some of those clothes. She remembered riding around town on her bike in those clothes, going to school in them, and now she might be leaving—forever. She lay on her bed, facedown, and cried. A good satisfying cry.

Mother knocked. "May I come in?" she said.

"Okay," said Rachel. Mother tiptoed in and collected the garbage bags.

One thing about Mother was that she almost never asked you what was wrong if she saw you crying. She simply tried to do something nice for you. If Daddy saw you crying—*whoa,* look out: Daddy would ask you what was wrong, and no matter what you said, he'd feel it was his fault, and in a minute he'd start crying, too. To Mother, it was as normal as laughing. You cried because you cried, that's all.

"Let's have a picnic with the Wymans," said Mother, and she called up Angie, and the two of them whipped up the meal in no time—Mother did chicken tacos, and Angie made sloppy joes, Fred made a pitcher of lemonade, Daddy brought home two quarts of Bluebird, one fudge ripple, one butter pecan, and Carol and Rachel made the taco buffet—chopped onions, green peppers, salsa, refried beans—and set the Wymans' picnic table.

Everyone took one taco and one sloppy joe, to be diplomatic.

"I love sloppy joes," said Daddy. "I like them better than hamburgers." He took a bite of his and brown juice dripped down his chin. "If we could figure out the secret of your sauce, Angie, we could open up a chain and get rich. Call it MacWyman's."

"The Fallen Arches," said Fred.

"Either way," said Daddy. "I think sloppy joes are the wave of the future. Easy to prepare. Tasty. Inexpensive. Fewer calories than hamburgers. By George, I think we

161

ought to make a couple thousand sloppy joes and sell them at the big Fourth of July affair."

Angie said she heard that the Fourth was going to be quite a shebang this year, what with the orchestra concert—she looked at Rachel and smiled. "I'm getting excited about it, and it's still a week away," she said. She turned to Mother. "Aren't you excited about it?" she asked.

"Yes," said Mother. "Looking forward to it."

"What an honor for the town!" cried Angie. "To have a violin player and the conductor! And both from one family!"

Mother smiled. "It's an honor until you think of what could go wrong, and then it's sort of an honorable headache."

"How about another of those beautiful sloppy joes?" said Daddy, trying to change the subject. He reached for the platter and offered Angie one, but she shook her head.

"What can go wrong? It'll be wonderful!" Angie said. "Imagine. All those people coming from all over—coming to Sandy Bottom—and to hear an orchestra! Won't that be a feather in our cap!"

"What are you going to play?" said Fred. "Old Glenn Miller tunes?" He was kidding, but Daddy didn't get it.

"No," said Daddy, "we'll play a Mendelssohn symphony and some of a Mozart piano concerto, the one that goes"—he hummed a few bars of the Mozart—"and wind up with a bang. 'The 1812 Overture.'"

"What is that?" said Angie.

Daddy looked up. "What is what?"

" 'The 1812 Overture.' "

"It's the one with the cannon," he said. "You'll know it when you hear it."

Carol leaned forward. "You're going to have cannon?"

"Spoke to the cannon people today and arranged for five cannons," said Daddy. "They'll put them in the high school parking lot. Everybody has to leave their windows open, so the glass won't shatter."

"It sounds lovely," said Angie. "I hope the weather cooperates. But Ingrid's not going to play the piano?"

"No," said Daddy. "She has retired from the concert stage, I'm afraid. We're bringing in a kid from Green Bay."

Mother smiled at Daddy. "The truth is, nobody asked me," she said. "But that's all right. I'm not sure I could follow this conductor anyway."

Fred stood up. "Who wants ice cream?" he said.

They ate their ice cream in Rachel's new garden, the fountain spraying and the water tinkling into the basin, and Carol said it was the prettiest garden she had seen.

They stood at the lilacs and said good night.

"How time flies," said Angie.

"A lovely evening," said Mother.

"Let's do it again," said Daddy.

"Absolutely," said Fred. The men shook hands, and Angie gave Mother a little hug.

Carol put her arm around Rachel's shoulders. "Thanks for coming to see my game," she said.

It *was* a lovely evening. When I grow up, Rachel thought, I will have evenings like this all the time. People sitting in the evening eating and talking together. Talking about normal things. Hearing each other make grammatical errors and silently forgiving them. *Them and us, we had a real good time.*

A DATE

*R*achel woke suddenly in the dark, sat bolt upright in bed, thinking she had heard a scream, and then she heard another one, from under her open window. She slid out of bed and saw the sliver of light under the door and opened it and stumbled sleepily down the hall to her parents' bedroom and slowly opened the door, just a crack, and looked in. They were asleep, back to back, breathing softly, and Mother had a pair of earphones on, so she could listen to the radio if she woke up in the night. Mother hated to waste a minute, and the public radio station broadcast Canadian and British programs all night, so if insomnia struck, she'd switch it on and lie there and learn something about salmon fishing or asteroids or aboriginal music in the Australian outback.

There was another scream, and another, and Rachel stood at the foot of their bed and said, "Dad—Mother," but there was no response. Then Rachel thought, Tomcats.

Two male cats had found each other and were squared off, fighting for domination and territory, and the screaming was simply one cat insulting another one, or chewing on his neck. There was nothing to do about them.

She tiptoed back into her room and looked out the window. She saw a flurry in the lilacs, two animals wrestling, and then the loser lit out across the Wymans' yard and the other chased it. There was a yelp in the distance, and then it was quiet.

It was three forty-five in the morning.

She lay awake in bed, listening. How cruel nature was, with cats battling each other to the death and hawks diving out of the sky to pluck up little rabbits from the corn stubble and cats capturing mice and torturing them. Not like the cartoons of happy critters cavorting hand in hand in the woods. It was constant warfare out there. And was mankind so different? Everybody pushing to get ahead, trying to be noticed, to get good grades, to move up the ladder so you can lord it over the others and make them do things your way. She knew she would never be good at that. She was a musician. A rabbit. Trembling in her burrow, peeking out, her pink eyes blinking. The hawks were up in the sky, circling, floating on the wind, their glassy telescopic eyes focused on the ground, and she could not see them up in the blue. But she couldn't live her life terrified, hiding in a hole in the ground. What could she do?

And then suddenly the room was bright. It was morning, and she smelled waffles and maple syrup.

It was Wednesday, the Wednesday before the Monday of the Fourth of July concert, and the first rehearsal was this evening. Mother had announced last night as she went upstairs with a raging headache that she'd had enough of Fourth of July and she'd be a lot happier when it was the Fifth of July. The Greens' telephone had been ringing for days, over and over and over, with people needing to know something about the Fourth. Daddy's meteorologist friend in Eau Claire had new information on the storm front in the Dakotas, moving east—the thunderstorms probably would arrive Sunday, and the sky should clear by Monday. The company that was renting Daddy the benches needed to know exactly how many. Was he expecting more than two thousand people? And how many of them would bring their own lawn chairs or sit on the grass? The bratwurst people needed a final estimate too, and the beer people and the ladies from the Lutheran church who were operating a pie booth wanted to know how many to bake. Daddy told them, "You could bake all year and never make enough, especially of the blueberry."

People called Daddy at the office and they called him at home. How many loudspeakers for the public-address system? What size canopy for the musicians' backstage area? Where should the portable toilets go? Mother and Rachel wrote down the messages on a yellow legal pad and soon it was half full of scrawls—"Library Used Book Sale: can they set up tables nr bandstand? Cotton candy. Yes or no? Call Bud abt when to spray for mosquitoes. Mayor wd like to lead crowd in Pledge of Allegiance, OK? Will VFW honor guard come up onstage or stand on ground? Prayer?"

A musician needed to line up a ride, and did Daddy have the phone number of that oboeist in Racine? Would there be food backstage or should the musicians bring their own? The man who was bringing the carnival rides from LaCrosse needed to know about electrical hookups and should he bring two Ferris wheels or just one? And what about the pony rides? The police chief called and Rachel answered: He was terribly concerned that a gigantic crowd would show up, and where would they park, and what had Daddy arranged as far as portable toilets? Rachel had talked to the portable-toilet man just a few minutes before, so she knew the number: twenty-four. You could handle two hundred people easily per portable toilet, according to the toilet man—and probably three hundred. He seemed to know exactly, down to the last gallon, how much urine is created per thousand people on a summer night. The police chief didn't think twenty-four toilets would be enough. And he was nervous about gangs. Motorcycle gangs. Drugs. Violence. "Motorcycle gangs don't usually show up for symphony concerts," Rachel said, trying to be positive. "We don't know that," said the chief. "Usually, it's when you think they won't show up, you look around and suddenly they're here." He thought he might need to call in some help from the Highway Patrol, and could the Fourth of July Dairy Days Committee help pay for that?

Rachel wrote it all down on the legal pad. The fact was, there wasn't any committee, it was all Daddy. Daddy was the sort of person who liked to run things and run them right, and that meant supervising everything himself.

Tuesday night, she got a call that made her laugh out loud. A man from the Zion Methodist Men's Club needed to know if the parking lot behind the square could be roped off a day early so their Dunk the Pastor tank could be put up. It would take a long time to unload it from the flatbed truck and fill it with water.

"You mean you *weren't* joking?" she said to Daddy over supper. "Reverend Sykes actually *is* going to let people throw balls at a target and try to dunk him?"

"Exactly," said Daddy. "But if only we could've gotten your Mother up there instead—we could've earned enough money to pay for everything!"

"Very funny," said Mother.

Mother woke up on Wednesday morning with a renewed intent to stop smoking. On Tuesday, she had worked so hard on the arts-center project, finagling a grant from the state Arts Board to match Mrs. Ferguson's and then persuading Mr. Sorenson down in Arizona to match both of them, and then she had ordered all of the music for the Zion choir for the fall from a choral supply house in Minneapolis, and engrossed in all she had to do, she simply had forgotten to smoke—only half a pack on Tuesday, she told them proudly, *ten measly cigarettes*. Surely she could reduce ten to five and then two, and—then the phone rang during breakfast, Grandma calling from Milwaukee. "Hi, Grandma," said Rachel, her mouth half full of cereal and toast. Mother looked around for a cigarette. Daddy stood up quietly and left the room.

"What's up with you people? Haven't heard a word from you. Your mother was supposed to call me. You sick or something? Did you forget the phone number? What's going on?" said Grandma. She talked loud. Rachel held the phone away from her ear.

"We're awfully busy, Grandma. There's going to be a big concert here on Monday, you know. Are you still coming on Sunday?"

"Yes, of course. What concert?"

So Rachel told her again about Daddy's orchestra, and as she did, she smelled the smoke. Mother was pacing the floor in her blue bathrobe, smoking her first cigarette of the day. Daddy had left for the office.

Grandma said something about people not having the sense that God gave geese and going off and getting into big projects instead of looking after their own health the way they ought to. Rachel said, "It's going to be wonderful, Grandma! Mendelssohn and Mozart and Tchaikovsky's '1812.' "

"Mozart!" harrumphed Grandma. She preferred Wagner, who was closer to her own personality. It was easy to imagine Grandma in a gold wig with braids and a helmet with horns, holding a spear and shield, standing among fiberglass boulders and screeching an aria from *Die Walküre*.

So Rachel passed the telephone to Mother, who sat holding it, smoking her cigarette and then another one, saying, "Yes, I know, Mother. Yes." Rachel knew she was getting Grandma's old lecture about WHY did they live in that miserable little jerkwater town when they could be living like civilized people in the city of Milwaukee in a nice house near Grandma and Grandpa's, and Grandpa would be *happy* to get Daddy a good job, he would be *tickled,* and Ingrid could *do* things with her life instead of wasting it away playing in that Baptist church— *"Methodist,"* said Mother. (Grandma didn't know about the battles with the school board and the war with Mayor Broadbent.) And, Grandma said, it would be awfully nice to have the three of them in Milwaukee as she and Grandpa faded away into the sunset—"We won't be around forever, you know, so you ought to see us when you can. When we're gone, you'll wish you'd seen more of us. And that's the truth, Ingrid."

By the time it was over, Mother had wilted down to a little pile of guilt—conversations with Grandma were hard on her. She went up to the bedroom and cried for a while, and when she came down, she had put on a nice white summer dress and painted her toenails. She sat down barefoot at the piano, her hands at her sides, and looked up at the ceiling with a faraway dreamy look on her face. She was counting softly to herself, then she gently raised her hands to the keyboard, breathed in lightly, and her left hand played soft pulsing chords and then came the melody in her right hand: the slow movement of the Mozart piano concerto. The same one the kid from Green Bay was going to play at the Fourth of July.

Rachel was washing up the breakfast dishes. It was a fine sunny day. She went out back and watered the daylilies and the daisies, which finally had half a chance now that the weeds had been cleared away. She thought about the rehearsal that evening. She thought, What if I stayed at home for the rest of my life as Emily did? Lived in my room and wrote poems on little slips of paper and tied them with ribbon and put them in a shoe box. I'd have a wall built around this garden so I could sit in it without feeling that someone was looking at me. I would wear a white dress. People would come to visit and Mother would serve them coffee and sit and talk with them and they'd be listening for the creak of floorboards overhead, looking for a glimpse of the mysterious Rachel Green, the elusive and ghostly Rachel, the saintly recluse who, every day, picks up her violin and plays a sad sweet tune, a tune for her unrequited love, the elusive Scott.

She tried to practice her violin, but she couldn't concentrate. She called Carol's house and Carol was asleep, said Angie. She flopped on the bed and tried to read *Moby Dick*. Mother had put it on Rachel's desk weeks ago with a note: "Now that school is over, you'll have plenty of time for reading, and here is a book that would be a very good use of your time. Love, your mother." Rachel read a few pages of *Moby Dick* and then skipped a few and then jumped thirty pages, looking for the scene in which the white whale attacks the whaling boat, but she couldn't find it. I'm sorry, she thought, but if this is a great book, then I'm Jascha Heifetz.

Mother was still at the piano. Now she was playing a fast movement of the Mozart concerto. Over and over she played a melody that went a little way and then turned around and came back. She kept stumbling on the same note. *"Grrrr!"* she said, and stomped her foot. Then she tried it again. It was perfect.

Rachel heard the phone ring just as she was about to go and work some more on the rock garden. Mother called, "Telephone!" from the bottom of the stairs. Rachel went to her parents' room and picked up the extension. It was Scott.

"Rachel," he said, "I know it's the last minute, but— could you go to a movie with me Saturday night?" He sounded nervous. "There's a drive-in called the Sunset about halfway between here and there. I'll pick you up. Okay? My mother said I could use her car. They're showing a couple of horror movies. You like horror? I do. Anyway, these're supposed to be pretty good. But we don't have to stay for both of them if you don't want. In fact, we don't have to go if you don't want to, we could do something else. I was going to ask you at rehearsal tonight but then I remembered that I have your phone number. How are you?" He was nervous, all right. Hadn't he ever asked a girl to the movies before?

She was going to say that she needed to ask her mother, but she decided not to bother Mother. Mother was busy. Mozart was rising up the staircase, a beautiful rainstorm of

Mozart, and the music seemed to say, "Sure, go to the movie, have a good time," so she said, "Sure. What time?" Eight o'clock, he said. And they said good-bye. And hung up. And then she sat down.

So she wouldn't spend her life in a white dress in a walled garden. A very handsome boy who was so much cooler than anyone she knew in Sandy Bottom wanted to come in his mother's car and take her to see a horror movie.

13

FIRST REHEARSAL

*R*achel's heart started to pound and her palms got damp when Mother pulled the car up to the curb alongside the high school and stopped. There was the sidewalk leading to the door leading into the school auditorium. A woman in a black short-sleeved blouse and billowy black silk pants was opening it, a violin case under her arm, and Rachel felt a little wave of panic: Was everyone supposed to wear black for rehearsal? Had Mr. Robbins said to wear black and she hadn't heard him? Had only she forgotten? Would she walk in and be the only one wearing the wrong clothes?

"There's no dress requirement for a rehearsal," said Mother. "But your father tried on five different shirts today, trying to find the most conductor-looking one. He

175

finally put on the black turtleneck. I think he's going to suffocate in it, but that's the look he wanted. So if you see someone in a black turtleneck, that's your father."

She kissed Rachel on the cheek and Rachel slid out, her case in hand, and slammed the car door. She wished Mother would drive away so that she could sit down on the iron railing for a few minutes and pull her courage together, but the car sat, idling, as Rachel walked to the door and pulled on the handle. Locked. She tried the other handle. It opened. Rachel waved and Mother drove off.

Inside was such a wonderful cacophony of tooting and scraping and tuning, Rachel had to smile. The door opened onto a gray cinderblock hallway, and the cafeteria tables along one wall were strewn with instrument cases and folders of music. Forty musicians jammed the hall, warming up and tuning and talking at the same time, and milling around like cows waiting to be milked. Three men stood puffing away on cigarettes, their heads tilted back, blowing thin pale puffs of smoke up past a NO SMOKING sign toward a vent in the ceiling where the smoke curled neatly in and disappeared. One of them looked at his watch. "I'm not staying one minute after nine o'clock," he said. A beefy bald man holding a French horn to his lips winked at Rachel as the door closed behind her, and he blew a long mournful note. He sat at the table, a piece of birthday cake on a napkin in front of him, and he wasn't wearing black; he wore a green-plaid polyester sportcoat with a big button that said I DIDN'T DO IT, and he had carefully combed his last surviving strands of hair across his shiny dome.

She tiptoed past him and squeezed through the crowd, past a couple trumpet players making blutzy sounds on their mouthpieces, until her way was blocked by a short fat man who looked at her, misery in his watery brown eyes, and did not move aside. He draped a handkerchief on the chinrest of his violin, put it under his chin, and said, "You're in the wrong place, kiddo. This ain't school orchestra."

"I'm looking for the conductor," she said firmly.

"What conductor?" Then he turned and said, "Hey, Larry, where's the maestro?"

A studious man with an old blue beret on his head turned and looked at Rachel and then at the violinist. His face was the color of cold potatoes, and thin, and a thatch of white hair poked out from under the beret. His bassoon rested on one shoulder like a rifle and he was chewing carefully on carrots and celery from a plastic container. A toothbrush poked out from his shirt pocket.

"Who?" he said.

"The conductor," said the violinist. "What's his name."

"His name is Norman Green," said Rachel. She looked past them for an empty place where she could put her violin case.

Larry shrugged and shook his head.

"Maybe Helen knows," the violinist said. He smirked and rolled his eyes and nodded to the left, toward an oboeist, slim and sitting perfectly straight, her black hair cut short, blowing a long A and watching the dial of an electronic tuner, adjusting her reed. The violinist plucked his A and Rachel could tell that he was slightly sharp. That was how violinists were. No matter how hard oboeists tried to find a perfect A, violinists always tuned a little higher, looking for that extra brightness.

Rachel liked oboeists. They were intense people, always worried about their reeds, whittling them with a knife, soaking them in water, sucking on them, and clicking the keys to make sure nothing drastic had happened to them in the last ninety seconds. Rachel had wanted to switch to the oboe once, she loved its soulful tones, but Mr. Amidore had discouraged her. "If it's hot, the oboe goes sharp, if it's humid the keys stick, and if it's cold the instrument could crack," he said. "You always have to nurse it. And the reeds—do you want to carve wood or play music? It's a pain in the wazoo. Stick to violin."

"Helen!" the violinist said, and the oboeist smiled at Rachel and said hi. "You're looking for Mr. Green?" she said. "He's looking for the janitor. There aren't enough music stands set up and the room is too hot. And there isn't a podium." She smiled and shook her head, as if this sort of confusion was utterly ordinary.

"Do you mind if I set my case down here?" said Rachel.

"Put it wherever you want."

Rachel set her case down and a woman with long blond hair who was reading a paperback book, a flute with a shiny gold mouthpiece across her knees, looked up, startled. She had cold blue eyes and wore long dangly silver earrings and a necklace made of shells and stones. "This is the wind-section table," she said. "Violins are back there."

"Sorry," said Rachel, again. "Bye," she said to Helen, who smiled sweetly. Rachel turned away. The long hallway led backstage, where she had stood a few months ago and watched Carol in *The Diary of Anne Frank,* sitting in the Frank apartment in Amsterdam, wearing a nice blue plaid skirt and white blouse and writing in her diary as the Nazi soldiers shouted offstage and banged on the door and the lights went dark and the audience gave her an ovation. Now it was bare, except for the black curtains and the row of old rope pulleys along the wall and the light board with the big wooden-handled switches. A street lamp left over from some long-ago play stood by the brick wall and a big box full of hats and a papier-mâché statue of a naked man sitting, his head in his hands.

The cellists had taken their seats onstage, and the basses were lined up behind them, rumbling and droning, but the violas and violins lingered in the wings. They stood, tuning, plucking at their strings, but mostly talking. A woman rubbed rosin vigorously on the hair of her bow, then she played one loud long note and a cloud of rosin rose up over the fingerboard. Another violinist played a flashy passage and then glanced around to see if anyone was listening. He was a little man, very dapper, in a white shirt and gray slacks and loafers, and he had the most incredible hairdo Rachel had ever seen, a real work of art— a cloud of white hair, combed up high over his bald spot, sprayed to make it stiff, and it didn't lie *on* his head—no, it lay *over* and around his head, a sort of birdcage of hair with his head inside it, and he had sprayed sparkles in it to catch the light. His head looked like a Christmas centerpiece. Rachel wondered how long it took him to construct the hair in the morning.

Beside the cardboard street lamp, a little apart from the others, stood a puffy-faced man with curly gray hair, who wore an old gray satin vest, his paunch riding comfortably inside. He studied the orchestra seating chart taped to the wall, a toothpick in his mouth, as he fanned himself with a piece of music. He turned as Rachel walked past. "Miss Green?" he said.

She nodded. He nodded back. "I'm Klonowski. I'm the concertmaster." He shook her hand limply. "You're his daughter, right?" he said, pointing to Daddy's name at the top of the paper. She nodded again. He nodded very slowly. "Well," he said solemnly. "We shall see."

Lester the janitor appeared from around the corner with Daddy right behind him. Daddy looked nervous. "I've got a rehearsal beginning in ten minutes," he said.

Lester waved his hand. "Don't worry, I'll take care of it. No problem, Norm." Then he stopped and sniffed. "I smell smoke!" he yelled. "WHO'S SMOKING! There is absolutely NO smoking in here! State law!" Then he spotted the three culprits in the hallway, exhaling into the vent. "Out! Outside!" he shouted. "I don't believe it! Get out! Now!" A vein on the side of his bald head was popping out, and his face was red.

"Oh get a grip on it, old man," said one of the smokers.

"Smoke? Vat eez problem?" said another in a thick Russian accent.

"Put it out!" yelled Lester. The smokers stubbed out their cigarettes in a tin can on the table. Lester scowled at them, shaking his head. "Buncha teenagers," he said. He was chewing gum; he shifted the wad to the other side of his mouth and looked at Daddy: "Whatcha need now? Music stands? Coming right up."

He shuffled off in the direction of the band room, and Daddy looked around and saw Rachel and said, "Hi, beautiful." And he turned and slipped through the black curtain onstage and walked to the conductor's stand in front of the orchestra chairs.

He looked nice in his black turtleneck, she thought, and his tan pants and black socks and wingtips. A white towel was draped over one shoulder. Exactly the right size towel for a conductor in rehearsal.

Suddenly, two of the violins headed out through the curtain for the stage, and then most of the others followed, including the man with birdcage hair. Rachel put her case on an empty chair and opened it and took out her violin and tuned it and picked up her bow and walked onstage. She saw Scott: He was already in his seat, in the back row of cellos, playing. He was wearing jeans and a white polo shirt that set off his tan. She tried to catch his eye but he didn't look up from his music. A woman in front of Scott was jabbing her bow into the back of the man in front of her. He turned around and said, "Hey Mabel! Knock it off!"

"Look, Jack, I don't exactly have X-ray vision, so move your chair over to the left about a foot," Mabel said. Jack got up grumpily and moved his chair. Rachel's chair was on the third stand of second violins, according to the seating chart posted backstage, and she slipped through a thicket of bows and sat down. Her stand partner, an older woman, plump, with gnarly hands, gave her a friendly smile. She wore a red sweatshirt that said NEVER MESS WITH MOMMA and jeans and sneakers, and on the floor she had a huge purse with pink and turquoise stripes.

"Hi. I'm Evelyn Carlson," she said. "So you must be Rachel. Nice to meet you." She opened the music on the stand, which was "The 1812 Overture," and clucked her tongue. "Last time I played this, they crammed the cymbals right behind me and it practically loosened my fillings. That's the lousy thing about playing second violin, you can wind up back there in the hardware department."

A man sitting on the other side of Rachel was playing a passage of Paganini—pretty sloppily, Rachel thought, and then he launched into a few measures of Brahms, which was even worse. Then he stopped and turned to her. "Hi, I'm David. Good to see a new face around here once in a while. Keeps the geezer element down."

Rachel introduced herself and because she couldn't think of anything else to say, she said, "What kind of violin is that?"

"Italian. Unknown maker. I'm trying to sell it, as a matter of fact. Know anyone who might be interested?" Rachel shook her head. "I've also got a couple of bows I'm trying to sell—want to try one? I'll bring a couple to the next rehearsal."

"No, that's okay. Thanks anyway." She turned toward Evelyn, to ask about the orchestra—did these people play together often and all know each other?—and David said, "By the way, if you ever want to buy a new case, I can get them wholesale. Let me give you my card." He handed her his business card. It had his address and phone number printed on it, and at the top it said in fancy script, *David Washburn—violinist extraordinaire*. Who would say that about *himself*?

"So who do you study with?" he asked her.

"Mr. Amidore down in Oshkosh."

"Rudy! He's an old friend of mine! Tell him hello from me, will you? How is he anyway? How's his mother? He and I were at Manhattan together, he's a great guy—got a heart of gold."

Rachel told David about her problems with playing the Mozart and he was friendly after that and didn't try to sell her anything else. She glanced toward Scott but he still wasn't looking her way.

The woman seated in front of Rachel sat down and said, "So what joys do we have to look forward to this time?" She opened the folder and glanced at the music. "Mmmm, well, the Mendelssohn's not so bad." And then she saw "The 1812 Overture" and groaned. "Oh, God help us. Shoulda known. Tchaikovsky! And we get to play his absolute worst piece. A lot of thrashing around, a little ballet music, and then comes the artillery. Not exactly music, if you ask me. But of course, nobody asked me."

Daddy stood up front, looking at the musicians, and now he tapped the edge of his music stand with his baton. It was white, with a cork handle, and he had bought it from a catalog company in Philadelphia for thity-one dollars plus five dollars handling and shipping.

"Sorry about the delay, but these things happen," he said. Lester was clomping around, distributing the rest of the music stands. People gave him a wide berth as he carried them around, clanking, afraid he might lurch at them and drop one and crunch their instruments. Daddy smiled nervously. "It is really great to be here, and I am looking forward to the best Dairy Days ever." Someone in the horn section made a mooing sound. Daddy smiled at him. "Let's get started with the Mendelssohn."

"We need an A!" someone called out from the wind section.

"Ah! Of course!" Daddy said, flustered, and nodded at Helen, who took a deep breath, and out came the A, a little wobbly at first, and then they all joined in. The sound swelled mightily and then gradually disappeared except for one violinist having trouble getting in tune—*waang— eee—waang*—and a bass player rumbled around for a moment, and then there was silence. Daddy was already perspiring.

"Excuse me, Maestro," called one of the horn players. Daddy looked up: "Yes?"

"I was just wondering, Maestro—in measure fifty-one, what are our notes? I think there's a mistake in the part."

Poor Daddy. He wasn't used to reading scores, it took him a while. Rachel knew he was stuck. He put his glasses on and leaned over to look at the music. "Mmm . . . let's see when we get there. We'll talk about it later. Remind me at the break."

Rachel hoped he didn't see the horn players smirking, jabbing each other in the ribs with their elbows. Daddy smiled. "Shall we?" he said. He pushed up his sleeves, raised his baton, and took a deep breath. "One and . . ." His arms shot out in front of him, like he was grabbing for something. The orchestra began with a stutter and someone in the front of the violin section yelled "Now!" and the violins came bursting in on the third measure with the tune, roping everyone in with them. Daddy looked startled. Rachel suddenly felt afraid for him. Real conductors weren't supposed to be *surprised* when the orchesta played, they were supposed to frown and glower and toss back their long hair and wave their arms and be brilliant. Daddy waved at the cellos, and a moment later they came in, and he poked at the trumpets, and one of them played even though it wasn't time yet. Rachel looked down at the music, a cloud of notes like gnats on the page, and what she heard didn't look like what she saw on the page. Out of the corner of her eye she could see that all the bows were going in the opposite direction from hers. She played up bow, and they all played down bow. She tried to correct herself, but everything was going so fast. And then she was lost. Evelyn whispered, "Measure eighty-two!" and stabbed her bow at the bottom of the second page.

Rachel found her place and started playing. When she glanced up at Daddy again, he was looking more like a conductor and less like someone reeling from a bad fall. It didn't sound like the Berlin Philharmonic, but at least it sort of sounded like Mendelssohn. Rachel loved this symphony. As she played, she could imagine walking across one of the bridges over the Arno toward an outdoor café and looking back over the city and seeing the sun sparkling on the roofs.

It was wonderful to be right smack in the middle of all this *sound,* and she was finding that if you didn't worry too much about the hard parts and get flustered, you could sail through them pretty well. She had never played spiccato this well in Mr. Amidore's studio, and if he thought she had vibrato like a cat, then he should hear her now. And just when she was thinking all that, she didn't see a rest and came charging in ahead of everyone, as loud as she could. One guy two stands ahead turned and said, "Bravo!" but Rachel kept right on playing. Maybe no one but Evelyn and David knew who had played in the wrong place.

The trumpets made a terrible bleating sound, and Daddy jumped. One of the trumpet players yelled, "Sorry!" but he didn't look sorry, he looked like it was all a big joke. The horn players were glancing sidelong at each other and laughing.

What a bunch of jerks, she thought. Just because they had to play so few notes didn't mean they had the right to make fun of the music—or Daddy. If it was all a big joke to them, then why didn't they go play in a circus somewhere?

Daddy waved at them to stop. He ran his hands through his hair and bent down over the music. He was breathing hard. "It says *piano,* people. Not so loud, okay? Once more."

A man behind her muttered, "Well if the guy would quit waving around like a broken windmill, maybe we'd play the dynamics." Someone else snickered.

But this time it sounded better. It was clearer. You could hear all the parts and when the tune passed from one instrument to another, it sounded more graceful, not like they were passing a hot potato. Daddy nodded and smiled and some of the violists perked up, and the tympani player waved his mallet and smiled at Daddy. The bassoonist looked worried, but it seemed to be a permanent expression with him, as if he had serious car problems to deal with and a houseful of relatives and the bassoon was just one more headache. One of the violists, a young man with arms and legs bent like a praying mantis, swayed from side to side when he played. Rachel was glad she didn't have to sit next to *him*.

Halfway through the movement, Mr. Klonowski stopped and waved his bow in the air. Daddy looked over and stopped.

Mr. Klonowski looked at the principal second violinist with disgust. "Emile, are you guys going to do my bowings or not?"

Emile said, "What? You want to play the lumberjack style? With all those downbows?" He lifted his bow to the strings and played a few notes, hacking away as if it were a square dance. The cellos laughed and shuffled their feet.

"Aw, go take a lesson," said the concertmaster. He shook his head and muttered something to the man next to him.

Daddy looked at his watch. "Can we go on now?" he said. "Measure 484!" he called out, and they played the rest of the movement. In the very last measure, one of the clarinets played one note too many when everyone was finished. Everyone burst out laughing, but Daddy just looked uneasy and said, "Good! Let's take a break!" and Mr. Klonowski yelled, "Fifteen minutes!" and everyone stood up.

Rachel was embarrassed. She had lost her place twice and played a lot of wrong notes and played in a rest: It was hard to keep your eyes on the music and keep track of Daddy at the same time. But when Evelyn stood up, her violin tucked under her arm, she touched Rachel on the shoulder and said, "Good job! You're doing just great!"

"I'm sorry I got lost a couple of times," said Rachel.

Evelyn laughed, "Oh, don't worry. You'll get the hang of it. Don't look up at the conductor so much. Just keep him in the corner of your eye. You'll get it. Who is he, anyway? Do you know him?"

"He's my dad."

"Your *father*!" There was a long pause, a little too long, as if she were trying to think of something polite to say. "How wonderful! Where does he usually conduct?"

Rachel thought, Oh, usually in the den, but she said, "Oh, just around. Here and there. Local stuff. He's pretty new at it."

Evelyn went off to get coffee, and Rachel followed. She saw Evelyn stop and chat with several people who then turned and looked at her, Rachel, so she could imagine that in a few minutes, the cat would be out of the bag and everyone would know she was the Conductor's Daughter, and then they would listen closely to how she played and hear her mistakes. She edged through the crowd, thinking maybe she should go outdoors so she wouldn't hear people say mean things about Daddy.

Little clumps of people stood backstage and in the hallway, talking and laughing. The remainder of the birthday cake was brought out—it was the birthday of one of the cellists—and the horn players sang "Happy Birthday" a half-step flat, deliberately flat, exactly one-half step all the way through—and everyone clapped. "Now if you guys could just play that well all the time," David said, and winked at Rachel. She was studying the seating chart on the wall, memorizing some of the names so she could walk up to people and talk to them.

Mr. Klonowski and Emile stood by the cardboard street lamp, exactly where they had stood before, with their backs to the wall, and told each other jokes. "What's the difference between a soprano and a terrorist?" said Emile.

"You can reason with a terrorist," said Mr. Klonowski. "How do you get a violin to sound like a viola?"

"Sit in back and don't play," said Emile. Mr. Klonowski frowned at Rachel as she walked past and stopped by the rope pulleys. She stood, wishing that Scott would come offstage and talk to her. Did he not want to be seen with her?

Katherine, a young violinist with big brown eyes and long black hair, passed around a large Tupperware container filled with homemade chocolate-chip cookies. "Thank you," said Rachel, politely. She stood by the rope pulleys, munching it. And then noticed Scott, a few feet away. He was running a comb through his hair. Next to him was his stand partner, a lovely young woman with long dark hair pulled back in a silver hair clip. Then he saw Rachel.

"Hey!" He stuck the comb in his back pocket and edged over next to her and whispered, "How's it going?"

"It's kind of hard, isn't it," said Rachel.

"It's a little tricky, but I was watching you. You look like you're doing great." He pointed at one of the bass players, who was shoving a cookie in his mouth. "I just wish those basses would quit rushing the beat, it's like having a stampede of elephants behind you."

"Do we look like we belong here?" Rachel whispered. "Or is there a big sign on our backs, saying 'Student Driver'?"

Scott laughed. "We belong just as much as anybody else," he said. "Look at them. What a bunch of oddballs."

He was right. You looked around the room and you saw Larry sitting in his chair whittling away at a reed and listening to something on headphones, and Marion, one of the violists, squatting on the hall floor, eating from a bowl of brown rice mixed with bean sprouts and water chestnuts, drinking from a bottle of brown water. Maybe it had vitamins in it. But for someone eating health food, Marion looked terrible, she was pale and haggard, long scraggly hair hanging in her face, and she chewed with her mouth open. And then there was the man with birdcage hair: She overheard someone say to him, "Stash, how many cats you got now?" and he said, "Eight." A man with eight cats was definitely off the far end of the normal chart. The percussion players were trying on hats from the props box backstage. The man with the cymbals was wearing a woman's straw hat with petunias around the brim and singing "Tiptoe Through the Tulips" in a falsetto voice and making flouncy gestures. What a nuthouse.

Scott's stand partner looked at Rachel coldly. "I hear you're from a really musical family," she said. She yawned. "So what do you think of this gig? It's kind of nickel-and-dime stuff, if you ask me, but summer gigs are always dopey, so—oh, well." She slipped away.

"By the way, I think your Dad is really great," said Scott.

"You do?"

"I do. He's very musical and I like his tempos. He's really not a bad conductor."

"Whew! I'm glad you think so," she said.

"What do you think?" Scott said, leaning close to her, whispering. "Do these people have other jobs? Or are they full-time musicians?"

Rachel thought that most of them probably were music teachers and did this once in a while, but some of them definitely looked like full-time players. They had that cool look that said, "So? I'm different. Is that a problem?"

Mr. Birdcage she could imagine as a strolling violinist in a restaurant with fake limestone walls and water trickling down them, playing "Malagueña" over and over. And you could probably find the trumpets playing in Polish polka bars in Milwaukee.

Suddenly, Mr. Klonowski clapped his hands three times and said, "Okay, let's go!" and they all trooped back onstage and took their places.

The second half of the rehearsal went better, she thought.

They played "The 1812 Overture." Daddy looked over at the cellos before they started, "Ready for this?" He smiled and yanked up his sleeves. There was a big solo part for them at the begining of the piece. The passage sounded like a hymn, a prayer, getting more intense with each phrase. Rachel shifted a little so she could watch Scott, and she could tell he was one of the best players there. He watched Daddy's baton and his head moved a little with the music and his hand moved easily up and down the fingerboard, not in a jerky spidery way like his stand partner. While everyone sat listening to the cellos, Evelyn leaned over and said, "You gotta count like mad in this one."

Rachel was glad she had practiced—the slow parts weren't so hard, but when things got wound up toward the end, Rachel had her hands full, she was perched on the edge of her chair, trying her hardest to keep up. Sometimes the music on the page looked like a simple scale, but when you added up all the sharps and flats it got complicated. This time Evelyn was the one who couldn't keep up. In the hard places, she kept stopping and pretending her violin was out of tune, or the hair on her bow needed tightening, or she would mark a bowing in the part; that way, she gave herself a breather. Evelyn turned pages because she was sitting on the inside; she set her violin in her lap, licked her index finger, and flipped the page over. Mr. Birdcage was trying to maneuver his bow through his hairstyle so he could scratch the top of his head with the tip of the bow, and the praying-mantis violist was faking a coughing fit every time they came to a hard part.

Daddy's conducting was getting really vigorous, his eyes were big, and his mouth made a little O, he was concentrating hard. His baton flew in loops and figure eights, he shouted at them "Yes!" and "Here we go!" and *"Yes! Yes! More!"* and he gave big swooping gestures to people for their entrances. The brass players were blasting away and getting red in the face, the percussion players were thumping and whacking, the strings were scrambling. Then Daddy threw up his hands and they all stopped, and he had the cellos and basses play their parts, which sounded like the rumble of heavy machinery, but it got better. At first the percussion sounded like a truckload of spare parts going through a plate-glass window, but they got it right eventually. Near the end, it got so loud some people stopped and plugged their ears. A final crash, and Daddy laughed out loud and said, "Better bring your earplugs for the performance! Remember, we're going to have cannons!"

At the end of the rehearsal, Daddy stood and beamed at all of them. "Great job, everyone! Thank you," he said.

"I know I shouldn't say this to a bunch of old pros like you, but: I'm new at this, and I must say, you make it seem not that hard." A bunch of people hooted and stamped their feet. "Next time we'll have the pianist here to do the Mozart, and please check and make sure you have parts for 'Star-Spangled Banner' in your folders. We have a tenor soloist coming for the Fourth. Thanks, everyone!"

The musicians cleared out quickly. Evelyn said, "See you Friday," and she was gone. Rachel waited for Daddy. He was collecting his music and listening as one of the violinists told him she couldn't be at the next rehearsal because of a family emergency. Rachel could tell it was all a big fib—how could it be an emergency if you knew about it two days ahead? But Daddy looked sympathetic and said he was sorry and told her to come play the concert anyway.

Then he saw Rachel. "How'd I do?" he said. She put down her violin case and put her arms around him and squeezed.

They heard Mother playing the piano when they pulled into the driveway, a Bach *Invention*, and when they came in the kitchen and the screen door slapped shut, the music came to a dead halt. Mother came bounding into the kitchen and gave them each a kiss.

"So, how was it? Everything went okay?"

"It was very, very good," said Rachel.

Daddy looked tired and happy. "I think it went okay. A lot of rough spots, but I tried to just give a clear downbeat and let them take it from there." He sat down in a chair and took a deep breath. "Sometimes it's best to let go of the reins and trust the horses to take you to the barn."

Mother's left eyebrow shot up. "And that worked, huh?" Rachel could tell she was curious. At the last minute, she had decided not to go to the rehearsal, though Daddy asked her to, said it would be a big help to have an objective pair of ears, she could take notes and help him with the dynamics and so forth, but Mother declined. "Too many cooks spoil the broth," she said. "I'll wait for the final product." But she was awfully curious.

Daddy was beat. He looked at the sheaf of telephone messages. The *Register* wanted to know when to send the photographer. The mayor felt it was extremely important to have the Pledge of Allegiance recited at the concert and felt that he was the logical person to lead it, so if Norman didn't have any objections, he would plan on doing that. And of course he would be making a few remarks. "Over my dead body," said Daddy. The woman he had hired to cater the supper for the musicians on the Fourth was down with strep throat, so he had to call Florence and ask her to ask some women from church. Florence asked what food musicians like to eat. "Everything. And lots of it," said Daddy. "Nothing too greasy, but remember: large quantities." He stood at the sink and ate coffee ice cream out of the carton.

"I remember the first time I ever heard that Mendelssohn symphony was in my junior year at the University, right after I met you," he said to Mother. "We'd eaten lunch together a couple times in the cafeteria and I asked you to a concert, and you said you couldn't go, so I

195

went alone, and then I spotted you two rows away, next to a guy with blond hair. He turned and talked to you and I could see that he was your date and that he was about the handsomest person this side of the movies. He was like a Greek god."

"He was about as smart as a boxful of hammers," said Mother.

"He looked at you as if you were the sun in his sky," said Daddy.

"He looked like that at every woman he met," said Mother.

"He obviously adored you. I remember his golden ringlets and his blue eyes. Obviously, he came from a background of some wealth."

"His father had a dry-cleaning shop in Sheboygan," said Mother.

"Anyway," said Daddy, "the Mendelssohn symphony was the first thing on the program that night. I listened to it, and I looked at the back of your head and his head and I was consumed with jealousy. I wanted to shoot him. It all came back to me, listening to it at rehearsal. A beautiful work, and so joyful, but to me, forever laden with dark meanings."

Mother snorted. "I ditched the guy at intermission the moment I saw you in the lobby and you and I talked and I practically threw myself at you."

Daddy winked at Rachel. "That was at intermission. But during the Mendelssohn, I was thinking about sailing away on a tramp steamer to South America."

He rinsed off the spoon and put the empty carton in the garbage. "Anyway, thank goodness for intermission. Good night, all." He kissed Rachel, and then Mother, and went slowly up to bed.

When he was gone, Mother said quietly to Rachel, "So how was it *really?* No train wrecks? Tell me the truth."

"It was really okay. It was a little rough at the beginning, but he got much better. I think you'll be surprised."

Mother looked out the window. "Daddy said that cellist from Oshkosh was going to be playing. Was he there? The one from your music school?"

"You mean Scott?" Rachel said.

"I guess so. You know, the one with the hair."

"What do you mean, 'the one with the hair'?"

"The one with the nice hair. Anyway, that's good there's someone you know in the orchestra." Mother paused. "What do his parents do?"

"How should I know?" said Rachel. She stood up and went to the cupboard and got a glass.

"I thought maybe he would have said."

"No, he didn't. Do you want me to send him a questionnaire? An application form?"

Mother's eyebrow went up again. "An application form for what?"

Rachel turned on the faucet and ran cold water into the glass. "I'm going to a movie with him Saturday night," she said. There was a silence. A sort of silent *thunk*.

"Oh," said Mother.

It was only an *oh*, a simple vowel, but Mother put a lot

into it, a whole paragraph or more, and Rachel heard it exactly, it said: *I have been waiting for your adolescence to happen, dreading it, knowing the inevitability of it, but then I got involved with other things and forgot, but now I will be paying very close attention, believe me. You might imagine that you can waltz out of the house anytime you like, no questions asked, but you are wrong. You and I will be having some very interesting conversations in the very near future.*

Rachel was tired. She lay in bed, in the dark, listening to the night, the distant whine of tires on Main Street, a song playing on a radio down the street. It was a big band, with a lot of saxophones, slow and mushy. Some old person, sitting on their porch, waiting for bedtime. There were no tomcats fighting. Evidently, the matter had been settled for now. She heard Mother's voice from down the hall.

She thought of writing to Phoebe but decided not to. If you write someone long letters and she sends you back an occasional postcard, it's a pretty clear sign. Phoebe had her own life to lead. Rachel wanted someone to write letters to. Grandpa would be nice to write to, but he'd never write back. Neither would Scott, she guessed. Men don't write letters, for some reason. It would have to be a girl. And then she thought: *Carol.* She could try out Carol. Maybe they couldn't talk to each other so easily but isn't that what letters are for? To say what you can't say face-to-face?

Of course it's odd to write letters to your next-door neighbor. But Emily Dickinson did it all the time. Her sister-in-law Susan lived next door and Emily wrote letters to her as if she lived in Wyoming. Emily was someone who knew

that vast distances separate people, even those in close prox-
imity, and that you try to bridge that distance in writing.

She got out of bed, lit her candles, and got out her stationery and pen.

Dear Carol,

Well today was it, the first orchestra rehearsal.
I sit on the third stand of second violins with a
woman named Evelyn. She's nice, maybe a little
past her prime in terms of playing, but okay.
Daddy is an okay conductor, not a living genius,
but good enough, which, considering he never did
this before, is amazing. As for the rest of the
orchestra, about half of them were grumpy and
growly, and the other half couldn't stop laughing.
The concertmaster is a grumpy old bear, but a
good player. The music is tricky, and it didn't
sound anything like Daddy's CDs. I guess that's
what rehearsals are for, to whip things into shape,
but this may take a lot of whipping. I'm babbling.
Sorry. I'm glad I play the violin. Oboe players sit
around carving reeds all day, they're as much into
crafts as into music. Trumpets don't get anything
interesting to play, a few big splats now and then
and that's all, and violas mainly play filler and sit
and look tired. Not like us violins, we get most of
the good stuff. I'm falling asleep. Is this okay to
write letters to you? I'm sorry I told you that I have
things to say and nobody to say them to. I'd like to
try to say them. One thing is, I think I'm going to

another school in the fall, a boarding school in northern Michigan and I'll miss you a lot. Once you said that we would always be friends, no matter what, and I hope that's so. I'll write to you again soon.

Lots of love,
Rachel

She folded the letter and put it in an envelope and wrote "Carol" on the outside and put it in her desk drawer. She blew out the candles and crawled into bed.

DREW

Daddy was wrapped up in the orchestra. He didn't talk at breakfast; he sat, eating his bran flakes and studying the music and making humming sounds and scratching notes to himself in the margin. The conductor's score was as big as an atlas, with all the different instrumental parts in it, and Daddy went off to work at the dairy with his big thick scores tucked under his arm. He sat in his office going over and over them, and came home and listened to recordings of the Mendelssohn symphony and the Mozart concerto and "The 1812 Overture," eating his dinner off a tray in the den, and following along in the score, scribbling notes in the margin. Florence called Thursday night to leave Daddy a message, that she had found forty temporary workers to scoop ice cream at the Bluebird booth for the Fourth of July. She told Mother that one of the supervisors had found Daddy in the men's room that afternoon, waving the baton and watching himself in the mirror. "Excuse me!" the man said, retreating backward, averting his eyes.

It was different now, Rachel thought, to sit in her garden, at the glass table, and drink cold lemonade and read a book. Before, she was only a kid whiling away a long summer, and now she was a professional musician, enjoying her day off. She was done with *The Blonde in Room 436* and was starting a new Pete Murphy mystery, *No More Soft Ballads for Belinda,* in which the wily detective had been called in to solve the mystery of a missing waitress named Belinda and within ten pages you knew that she was dead and that the culprit was a folksinger named Jon who played in college coffeehouses and had long soft brown hair. Pete Murphy was very dubious about folksingers with long brown hair, especially if it was soft.

Rachel wondered if Mother had ever read trash novels, and guessed that she had. Those drippy duets they had played a few weeks before—anyone who loved them as much as Mother did certainly must enjoy an occasional bad novel too. Probably Mother was hiding this, not wanting to lead her daughter down that path, wanting her to read *Moby-Dick* and *Jane Eyre*. Florence, on the other hand, made no bones about trash. She loved *The Bridges of Madison County*. Florence was a major consumer of trash. Since her fiancé had left her all those years ago, she lived alone with her toy collie, Tess, and ate cherry creams and was addicted to trash novels in which handsome sensitive men with abdominal muscles like corrugated steel gently took older women in their arms and made them feel things they had never felt before.

It's different with me, though, thought Rachel, filling her glass with lemonade. When you have to go to work the next day rehearsing Mendelssohn, you can allow yourself a little Pete Murphy in the afternoon. Pete was on Jon's trail, following him from college to college, sitting in the coffeehouses, watching him sing "Black, Black, Black Is the Color of My True Love's Hair," waiting to nab him.

Drew Johnson came to the second rehearsal, on Friday morning. He and his mother walked through the crowd of musicians tuning up in the hallway, who stopped to stare as they passed by. Mrs. Johnson was hard to miss. She stood six feet tall in her high heels, her short black hair was slicked back on the sides with a shiny pomade, she was broad in the shoulders and broad in the rear, and she wore a canary-yellow suit under a bright green plastic raincoat. She carried two bulging shopping bags and led a toy poodle on a leash. The dog was white. Behind her came Drew, in a little blue suit with a white carnation in the lapel, his brown hair watered and parted and severely combed, his face pale, as if he had been hauled from his deathbed.

Mrs. Johnson had a look of command about her. She plowed through the crowd and when she got backstage, she set down her shopping bags and looked around at Mr.

Klonowski and Emile and Evelyn and some of the wind players and Rachel, all busy tuning and talking, and then she spotted Scott, the only person in the vicinity who was not holding an instrument, and held out the dog's leash to him and said, "Would you mind watching Michelle for a moment, thank you," and then parted the curtain and walked onstage, leaving Drew with the bags.

Evelyn said to Scott, "We forgot to tell you—you're the animal handler, too."

"Yes," said Emile, "if you can play cello, then we figure you're good with dogs."

The dog sat, her eyes fixed on the fold in the curtain through which Mrs. Johnson had gone. Drew turned to Rachel and smiled a faint sickly smile and whispered, "May I have a chair, please?"

She brought him a chair and he sat down, slumped back, and whimpered softly. He drew a deep breath, as if trying to collect himself after a harrowing experience.

"Is this the pianist?" Mr. Klonowski asked Rachel.

She nodded. "His name is Drew."

Mr. Klonowski looked at the boy and scowled. "What's his problem?"

"He's probably just a little nervous," said Rachel. "He'll be all right."

"I hope the dog isn't part of the act," he said.

Then Mrs. Johnson's voice boomed from the other side of the curtain: "I don't care if the concert *is* in a band shell, Mr. Green. Drew needs a dressing room! I thought I made this clear. He can't share a common space because he needs to lie down when he isn't playing! He has a sugar imbalance, as I told you on the phone."

"There aren't any dressing rooms at the band shell," said Daddy, "but let me see about getting a camper or an RV for him."

"Whatever," she said, "but it must have quiet and it must be dark. Curtains are an absolute must. Absolutely. I have to keep him in a quiet, dark place for an hour before he performs, where I can regulate his sugar intake and keep him hydrated."

Then she opened the curtain and came backstage. She saw Drew, half collapsed in his chair, and looked around at the musicians. "You haven't given him candy, have you?" she said. She took Michelle's leash from Scott—"Thank you," she said—and hoisted her shopping bags. "Come, honey," she said. "We have to sit in the auditorium. No dressing room today. I'm sorry, lambie. Just make the best of it."

They sat in the first row of seats while the orchestra played Mendelssohn, Mrs. Johnson in her yellow suit, legs crossed, and Michelle on the seat next to her, and Drew spread out across three seats, the green plastic raincoat over him, a sleep mask over his eyes.

Evelyn nudged Rachel and whispered, "The kid is a zombie. You see him backstage? His eyes are like pee holes in the snow." That got Rachel giggling, and Daddy gave her a severe look.

The last part of the symphony was a little ragged, but they ended together, and Daddy looked out over the orchestra and smiled. "Thank you!" he said. "It's starting to come together very well, I think. This is going to be a top-notch performance. Just keep in mind that it'll be outdoors, so let's have plenty of sound. Don't get too soft. Let's take a break."

"Hold it!" said Emile. "I have an announcement to make. Whoever's tapping their foot back there, stop it!" He turned and glared at the violins. "This isn't marching band."

At the break, Rachel stood up and looked out into the auditorium, and there, sitting in the back row, were Carol and Valerie and a couple of other girls from the softball team. They waved at Rachel and she waved back and climbed down the stage steps to say hello to them. Drew was sitting up now, and his mother was doling out pieces of chocolate to him. She gave one to Michelle too.

Carol came bounding up, grinning.

"How long have you been here?" asked Rachel.

"Got here when you started playing," said Carol, "Wow. This is really cool! I didn't know you were that good! I mean, I knew you were good, but I never knew you were good like that. Gosh, you were really playing fast stuff. And your dad. He really looks great. He puts so much *emotion* into it!"

Valerie gave Rachel a cool look. "It sounded good," she said. "But are there a lot of mistakes in there that, like, the average person wouldn't notice? It sounded like there might have been in that fast part."

Rachel gave her a cool look right back. "I think it's a pretty good orchestra," she said. "How was your game?"

"We lost, but it was close—eleven to nine," said Carol. "Valerie hit a home run with two on. Really poked it."

Valerie smiled modestly. "And Carol stole home, which was way cool," she said, smiling at Carol. "Their catcher wasn't paying much attention, and she tossed the ball back to the pitcher as Carol came streaking in and *bam,* ran right into her. It was awesome."

The teammates grinned at each other, and Valerie slapped Carol on the back. "My homegirl!" she said in a tough voice. "My main woman!" They all laughed. Rachel wished they would leave. Carol was the only one of them she liked. But they were a team and Carol had to be loyal to them, she supposed.

Valerie leaned forward and whispered to Rachel: "Who's the nerd?"

Mrs. Johnson led Drew by the arm up the stage steps, as Lester and Daddy rolled the piano out from the wings. They parked it in the middle, braked the wheels, and rearranged the orchestra chairs to make room for the conductor's podium.

"He's the pianist," said Rachel. "He's from Green Bay. He's thirteen."

Drew sat down on the padded piano bench and turned the two big knobs on the sides to adjust the height. He cranked it up a little, and then down a little. Then he bounced on the seat and raised it again as Mrs. Johnson watched.

"Is he good?" asked Carol.

"He's supposed to be," said Rachel. "I don't think he's feeling so hot right now, though. Poor kid. He's pretty scared."

When the orchestra filed in from the break, Drew still hadn't gotten the bench adjusted. The musicians took their places and retuned, and Daddy stood at the podium and smiled patiently as Mrs. Johnson took over cranking the bench and said, "How's that?" and Drew said, "I don't know," and then she cranked it down. Finally, he waved her away with a groan. She pulled up a folding chair next to him, and sat down. Michelle sat on the floor. Mrs. Johnson looked up at Daddy and nodded.

Daddy rapped on his music stand and said, "I'd like to introduce our piano soloist, a very talented young man, Mr. Drew Johnson," and there was a big hullaballoo of clapping and foot stomping.

Drew stood up and bowed stiffly, and then sat down. And then got up and adjusted the bench again. He leaned over and said something to his mother in a low urgent voice.

"We'll be right back," Mrs. Johnson announced, and she led Drew offstage. They all heard her ask Lester which way the bathroom was. The horn players snickered.

"Okay, let's play a little without the pianist," Daddy said.

Mr. Klonowski stood up. "Does everyone have a mute? The music is marked *con sordino*." Several string players leaned over and fumbled in their cases looking for mutes.

Mr. Birdcage piped up, "But we're playing outside, they're not going to hear a thing if we use mutes."

Daddy said, "I think he's right. Let's try it without."

Daddy raised his baton and counted silently and gave them an upbeat. They started playing what was supposed to be a gentle pulsing beat, but it sounded more like a pack of dogs tugging at the leash. Daddy stopped them and looked over at Emile in the second violins. Emile shrugged. Mr. Klonowski glared at him: "You've got about six different tempos going on over there. Can't you people read music?" Emile was about to say something back but Daddy rapped on his stand with the baton. "Okay everybody, I know it's a long rehearsal, but let's concentrate." This time everything worked. Everyone was together at the beginning and the wind players who had been cutting up in the Mendelssohn were watching Daddy, and the violins sounded smooth and glorious when they came in with the tune.

Drew and his mother returned. His jacket was off now, and his shirt was wet under his arms and down his back as he plopped down on the bench. Evelyn whispered, "It's out-and-out child abuse."

Mrs. Johnson sat in her chair and smiled at Daddy and mouthed the words "Thank you."

They started again. Drew sat very still, his arms at his sides, his head bent over the keys. The orchestra was making a lovely bed of sound—a perfect place to set down a solo. Daddy leaned over and gave Drew a huge cue when it came time for him to play, and he didn't play. There was nothing. He didn't even move. He was staring down at middle C.

The orchestra stopped. "Drew?" Daddy said. "That was your entrance."

Drew looked up in terror. Mrs. Johnson smiled at Daddy. "I'm sorry, but I don't think he can see you very well from where he is, Mr. Green." And so Daddy moved his music stand on the podium so that he was almost facing Drew.

"Poor kid," said Emile to his stand partner. "He looks scared, like he never saw a piano before in his life."

"Bet you a dollar the kid is about to lose his cookies," said David.

Evelyn leaned over to Rachel and whispered, "If you ever wondered what *real* stage fright looks like, this is it, a classic case."

They started again, and when it was time for Drew to play, Daddy looked straight at him and pointed and Drew plunked the keys, very softly and hesitantly, so you could barely hear him. His hands shook, he drifted behind the beat, and then he had a memory slip right in the middle of the big melody, the main theme, and played a few bars that sounded like Stravinsky and then repeated them. Daddy waved and the orchestra stopped.

Mrs. Johnson jumped up. "This piano bench is still not working right," she said. "If we could take *two minutes* and get it so it doesn't wobble, we could save ourselves a lot of time here."

So Lester had to come in with a piece of cardboard and snip off little squares for shims and put them under the legs of the piano bench. Four legs, four shims.

"The kid doesn't need a bench, he needs a bed," said David.

A flute player turned around and said something to the horns and they laughed, and then an oboeist played a honk, and all the winds chuckled. Drew stood by the piano, holding on to it as if he were about to fall over in a dead faint. Michelle was standing now, looking around anxiously, whining. Just as Lester finished the bench operation, Mrs. Johnson said that she thought Drew needed a glass of water, so Lester went off to fetch that. Michelle barked at him.

Daddy stood, arms folded, and gave Mrs. Johnson a stern look, and then he bent down and put a hand on Drew's shoulder. "Let's take a run at it, pal, okay? Once you get into it, it'll all come back to you. Don't think too hard about it, just let the music come out."

Mrs. Johnson rooted through one of her shopping bags, and came up with a big chocolate cookie and handed it to Drew.

Daddy sighed. She shrugged at him. "Have you ever read about blood-sugar imbalance, Mr. Green?" she said. Drew chewed his cookie slowly. There was snickering around the orchestra. A cellist played a few bars of "Twinkle, Twinkle, Little Star" in a minor key. Finally Daddy said, "Could I have it quiet? *Please*."

They tried again. The orchestra sounded beautiful, very elegant and serene, and Drew played as if he had been programmed, the melodic lines were perfectly flat and straight, and there was a glitch on his hard drive, and he repeated a phrase where he shouldn't have, and when Daddy turned to correct him and saw his pale pinched face and stricken eyes, and his large mother in yellow camped nearby, holding a cookie, Daddy was speechless.

"There's a very bright reflection on the piano lid," said Mrs. Johnson. "It's extremely distracting. I wonder if we couldn't cover the lid with black cloth. It's shining right in his eyes. And could we have that glass of water? Unchlorinated?"

Daddy stood, arms folded, eyes closed, as Lester laid a piece of curtain over the lid and taped it with silver duct tape. Then Mrs. Johnson wanted black duct tape, so he went and found a roll of black tape. He also brought a bottle of spring water, unchlorinated. Mrs. Johnson checked the label to make sure.

The musicians were enjoying this spectacle, especially the wind players. They watched Daddy's face, his closed eyes, his mouth twitches, his jaw clenching, waiting for him to explode and turn around and tell this witch to get out and take her dog and her wretched child with her— they were looking forward to that happy moment. But they didn't know Daddy. Rachel could see how hard this was for him, a man who believed in politeness and generosity at all costs. It wasn't in Daddy's makeup to *ever* turn around and yell at someone. Daddy hated confrontations, especially with women. It was all he could do to rap on the music stand and ask for quiet.

On the fourth attempt at the Mozart, Drew simply stopped halfway through and looked at his mother, and she jumped up and said, "Mr. Green!" The orchestra stopped. "Mr. Green, I'm very sorry," she said, "but Drew needs to take a break now." Rachel looked at Daddy and thought, Get tough now.

"Let's finish this," Daddy said sharply. "Okay, Drew?" He glanced down at the boy, and Drew went to pieces. He put his head down on the keys with a loud *thwankkkk* and sobbed for all he was worth. He sobbed louder than he had played the piano. He made terrible shuddering honking sounds, a *"Hwah-hwah-hwah"* like the sound of a board being pulled off a wall, the nails screeching, and all of the musicians stared straight at their music, embarrassed for him.

Mrs. Johnson rose from her chair and stepped toward Daddy as if she were about to whack him with her shopping bag. "This is outrageous," she said. "There has been absolutely no consideration here from the very beginning. I don't think you have any experience whatsoever in dealing with younger talent, Mr. Green. You have pushed and pushed and pushed, and you have shown a very belittling attitude toward me and my son, and we have taken about all we intend to take for one day." She bent down over Drew, who was still sobbing. "Come, lambie," she said. "Mommy's sorry. Mommy's going to take you home now." She pulled him up by his arm, and held him close to her, and picked up the shopping bags and managed to bend down and get Michelle's leash. She got her green raincoat off the chair, and she made a grand exit, glaring at Daddy, towing the dog, who was also glaring at Daddy and snarling, and helping Drew, who clung to her, his face buried in her yellow jacket.

Just then a horn player, who had been holding back his laughter, couldn't hold it any longer, and it came bursting out of his nose.

Mrs. Johnson stopped and glared at him. "I hope you roast in hell," she said. Then led Drew out through the back curtain. And then the back door slammed. And then it opened again and her voice yelled, "You won't be seeing *us* again!" And then the back door slammed again.

And then the orchestra broke up for good. The horns exploded into screeches of laughter, and the brass players fell over each other, and Mr. Klonowski laughed so hard, he bent down and put his head on his knee, and Emile turned red laughing, and even Mr. Birdcage. Daddy stood looking at them solemnly, and then he smiled a little, and then he had to laugh, too.

"What's the difference between a stage mother and a rottweiler?" yelled David. "Jewelry."

Daddy rapped on his music stand. "I'm very sorry. I don't know what to say except that I still want to do the Mozart on Monday—" There was a buzz of talk. "That's right. So make sure you bring *all* the music. Okay? Monday. Seven P.M. sharp. The dress is black and white. Don't forget to pick up your parking permits on the table backstage. That gets you into the lot behind the band shell. There will be supper for everyone at six P.M.—fried chicken, salads, beverages, the works—any vegetarians, let me know and we'll have a vegetable platter for you. Okay? It's going to be a terrific concert, and a big crowd will be there, and don't forget—for a lot of these folks, this will be their first exposure to classical music, so we want this to be really good, which I know it will be. Oh, and by the way, just so you know, we'll start with 'The Star-Spangled Banner,' with the tenor soloist. No need to rehearse that. Thank you, everyone, for all your hard work."

"Thank *you*!" called Evelyn.

Mr. Klonowski jumped up. "Excuse me, Maestro, but how can we do the Mozart without a rehearsal?"

Daddy looked at him, and smiled. "Because you've played this so many times before and because you're good musicians."

"But what about the pianist?" said Mr. Klonowski.

Daddy laughed and waved his hand. "She can play this in her *sleep,*" he said. "I know, because I sleep with her."

15

THE NEW SOLOIST

*O*n the way home, Rachel waited for Daddy to say something, but he only hummed a tune from the Mendelssohn, tapping his fingers on the steering wheel. He drove slowly along Main Street, and they stopped at a red light. Daddy pointed across the street to the flashing green COCKTAILS sign hanging in front of The Tip Top Tap, four motorcycles parked out front. Daddy pointed to it and laughed. "Your mother and I went in there one night the first week after we moved here, looking for a little elegance, a glass of white wine, a piano playing Cole Porter, and it was like a scene out of Dostoyevsky. Great big guys in overcoats staring into their beer. The bartender was a woman with a voice that could remove wallpaper. Like that Mrs. Johnson. Quite a woman." He turned left into the alley alongside the dairy and parked in back. "Got to copy the Mozart for your mother in case she doesn't have it," he said.

Rachel followed him up the back stairs to his office. She hoped he knew what he was doing. She couldn't imagine Mother saying yes to this. It was all too bewildering. She sat down on the floor by the copier. "Tell me again why you and Mother moved to Sandy Bottom?" she said.

Daddy turned on the photocopy machine, which hummed to life. A red panel flashed, that said WAIT.

"Got a job offer from a man who believed in me. Mr. Sorenson. This was his office. He sat behind that desk, I sat in that chair." Daddy pointed to a heavy oak armchair against the wall. "I had graduated from the University with a double major—English and music history—and your mother and I had been married a year, we were living in a tiny apartment with an enormous piano, and we were expecting you any minute. Your grandpa had offered me a job, but I didn't want that. I knew I had to be on my own. The college placement office said there was a job running the audio-visual program at a high school up north. I said I didn't know anything about audio-visual and they said, 'Awww, you can learn everything you need to know in a week.' Well, I didn't want a job that could be mastered in one week, don't you know, but I came awfully close to accepting it, and then a former girlfriend told me about a dairy in Sandy Bottom that needed a manager. A person tends to distrust advice you get from a former girlfriend, but her aunt was from here and said it was a nice town, nice people, so I came up here to see Mr. Sorenson, and I told him: 'I don't have a dairy background, I don't know one thing about milk or making butter or any of it.' He said, 'I don't care. I've got people who know everything about that, they've been doing it all their lives. I need someone to manage. Someone who can see where this company needs to go and lead us there. Someone smart who also likes people.' He said, 'These are good people here. Anybody who makes fun of small-town people doesn't have his head on straight, in my book, but they need leadership, like anyone else.' He was gruff, but he was a good man. An interesting man. Never married. He was a bird-watcher. He collected old books. He was an odd duck, but you know, you can be an odd duck if you do your job and make a contribution. He taught me that. And that's how we got here, and here we are, and let's get the Mozart copied."

He turned and opened the copier lid and put a page of music on the glass, and Rachel came up and hugged him from behind. "I love you," she said.

"I love *you,* beautiful," he said. "You're really sounding good in that violin section. You're terrific."

"Am I playing too loud?" she said.

"No. You sound terrific. You're playing great. Evelyn and David said so too. David said that you're a joy to sit next to."

Rachel could feel her face get warm and tingly. It was one thing to get a compliment from Angie or Carol, but to know that fellow musicians had said they liked your playing—that really meant something.

"So which piece do you like better, Mendelssohn or Tchaikovsky?" Rachel said.

"Well, they're two completely different works."

"I *know*. That's why I'm asking."

"Mmmm. I'd have to say Mendelssohn."

Rachel said, "Good. Me too. When you play the Mendelssohn you imagine he was a friendly type of person to have around, don't you? The Tchaikovsky is so big and loud. All those big crescendos and you think this *has* to be the end, but it just keeps going."

Daddy laughed. "Glad we have the same musical tastes."

Daddy copied each page of the Mozart onto stiff white paper and then taped the pages together to make a book. "What makes you think Mother is going to do this?" said Rachel.

"Oh, she will," he said. "You leave her to me. I've been married to her for fifteen years. I've got her figured out."

When they got home, the house was quiet. There was a note on the kitchen table: "At a meeting, errands afterward. Sandwich makings in fridge. XXXXXXOO."

Rachel told Daddy she wasn't hungry. And she wasn't. She was getting worried. It was fine for him to be all upbeat about the Fourth of July—he was the conductor, it was his job to be positive—but she, Rachel, had a hunch that the concert was unraveling before their eyes. How could Daddy have been so naive as to hire a zero like Drew Johnson to play a Mozart piano concerto? It made her wonder what else could go wrong.

She had imagined that playing in an orchestra would be quiet and serious, with dignified people pursuing their art, but it was more like a rodeo, with a few dozen cows and horses romping around and bellowing and whinnying and poor Daddy trying to keep them fenced in. The violinists crabbing at each other about bowings and the wind players talking out loud and doing dumb things, like asking, "Maestro, what note do I have in measure ninety-eight?" when they knew perfectly well they didn't play in measure ninety-eight. And now Daddy expected Mother to come sailing in without rehearsal and play the Mozart and save his skin.

When Mother came home, Rachel was in her room. There were murmurs of conversation, the refrigerator was opened and closed, and there were more murmurs. Rachel could tell from the low tones that Daddy was talking and Mother was listening. He murmured and paused and murmured and Rachel sat, not moving a muscle, and then Mother said, *"What!"*

(Mumble mumble murmur murmur.)

"You must be kidding!"

More mumbles. More murmurs. Some murbling and mummering.

"Oh Norman. What am I ever going to do with you?"

It didn't seem like a good time for Rachel to go downstairs. It was their discussion, not hers. But she opened her bedroom door so that she could hear better.

Mother was saying that she *hoped* he understood what an *impossible* thing he was asking her to do, to prepare a

220

Mozart *concerto* in *two days*—did he *realize* the work that this *entailed*, because if she was going to do it, she was going to do it *right*, all three movements, and no, she was *not* going to play from a score, she would of *course* do it from memory—and Rachel realized that Mother was protesting her way into playing the concerto—she could *not* get this concerto together *and* manage things around the house, so if he expected her to play on Monday, there would be *no more telephone messages* and he and Rachel would have to cook and clean up and do their laundry, that she, Mother, could not be expected to run a household *and* do justice to the Mozart, and when Mother was done protesting, Rachel heard Daddy murmur his thanks. There was a tender silence. Rachel hoped he was kissing her. Mother would do the concert because it was important to Daddy, and he had asked her to, and she loved him.

And now there was more quiet murmuring. Mother got up from her chair, and some dishes clattered. Daddy walked down the hall and into the den. Mother walked into the dining room. The piano bench scraped. There was silence. And then Mother played the first movement of the Mozart.

She played it briskly, full steam ahead, and so naturally, as if it were simply a conversation, only with music instead of words. Then she paused and went back and did it again. Rachel heard Daddy coming up the stairs. He stopped in her open doorway.

"You did it," she said.

"Your mother is a good-hearted woman," said Daddy.

"So what did you say to bring her around?"

"Didn't have to bring her around. She always wanted to play the concert, she just didn't know it."

"Okay. How did she find out that she wanted to?"

Daddy stepped into the room. "It's like this," he said. "Your mother only pretends to be from Milwaukee. Actually, she's a true Sandy Bottomite at heart, and a true Bottomite would never play a concert by her own choice—it might look as if she was showing off—but she would *gladly* play it if someone really needed her to. So all I had to do was show her what a deep hole I was in, so she could come to the rescue. See how that works?"

"How hard did you have to beg?" said Rachel.

"Not begging," he said, sitting on the bed. "Bargaining. I got off rather lightly. I told her that she was my last hope and if she didn't do the Mozart, I'd have to substitute a Stephen Sondheim medley. Your mother is not a big Stephen Sondheim fan. And I told her that if she did do it, I'd get behind her arts center a hundred percent. And I told her that this fall, we could either buy a new house or go to Italy. She chose the house. So—I'd say it was quite a reasonable deal."

Rachel took a deep breath. "I've thought about it, and—I mean, I'd still like to play in the orchestra and everything, but if Mother needs me to turn pages for her, I'd be happy to do that."

Daddy put his hand against her cheek. "That's sweet of you," he said. "But she's not using music."

Rachel shook her head. "Between now and Monday

222

night she's going to memorize an entire concerto? Are you crazy? It's at least a half hour of music."

"She's a trouper, isn't she? Actually, she already knows it. She's playing from memory right now." Rachel listened; Mother was going over the first movement again.

"She played it fifteen years ago at a Young People's concert with the Milwaukee Symphony. She was five months pregnant with you. A few months later and she wouldn't've been able to reach the keyboard. So this is probably the first music you ever heard, sweetie. You lay there in the dark in your little tank, thinking you'd be a fish forever, and this music came booming through the abdominal wall, and it said, 'Hey. You. There's a whole other world out here and it's better than in there.' Mother said that during the concert, you were kicking her so hard that she almost started playing your tempo instead of the conductor's."

Rachel and Daddy ate supper at the glass table in the garden as Mother worked away, and after supper, Daddy went in the dining room and laid his score across the piano and kept time with his baton, singing the orchestra part in a loud voice—"*Dee-dee-dee-dee da-da*"—so Mother could rehearse her entrances. Rachel got out her violin and joined them, playing the second-violin part. Mother looked up. "Thank you, dear," she said. They did the concerto three times, and then Mother said, "Enough. I'm going to bed. Thanks, everyone." And she went straight upstairs. She lay in a hot bath for a while and went to bed.

"I believe this calls for a little celebration. How about

some ice cream," said Daddy. Rachel got out the ice cream and made two chocolate mint sundaes. They stepped out the back door. There was an almost-full moon, big and gold, in the treetops. They turned the chairs at the glass table to face the moon and sat and gazed at it.

"Good ice cream you people make," said Rachel, licking the back of her spoon.

"What do you say we go out for dinner tomorrow night," said Daddy. "I know a nice place called The Farmhouse where we can have a steak. We could even take the piano soloist if she wants to go."

"I can't," said Rachel. "I'm going to a movie tomorrow night. With Scott."

"Oh," he said. He was a little hurt. She could tell.

"You mean Scott the cellist in the orchestra? The one from Oshkosh?"

She nodded.

"What movie?" he said.

She said, "Some horror movie. He's going to come pick me up at eight and we're going to a drive-in."

Daddy was quiet. It was that sort of *busy* quiet of someone who thinks he ought to say something and is trying to think of what it is. She ate her ice cream, her bare legs up on the cool glass top. The moon was so bright that the oak tree made a shadow, and the backyard of the family across the alley was lit up so she could see the strips of grass clippings where they had mowed the lawn. She couldn't remember the family's name, but Mother said they went to Zion Methodist and were nice people. Strange to live so close to them and not know them, except vaguely, to wave to and say hi. They were young and had two babies, whom the mother sometimes parked in the backyard in strollers while she lay on a chaise longue and read magazines. She was pretty, with bright red hair. Her husband came home wearing green coveralls. Maybe he was an auto mechanic.

It seemed right that you ought to walk across the alley and meet them, and if they invite you to sit down, then sit down and find out who they are, where they come from, the names of their children, where he works, what magazines she reads, but is it really any of your business? Emily would say no, it isn't. Amherst was full of people she didn't know from a bale of straw. It's your business to live your own life and to be close to a few people and you don't have to worry about the others, unless they come screaming up to your house with their shirts on fire and then, of course, you roll them up in a rug and put out the flames and call 911. But otherwise, it's okay to stay in your corner.

"What are you thinking?" said Daddy.

She said, "I'm thinking that I might like to go to Interlochen."

"I see," he said. And he was a little bit hurt again. Twice in two minutes.

"I suppose it would be a wonderful opportunity for you," he said, sadly.

Rachel woke to music on Saturday morning. Mother was practicing. It was the third movement of the Mozart concerto, and she was taking it at top speed, whipping through the long runs, forcing her fingers to play the notes before her mind could think to tell them to.

Daddy was in the bathroom, shaving. The door was open. Rachel stood and watched him pull the razor along his throat, the band of skin appearing in the white foam. He drew his mouth down into a frown so he could shave his upper lip. He shaved under his nose and shaved off something between his eyebrows and set down the razor. He leaned down over the sink and cupped his hands full of water and put his face in it and blew like a whale. Rachel handed him a towel.

Rachel fixed a bowl of bran flakes and blueberries for breakfast and noticed, beside the telephone on the counter, an answering machine. They had never had one before—Daddy thought answering machines were rude, everyone knew you were using it to screen your calls and not have to talk to people you didn't want to talk to. But there it was, the phone plugged into it, the ON light glowing, and a note from Mother lay there too.

Rachel—I am going to be busy today so can you make dinner tonight? And can you entertain Grandma and Grandpa when they come Sunday night? Thank you. I love you. Mother.

Rachel practiced that morning, and a little more in the afternoon. When she started fixing dinner, Mother was still glued to the piano bench, practicing, and Daddy was on the phone, telling the mayor that no, he had not heard any rumors about someone who planned to burn the American flag at the concert, and, no, the mayor shouldn't

226

worry about it. Then the mayor said a bunch of things. The voice in the telephone sounded to Rachel like a talking mouse. "No," said Daddy, "we've decided not to read the Declaration of Independence. We have an hour of wonderful music, and I think that's enough for people, and an hour is as long as I want to ask them to sit and listen."

Daddy was making loops and triangles and checkerboards on a piece of paper with a black felt pen. "Mayor, you're absolutely right. I couldn't agree more," he said. "Our young people today—I don't know. Somehow the things you and I learned—hard work, responsibility—kids today are missing out on. That's the beauty of music, it inspires kids to work hard. Because in music, unlike politics, you cannot hide laziness. And that's why we need arts in our communities, and that's why I think this arts center is a great idea."

Daddy winked at Rachel. "Yes, sir. The evil today, if you ask me, is parking lots. You build a parking lot and you're making a passion pit. Kids park in cars and the next thing you're talking about teenage pregnancy and single mothers and welfare kids. Look up the statistics, and you'll see. There's an illegitimate child born every year for every parking lot in America! It's true!" And then he put down the phone. "It was too much for him," he said. "He hung up when I got to illegitimate babies. Guess I struck a chord."

Daddy called his meteorologist friend who told him that the storm system was in North Dakota now and might arrive in central Wisconsin around Monday afternoon or early evening. "Not what I was hoping to hear," he said to Rachel. "But no matter what, even if we get ten inches of rain, it's worth it just to hear your mother play that Mozart."

From behind the dining-room door, they heard Mother playing the achingly beautiful, slow movement of the concerto. Mother was at her best when she was up against a big challenge, Rachel thought, something that got all her attention, and now, faced with an impossible deadline to play Mozart in a band shell in a town where people didn't care for Mozart and a lot of them didn't care for Mother, she was making Mozart sound like angels hovering overhead, blessing the gardens and the yards and the bedrooms and kitchens of the earth. Daddy was right. No matter what, the music was the thing.

16

SQUASH

Scott's mother's car was a white convertible with a bright red top, and it pulled into the Greens' driveway shortly before eight, about half an hour after Rachel had begun looking for it. She had taken a nice long bath at six o'clock, while Mother and Daddy were rehearsing downstairs, Daddy's *"Dee-dee-dee da-da"* starting to sound a bit frayed at the edges, and Mother saying, "Norman, please. You're dragging. Tempo!" Rachel lay in the bath and thought for the first time about the rest of her summer, Summer After the Fourth, when she would go off to Menomonie and Eau Claire with the orchestra. Would Daddy still conduct? She hoped not. It was terrible to hope not, but she wanted to go off alone. Scott would be there. And they'd play in Oshkosh too, his hometown. Maybe he would ask her to stay over at his parents' house after the concert. Yes, of course she would. And then August—perhaps she could invite him to visit Milwaukee and the two of them could stay at Grandma and Grandpa's and go to movies and concerts.

Daddy knocked on the door. "How late are you planning to stay out?" he said through the door. "I hate to be the worrying father, but—when are you going to be home?"

"By the dawn's early light," she said.

He groaned. "Please. No humor. I'm not in the mood."

He asked her again as she was getting dressed. She put on a bra and panties, a khaki cotton skirt, and a dark green short-sleeve jersey top. She was sitting on her bed studying a lineup of her shoes, trying to decide between sandals and boat shoes, when he knocked again. "I'd sort of like to get this issue resolved," he said. "When are you going to be home?"

"I'll ask Scott," she said.

"I'm asking you."

"When do you want me home?"

"How about midnight?" he said. "I mean, you're fourteen years old."

"That's fine," she said.

"I mean it. Midnight. Twelve-thirty is no good. One o'clock I'm going to be really upset. I mean it."

Poor Daddy. He tromped downstairs, muttering to himself, and when Rachel came down, he had opened the dining-room door and poked his head in and was saying, "Don't you think fourteen is a little young to be dating?"

and Mother yelled, "Norman, deal it with it yourself. She's your daughter, too. Go! Out!" and he retreated to the kitchen. He looked up mournfully as Rachel came in, her hair nicely tousled (she thought) using a gel she had borrowed from Carol, her lips a glossy pink, her nails too, and her body lightly dusted with talcum and faintly sprayed with a perfume from Mother's vanity, called Eve.

"I wish it were possible to *meet* this guy before he comes and hauls you off into the night," said Daddy. "Is that too much to ask?"

"You've met him. Several times. Scott. The cellist. Remember?"

Daddy threw up his hands. "I don't mean shaking hands and saying hello," he said. "I mean *meet* him. Get to know him. Find out what he's like."

"He's really nice," said Rachel.

"Can he drive a car in a sensible manner?" said Daddy. "Or is he going to be racing around at eighty miles an hour down country roads with the headlights off? I'd like to know."

"Once you've driven with Mother," said Rachel, "what's eighty miles an hour?"

Daddy threw up his hands again. "I am not joking," he said. "Does the guy drink?"

"Drink?"

"Drink. Liquor. Alcohol. Hooch. Booze. Is he going to get you off in a drive-in somewhere and get tanked up on gin and drive you home at eighty miles an hour and wind up running head-on into a tree?"

Rachel saw a car come around the corner from Prairie Avenue and slow down as it approached, but it didn't turn in the driveway.

"Don't be ridiculous. Of course he doesn't drink."

"I wish I shared your confidence," he said. He got up from the table and walked to the refrigerator. He opened it. Then he closed it and walked back and sat down. "I never knew how hard this was going to be," he said. "If I'd known, I would've been a lot easier on my parents, believe me. You have no idea. Being a parent is just full-time worry. It's a life of constant prayer. It's not for the timid, take my word for it."

That was when the white convertible pulled in. Rachel wondered why the top was up on a warm, sunny summer evening. Scott got out. He wore a blue button-down shirt, the sleeves rolled up, and tan chinos and penny loafers. Pretty preppy, thought Rachel. Just the right look to reassure an anxious parent. Blue button-down shirt, tan pants—one look tells you the boy is heading for a career in banking.

She opened the door. "Hey," she said. "On time. A professional musician." He came in and was leaning forward to give her a friendly kiss on the cheek when he pulled back, seeing Daddy out of the corner of his eye. "Good evening, Maestro," he said, reaching out to shake Daddy's hand.

Daddy stood up. "Hello, Scott," he said.

"Sir," said Scott, "I was telling Rachel the other day how much I like your tempos."

Daddy looked at Rachel.

"I can't believe, sir, that you've never conducted before."

Rachel put her hand on Scott's elbow. He turned. "It's a pleasure being in an orchestra like this, sir. And now I understand that Mrs. Green is going to step in as soloist." Scott listened for a moment to Mother playing the slow movement in the next room. "I'm looking forward to it," he said solemnly.

Rachel squeezed his elbow. "Let's go," she said. She kissed Daddy good-bye. He seemed stunned by all the flattery.

"Midnight," he said.

"Absolutely, sir," said Scott.

"What was that all about?" Rachel said as she climbed into the car. It was new and had black leather upholstery and a deep black carpet. "You don't have to butter up my dad."

"Sorry," said Scott. "I was trying to put him at ease."

They pulled out on Prairie Avenue, and Rachel asked if he wanted to stop and put the top down. She had never ridden in a convertible and she wondered how it felt, to be in the open, the wind rushing past, the sky overhead. He said something about it not being as safe with the top down. "You roll over and you're a goner," he said.

She didn't see that a canvas top and some thin steel ribs could be much protection in the event of a crash, but she didn't mention it: She could see why he wanted the top up—it was to keep his hair from getting mussed up. He had the most perfect hair she had ever seen on a boy, perfectly clipped, every curl in place, the sideburns trim, a perfect border on the back of his neck. She wondered how long it took him to do it and what kind of gel he used.

"You look terrific tonight, by the way," he said.

"So do you," she said.

"Have you lived here all your life or did you move here from somewhere?" he said.

"My parents moved here when I was about two months old," Rachel said.

The conversation lagged there for a minute. He sped up as they left town on the road along the river, past the truck farm, but compared to Mother, he was only coasting.

"Are you having a pretty good summer?" he said.

"Not bad, considering there's not that much to do around here. I'm glad I'm playing in the orchestra."

They talked about the other musicians. "Can you believe the guy with the birdcage hair?" said Rachel.

"I love it. Old swirly head. And your stand partner. She makes really weird faces when she plays. Her face gets all scrunched up like a raccoon."

"Really? I can't see her. I don't make faces, do I?"

"No. You look good when you play."

"The people around me are funny. I try not to laugh, but sometimes I can't help it. Isn't it crazy the way the concertmaster and Emile yell at each other and then at break they hang out like long-lost pals?"

"It's great, isn't it?" said Scott.

"The cellos sound really good at the beginning of the Tchaikovsky. Is it hard?"

"No, it's not that bad," he said. "Of course it would help if everyone looked at the conductor once in a while, and didn't just go off hiking at their own pace. Did you know Tchaikovsky was a real scaredy-cat? He was deathly afraid of thunder and every time there was a big storm he crawled under his bed and cried?"

"I read in a book that he cried all the time."

Scott was silent, thinking about something—crying or Tchaikovsky or cellos.

"Do you go to a lot of movies?" he said, finally.

"No. There's only one theater in Sandy Bottom, and they usually show some action movie, you know, a lot of explosives and automatic weapons. Arnold Schwartzenegger stuff." She thought, This is not an easy conversation to keep up.

The drive-in was on a hill, and you approached it through a gate, where the ticket-taker sat in a gatehouse, and up a long drive lined with little lamps. Scott parked in the middle of the lot, the front wheels sitting on a slight ridge so the movie screen filled the windshield. The movie was starting as he shut off the engine, the titles rolled up on the screen. He reached up and unfastened two handles at the top of the windshield and pushed a switch and a motor hummed and the canvas roof rose up and folded itself backward. "There," he said. "The big sky." On a steel post by each parking spot was a little loudspeaker that you could lift off the post and put on the dashboard. He turned up the volume and a creaky old woman's voice said, "I know you think I'm strange, but once I was like you. Yes. Very much like you."

The movie was called *Squash* and it was about an old lady named Eloise who lived alone in a big spooky house in a little town, who, many years before, had had a fiancé named Norman—Rachel shuddered at the mention of Daddy's name—who had died in a terrible accident. Some boys had dared him to go over a waterfall in a canoe and he had done it and was drowned—you saw this in a flashback—and as a result, Eloise hated young men. She hated young people generally. She watched through the venetian blinds as they passed her house and cursed them and every summer she got her revenge when she planted a big garden behind her house. The garden looked like a South American rain forest. Eloise's specialty was squash, an extraordinary breed of squash that, by night, became an aggressive carnivorous plant. In her garden she had an arbor, with a glider swing, and when young people sneaked in there at night to sit in the swing and neck, you heard the rustle of vines as the squash went berserk.

Thorny vines slithered up between the slats of the swing and grabbed the boy and the girl, to a shrill violin accompaniment, and the boy yelled and a vine went right down his throat—Rachel clutched at Scott then—and immediately the two were covered with vines and you heard munching and dripping and slurping and there was the glitter of blood, and Rachel turned to Scott, and he kissed her.

He kissed her smoothly on the lips and put his hand against her cheek. She closed her eyes. He stroked her neck and he put his nose against her hair and sighed.

"I've wanted to kiss you for so long," he said. "I wondered what it would be like."

She kissed him. She put her hands on his shoulders and gently touched her lips to his.

The police had come to the old lady's house and asked her a few questions about the shoes and clothing they had found in her arbor, and she said, "Oh, well, you know those boys—heh, heh, heh, heh," and the police chuckled knowingly, and the old lady chuckled, and the next thing you knew, it was night again and another young couple was sneaking into the garden, and the squash was getting restless.

"I like kissing you," she said. He kissed her again. She opened one eye and saw that the boy on the screen was kissing the girl, and it made Rachel laugh.

"What is it?" said Scott.

"It's nothing," she said. "But if we should be eaten alive by giant plants, I want to say thanks for a really good time."

17

FOURTH OF JULY

*S*unshine streamed through the curtains when Rachel woke on Sunday. She lay and thought about Scott, sweet Scott, and thought, I have now been kissed by a boy on the lips, a boy who meant it and wasn't only kidding. She got up and brushed her teeth and looked at herself in the bathroom mirror. This face, she thought, has been kissed by a boy, not just once but over and over.

Mother had found a replacement organist for church that morning, and when Rachel came downstairs, it was eleven o'clock and Mother was scrambling eggs and frying bacon. Daddy sat at the table. A voice in the answering machine was saying, "Can you get back to me on this by tonight? I'd appreciate it." And a click.

"How was the movie?" said Daddy.

"It was good. People being eaten by gigantic vines."

Rachel stood behind Mother at the stove and put her hands on Mother's shoulders and then her neck and pressed the muscles leading up to the base of her head.

"Don't get her too relaxed," said Daddy. "She plays better when she's wound up."

Mother served up the scrambled eggs onto three plates, with the bacon on two of them, and set the plates on the table. She poured herself a cup of fresh coffee and looked out the back door toward the Wymans', and then she turned to them and announced, "I love this concerto. I never realized how much until yesterday. I used to look down on it as some sort of claptrap because it was so popular, and I was wrong. It's a wonderful piece of music. And that's the truth."

It was a peaceful day. Mother played and Rachel went over to the Wymans' and played Scrabble with Angie and Fred—Carol had a softball game—and when Rachel came home, Mother was upstairs taking a nap and Daddy was making dinner. She had never seen him cook before. He was making meatballs and a tomato sauce for spaghetti.

"I trust you got home at midnight last night," he said. "I fell asleep at eleven."

"Twelve o'clock, sharp," she said. "I got out of the car and it suddenly turned into a pumpkin and a mouse ran out of it. So I guess you need to find yourself a new cellist."

"I'm sorry if I was a little hard on you. It's this concert. I haven't been this excited since the night Segovia played the Lyceum. Did I ever tell you about that?"

"No, you didn't," said Rachel.

"It was my freshman year, and I had a part-time job stagehanding at the Lyceum.

"It was a gorgeous old hall with gilded brass and paintings of naked goddesses and nymphs floating around the ceiling and it was where all the big artists played, and that year Andrés Segovia, the great guitarist, came and played with the Symphony. He was the first one to transcribe all those Bach keyboard pieces for guitar, you know. He was a genius.

"Segovia came to town, a solemn man with long wispy gray hair. And that night, we're all set for the concert, the orchestra is onstage, and the conductor and Mr. Segovia are in the wings. The house lights dim, and Abe, the stage manager, looks at Mr. Segovia and he nods, and Abe says—as he says to every soloist—'Toi toi,' which I think is Romanian for 'Kick 'em in the pants,' and he opens the door and Mr. Segovia marches out onstage, followed by the conductor, and there's a huge ovation, and then silence. A long silence.

"And then we hear footsteps and it's Mr. Segovia. He's coming offstage. Abe opens the door. Mr. Segovia points up and says, 'Fan.' Abe thinks for a moment and he looks at me. 'Norm,' he says. 'Run up the ladder to the fly gallery and turn off that ventilating fan up there. It's bothering the maestro.' So off I go.

"That ladder goes straight up the wall eighty feet up, no safety guards, and I go up trying not to look down, and I walk out on a catwalk about two feet wide over the orchestra, and out in the middle is a long chain hanging down from the roof where the ventilator is, and I pull the chain and the ventilator fan stops. And right then, the audience bursts into applause, and I look down and eighty feet below me, out comes Segovia with his guitar and sits down on his stool and he tunes again. And now I don't dare take a step for fear of making a noise.

"So I lay down on the catwalk, face down, my arms wrapped around it, and I watched through the grill, eighty feet in the air, the entire concert. There was a slow Bach piece that was so wonderful, I got tears in my eyes—you know me—and all of a sudden one of my tears dropped. I watched it fall eighty feet. It was a big teardrop and he was bald on top and it was aimed straight for that big pink head, but the audience must've all exhaled at the same time—missed him by inches."

Rachel looked Daddy straight in the eyes. "Aren't you nervous?" she said.

He grinned. "Think I should be?"

"*I'm* nervous and I'm only in the violin section," she said.

At six o'clock, Grandma and Grandpa's Lincoln pulled in the driveway, and Daddy and Rachel ran out to help them in and carry their bags upstairs and get them both situated, always a long and involved process, though today Grandma was on her best behavior. She had been warned by Mother to stay out of the way, and when Grandma was reprimanded, she went to extremes trying to make you feel guilty. If you asked her to please be quiet, she would be silent for hours, until you couldn't bear it and begged her to say something. So her reaction to being told to stay out of the way was to go straight to the tiny spare bedroom and close the door and not come out.

The four of them ate Daddy's dinner, with an empty place for Grandma, and Grandpa asked how the big concert was coming.

"It's going to be a good show," said Daddy. "I think we may get a couple thousand people." He turned to Mother. "Did you know that Florence invited her entire family? They're coming down from Port Wing.

"The employees threw a party for me Friday," he said to Grandpa. "During lunch hour. It was nice. They gave me a bottle of champagne and a big plaster bust of Beethoven with a white paper Sandy Bottom Dairy cap on his head. So how can it not be good with people like that cheering us on? I ask you."

Grandpa said, "Well, that's right, Norman. Good for you." He looked at Mother. "I have to tell you, Ingrid. Thank you for playing the Mozart. It means a lot to me."

"I haven't played it yet," she said.

"Nonetheless. Thank you."

Grandpa talked about his mother, who had been a piano teacher in a little town in southern Illinois, and how his father had fallen in love with her, but was too shy to ask her to a dance or even to take a walk. He was a butcher, straight off the boat from Germany, ashamed of his poor English. But he couldn't get her out of his mind and so— Rachel had heard this story before, many times, but she loved it, especially this part—"So," Grandpa said, "he asked her for piano lessons. He took lessons every Saturday afternoon after work. He swept out the butcher shop and walked to the Davis house and went in and played his lesson for her. And by golly, he worked hard on them! Oh yes! He was out to impress her! And eventually he did. It took him four years of lessons, but eventually he got to where he could ask her to marry him. And I suppose his English had improved by then too."

"If I'd had my wits about me," said Daddy, "I should have taken lessons from Ingrid."

Rachel was sleepy, all of a sudden. She put her head against Grandpa's shoulder and closed her eyes, as he went on to tell his story about the Boesendorfer piano and why he had bought it. She fell asleep. She woke up as he told about the piano being raised by the crane to the third floor, and then Daddy was leading her by the hand up the stairs toward bed.

And then she awoke and he was standing in the door of her room, beaming, a cup of coffee in one hand and his baton in the other, his lips pressed together as he trumpeted reveille. His hair was still wet from the shower, and his chin was bleeding from the razor. "Today's our big day," he said. "Our debut. Or our debacle. What do you say? Shall we do it?"

Rachel showered and brushed her teeth and got dressed and came downstairs for breakfast. Grandpa sat at the table, exactly where he had been the night before, reading a book. He looked up when she came in, his blue eyes sparkled, and he held out his hand. "Hi, Grandpa," she said. He put his hand on her neck and pulled her head down and kissed her on the cheek.

"How's my favorite violinist?" he said.

He had put on a white shirt and red suspenders and blue seersucker trousers. He wore a red polka-dot bow tie, and his thin white hair was slicked straight back. A pack of cigarettes lay unopened in the middle of the table, next to the napkin rack.

"Where's Mother?" she said.

"She went for a walk."

"And Grandma?"

"Your grandmother is making herself beautiful. And I'm sitting here waiting to admire her."

When Mother returned, she looked flushed and happy. She drank a glass of water and mopped her brow and said, "It looks like it's going to be good and hot today. So I told the piano movers to come right away."

"Piano movers?" said Rachel.

"Of course. What piano did you think I was going to use?"

"But—don't you need it to practice on?"

"Why would I want to practice today?"

And just then a big truck backed up the Greens' driveway and stopped, and two burly men with leather straps around their necks came to the back door. Mother showed them into the dining room. One of them whistled. "A Boesendorfer," he said. "Wow. Don't see too many of these around." They put a quilt over it and fastened the straps to either end, and managed to ease the great black piano sideways out the front door and down the walk and onto the truck, and then it was gone. "It needs to sit outside for a few hours and acclimate before they can tune it," said Mother.

"Is somebody going to guard it?" said Rachel.

"There are fifty people down at the park, working," said Mother. "Hard to walk away with a piano and not have one of them notice. There are people hanging bunting in the trees and people hooking up garden hoses to make drinking fountains and people cooking big pots of *beans,* for crying out loud. There are people setting up benches and people blowing up balloons and tying them to the benches. One thing about your father—he certainly knows how to get people to work for him."

The phone began ringing before noon. The weather watcher reported that the storm front was veering to the north and would miss them. The bratwurst man asked if it was okay if he substituted Polish sausage for some of those bratwursts. The tympanist asked if he could get six tickets for his family. "It's a free concert," Rachel said. "You can bring everybody."

"Yes," said the tympanist, "but isn't there a reserved section of seats that's—you know—roped off?"

"I don't think so," said Rachel. "First come, first served, I think."

Actually, Daddy said, there was one row roped off for Mayor Broadbent and his family and the members of the town council. The old men who wouldn't donate a dime for the concert and were trying to tear down Mother's beloved Ramsey Building would sit in the second row and watch her play the Mozart concerto.

"That's one thing about politicians," Daddy said. "They'll fight you tooth and nail when you try to get something done, and then when you finally do it, they'll try to take credit for it."

The phone rang and rang, and Grandma came downstairs all powdered and pink and Grandpa jumped up and fussed over her, and Grandma sat at the end of the table and began to issue commands. "Norman dear, do be so good as to find me my purse. Rachel, come let me give you a kiss. Rachel, do you think there might be one of those strawberry yogurts in the refrigerator? Darling, could you put some in a bowl and put Grape Nuts over it? Thank you, darling. Ingrid? Where's Ingrid?"

Mother had disappeared again. And when she had put the yogurt and Grape Nuts in the bowl, Rachel slipped quietly out the back door and into the backyard.

Grandma's voice was not easy to listen to. It was firm and queenly, and it rose and fell, and she talked about a visit to her internist as if describing a meeting with the prime minister. Grandma kept close contact with the workings of her innards, and could give long descriptions of grim things that might someday happen to her.

Mother sat in the garden. She looked up as Rachel sat down next to her and said, "I'm not like her, am I? Tell me I'm not like her."

"I think you have a ways to go yet," said Rachel.

She turned on the faucet and the little fountain began to burble and tinkle, beside the red begonias in the brown pot. The daisies in the rock garden were big and white, and the honeysuckle vines on the side of the garage bloomed. Rachel sat in one of the cast-iron chairs and pretended to read a book until the sun made her drowsy, and then she spread a blanket out in the shade and lay down and fell asleep.

When she woke up, Carol was sitting beside her. "Hi," she said. She looked sad. She said that she and Valerie had had a fight. She said she didn't want to talk about it. She said the fight was over something really dumb. It was too dumb to talk about.

"We were at her house fooling around with makeup and stuff, and she said I ought to cut my hair really short. Like a buzz cut. And I said 'I don't think so.' And she got all serious about it. She said that I needed a new look. She went and got hair clippers. She says, 'What do you have to lose? It'll grow back. You do me and I'll do you.' She was serious. Isn't that weird? She couldn't believe that I didn't want to have all my hair cut off."

"You'd be terrific no matter how short your hair was," Rachel said. "You've got a great-looking head."

Rachel lay on her back and looked up at the trees. She tried not to feel happy about Carol and Valerie having a fight. She wished it would be evening so she could go and play the concert.

Daddy left at five-thirty, to make sure the orchestra chairs were set up right. He wore a tuxedo and black tie, and Mother had put gel on his hair and combed it back and trimmed his eyebrows and shined his shoes. Grandma and Grandpa were taking a nap, and Angie Wyman would pick them up at quarter to seven and drop them at the park where Daddy had a bench ready for them next to the mayor, a bench with comfortable cushions so Grandma wouldn't get too stiff while sitting. Mother sat in Rachel's room as Rachel got into her black trousers and blouse. Mother was dressed in a lovely blue gown, silky and shimmery, and her hair was braided and wound into a bun in back. She had put on mascara and eyeliner and a pale pinkish lipstick—Rachel hadn't seen her use makeup since the trip to Italy, when they ate dinner at an especially nice restaurant. Mother wasn't a makeup-type person. But tonight she looked so lovely and elegant. Rachel stared at her in the mirror as Mother blotted her lipstick and dabbed perfume behind her ears. "I hope he doesn't take the Mozart too slow, that's all I hope," said Mother. "I can play it faster but I'll never make it if I have to crawl through it."

Mother put her high heels in a bag and put on a pair of loafers, and Rachel picked up her violin, and they walked to the park. Division Street, which was the county road coming in from the east, was jammed with traffic. People along Division and Maple Streets were charging cars a dollar to park in their driveways and on their front lawns, and boys stood halfway in the street, waving red flags to bring in the customers. At the intersection of Division and Main Streets, the chief of police himself stood and directed traffic, his face red, a silver whistle in his mouth, wearing a bright orange vest and white reflective gloves.

"Once a year that man gets to direct traffic and this is his day," said Mother. "He looks like Napoleon, doesn't he? Except for the vest."

The sidewalk along Main Street was thronged with people, families in shorts and T-shirts, carrying lawn chairs, ice chests, picnic baskets, little American flags. When people saw Rachel and her violin case, they immediately smiled and said hi. A woman called her name, and Rachel turned and there was Mrs. Erickson, in shorts and T-shirt, holding hands with Mr. Erickson, a tall bald man with dark glasses. It was always shocking somehow to see a teacher outside of school, going around like a normal person. "What do we get to hear tonight?" said Mrs. Erickson.

"Mozart and Mendelssohn and 'The 1812 Overture,'" said Rachel.

"When was that '1812 Overture' written then?" asked Mr. Erickson. Rachel smiled at his attempt at a joke.

She said, "It commemorates the Russian victory over Napoleon in 1812. Tchaikovsky wrote it around 1880, I guess. Watch out. It's loud. But it has a nice long pretty part too."

The park was almost full of people when they arrived. Rows and rows and rows of benches and behind them and on the sides people sat in clumps of folding chairs or on blankets. Mother pointed and Rachel looked: A crowd of people stood around a big blue tank, water slopping over the rim. Sitting on a chairlike contraption over the tank, his clothes drenched, water dripping from his hair, was Reverend Sykes. He waved at them and sort of smiled, but it was a forced smile. He looked as if the Dunk the Pastor idea had been fun at the beginning and now was wearing thin. And as he waved, a boy hurled a softball and struck the bull's-eye, and the seat of the chair collapsed and the poor man toppled into the tank and water spilled over the edge.

Smoke drifted across the park from the barbecue pit at the bratwurst stand, where the Lutheran Men's Club was roasting brats and cooking up onion rings in cauldrons of hot fat. The aroma of sweet pork and corn oil and charcoal combined with the sugary smell from the cotton candy booth and the smell of suntan lotion, and new-mown grass and car exhaust and beer and cigar smoke. Beyond the park, in the middle of River Street, a Ferris wheel turned slowly as benches full of people rose up over the trees and descended. The trees and the band shell were decked out with red, white, and blue ribbons and bunting, and a big American flag hung down over the stage. Mother and Rachel walked through the crowd toward the band shell, and Rachel heard Lonnie call her name, and she waved to him. Fred Wyman had set up three lawn chairs right in front, and he was there alone. Carol was scooping cones at the ice-cream booth, he said. "You don't look nervous," he said.

"I'm not," said Rachel. "It's going to be fine."

None of the musicians were on stage yet. They were all behind the band shell, around a long table where some women from the dairy had laid out a big buffet supper for them, fried chicken and pasta salad and cherry Jell-O and rhubarb pie.

Mother went off to find Daddy, who was sitting in his car, looking at the score, and Rachel got a paper plate and helped herself to some chicken and pasta salad, and then up came Evelyn, in an ankle-length black chiffon skirt with a lacy blouse and heels three inches high. She gave Rachel a hug. "I don't know if I can play or not," she said. "I've had three helpings of onion rings and I had to throw fifteen softballs before I could drop that bozo in the tank." Mr. Birdcage was eating a bratwurst; Rachel noticed that his hair contained red and blue sparkles. All the string players seemed to be in a festive mood, even Mr. Klonowski, who gave her a kiss on the cheek and said, "Isn't this great?"

But the wind players stood under a tree, their instruments out, looking worried. Helen, the oboeist, honked a few notes, shook her head, and said to a flute player, "It's not so bad for you, but it's absolute murder for an oboe."

"I have trouble concentrating when I'm this hot, I get so dizzy," said the flutist.

Larry stood under a tree with his bassoon tucked under his arm. He wiped his brow with a hanky. "Not getting any cooler, is it," he said in a whiny voice.

One of the trumpet players had spilled his dinner down the front of his shirt and he was wiping it off with a wet napkin, and the others were laughing at him.

As Rachel stood by the band shell, eating, Mother and Daddy walked past, hand in hand, and didn't notice her.

They stood by the steps to the stage, talking in low voices. Mother looked at him and smiled brightly and kissed him on the cheek. He put his hand around her waist. The mayor and his wife walked up, and the four of them stood together, and the mayor's son took a picture of them. And then one of Daddy shaking hands with the mayor. The mayor wore a bright green plaid sportcoat and yellow pants, and he wore a white straw hat on top of his black toupee. He saw Rachel and came over and shook her hand. "This is a proud day for all of us," he said. "A very proud day."

Rachel saw Scott, sitting on the bumper of a pickup parked on the grass, playing runs and scales on his cello. Rachel went over to him. "How are you?" he said.

"My dad is making his conducting debut in twenty minutes and my mom is the soloist. I ought to be nervous, I guess."

Scott looked toward the crowd. "You think these people are really up for this much Mendelssohn and Mozart? I mean, it's going to be at least an hour long. They're probably expecting the theme from *Star Wars* and a medley of tunes from *Cats*."

"Maybe they'll think the Mendelssohn is from a movie and the Mozart is Andrew Lloyd Webber."

Rachel took her violin out and played a few scales, and then Mr. Robbins came around and said, "Five minutes. Five minutes, everybody. Musicians onstage."

Rachel climbed the stairs onto the stage of the band shell and found her seat. She said hello to David, on the other side of Evelyn. It was crowded, so there was a lot of rearranging of chairs and stands.

"Hey! Get that thing out of the back of my head, will ya?" said Emile. The girl behind him pulled her stand back.

A cellist stood up and said to the bass players, "There is no *way* I can play with you guys breathing down my neck, so move back!"

The bass players snarled right back at him. "What are we supposed to do? Go home?" said one. "We're back as far as we can go." So all the cellists moved up closer to the podium. The piano sat front and center, the lid down, and the podium was upstage. The space across the front of the stage where Mother would walk to get to the piano was only a few feet wide.

The first trumpet player said, "I can't find my part to the '1812'! Check your folders, everybody."

A violist turned and laughed at him. "Why would *we* have a trumpet part? We're musicians."

"Never mind! Here it is!" The trumpet player pulled it out from behind his folder.

Finally, everyone settled in, and the orchestra quieted down. Mr. Klonowski stood and leaned over the piano and plunked an A, and the orchestra tuned. Evelyn whispered, "Your mother looks absolutely gorgeous." And Rachel looked, and there was Mother standing at the edge of the crowd in her blue dress. She wasn't smoking a cigarette. She was smiling.

And then it was silent. The Ferris wheel had stopped

and the Dunk the Pastor and no horns honked and the sea of faces became still. "Big crowd for a little town, isn't it?" said Evelyn. Rachel nodded. Some people had backed their cars in at the other side of the park and were sitting on the roofs. There were people on the roof of the drugstore across the street and the Dew Drop Inn Café. Rachel shaded her eyes and looked for Grandma and Grandpa and saw them sitting next to the mayor in his green-and-yellow outfit. Grandma wore a white summer dress and a big white hat. The people behind her craned their necks to see around it. Grandpa appeared to be asleep.

And then a wave of applause started in the front rows and spread out all over the park, and Daddy marched out onstage, followed by a fat man in a blue suit. "Who's that?" Rachel whispered. "The tenor," said Evelyn.

And then Rachel looked at the music stand and there, on top of the Mendelssohn, was a sheet marked "National Anthem." "I don't remember how this goes," she whispered. And then Daddy gestured to the orchestra to stand and everyone stood and the applause got even louder.

"It's easy," said Evelyn. "Just follow me."

Rachel felt a little knot of panic in her stomach. Oh boy. Just imagine—you come to your first orchestra job and you mess up on "The Star-Spangled Banner." And then the orchestra sat down, and Daddy looked out at them and smiled and raised his baton. The tenor puffed out his chest, and then they were playing the National Anthem, and the crowd rose to its feet. Rachel's bow felt wobbly, so she played louder, which was what Mr.

Amidore had said to do if you felt nervous: "Makes the bow stop shaking," he had said. And it did. The fat man sang into a microphone and his voice echoed off the buildings and bounced back. He was a little flat and he got a little behind on the words, and when he came to the high note on "the land of the *free*" he slid up to the *free* and hit it right on the money and then held it a little too long. It cracked and it sounded like Tarzan calling to his jungle friends. Evelyn laughed out loud. As he neared the end, a huge cheer rose from the crowd. People yelled and whistled and clapped and the fat man took a bow and waved and left the stage and on came the mayor.

Daddy had tried to be firm with the mayor, who had wanted to lead the crowd in the Pledge of Allegiance and read some of the Declaration of Independence and also talk about the importance of local government in protecting our freedoms, and Daddy had said no, that this was a concert, and that the mayor should simply come out and thank the many volunteers who had worked so hard to make the day special. The mayor came out, and Daddy turned and shook his hand and smiled as the mayor welcomed everyone to Sandy Bottom and said what a privilege and an honor and a pleasure this was, and so forth, but Daddy's smile faded away as the mayor reached into his pocket and pulled out a sheet of paper. It seemed to have a lot of writing on it.

"The Fourth of July is a day when it behooves all of us to pause for a moment and consider the foundation of freedom that was laid so ably by our Founding Fathers in

1776," he intoned. He said something else about not taking these freedoms for granted and said that all of us owed a great debt of gratitude to those who had given their lives to defend freedom and also to those who gave their time in government service, and just then Daddy looked over toward the band-shell door and nodded, and Rachel looked and saw Lester reach down and pull something, and suddenly the mayor's voice was not amplified any more. It was just a tiny voice. And just then Daddy began clapping and the audience clapped, not as loud as before. The mayor bowed. He turned and said something to Daddy and then he waved to the crowd and left.

And then it was time for the Mendelssohn. Daddy grinned and raised his arms. "Here goes!" whispered Evelyn. And off they went. The orchestra had never sounded better, Rachel thought. Everyone was trying twice as hard, no goofing around like in the rehearsals. Rachel's fingers flew up and down the fingerboard, and she didn't get lost once. Daddy hardly looked down at his score; he seemed to know the symphony by heart, and his beat was steady and precise. The audience clapped after the first movement, and Daddy turned and smiled, and then started the second. People actually were listening, rows and rows of them, and people stretched out on their blankets looking up at the sky, so peaceful and idyllic, and a few little clouds drifting across the blue sky, and nobody yelling, nobody honking, everybody sitting and letting the music sweep over them. It was magical, she thought, how *concentrated* they all were, even Mr.

Birdcage—every eccentric and nutcase and comedian, everyone bent to the task and pulling together—I love this, she thought, as they played the third movement, so light, so delicate—I could be happy doing this—and then they leaped into the final fast movement and she couldn't think, she just played.

At the end, thunderous applause. Daddy bowed and left the stage and came back and got the orchestra to its feet, and bowed again, and Rachel saw Carol and Angie and Fred standing, clapping, cheering, and then the entire audience stood. They cheered and cheered, and Daddy came out for a third bow. He was perspiring and the hair gel was staining his collar but he looked like a man who was having the time of his life.

Then it was silent again. Lester came out and propped up the piano lid. "Is this your mother's debut too?" whispered Evelyn. "Sort of," said Rachel. She could see Grandma and Grandpa looking anxiously up at the stage. And then came the applause as Mother and Daddy came onstage. Mother's blue silk dress looked even more stunning under the bright lights. She put her hand on the piano and bowed to the audience and sat down. She adjusted the bench and nodded to Daddy, and he raised his arms and counted softly to himself, and gave the downbeat, and off they went. Mother sat, head bowed, swaying slightly with the music, and then suddenly raised her hands to the keys and began playing.

Rachel could hardly breathe, it was so perfect. Every phrase sparkled. You listened and you didn't worry for an instant about the pianist, you simply heard the music, so bright and warm and natural, and when they came to the cadenza, the musicians put their instruments in their laps and no one moved as Mother's fingers raced up and down the keyboard, not missing a note. The audience listened so intently, and at the end of the movement no one clapped, there was only a little shuffle of people rearranging themselves in their chairs, and then Daddy began the slow movement.

Mother had said last night, "If I have a memory slip, it's going to be in the second movement." And for a moment Rachel worried that she'd forget, and have to start over, and of course it's the mistakes that everyone remembers afterward, not the great stuff, but Mother didn't falter. Not one little wobble, not one wrong note. She played like an angel. The music floated along, so sweet and sad, like a beautiful story that Mother was telling, a story without words, a story about deep longing and the love of beauty, and then they jumped into the last movement, a sort of lighthearted dance after all that poetry, and then it was over. There was silence. The audience sat, hypnotized, and so did the musicians, and then Mother looked at Daddy and he smiled at her and reached over and took her hand, and pulled her to her feet and then the applause started. People were clapping like crazy. They were standing and cheering, and the orchestra stamped its feet on the stage and Mother put her hand on the edge of the piano and bowed gracefully, not too low, and Daddy kissed her. And Rachel was surprised to see the glitter of tears in her eyes. She bowed again. Did she see the Wymans, the Sykeses, the Ericksons—even the Broadbents—all standing, clapping? She made an elegant exit, holding Daddy's hand.

"That was incredibly beautiful," whispered Evelyn. Rachel thought so, too. Mother and Daddy came back for one more bow. Daddy's face was glowing. He was so *proud* of her—Rachel wanted to cry—the way he took Mother's hand and kissed it and presented her to the audience, clapping, clapping, clapping.

There was an intermission now, so that Lester and his crew could lift the piano offstage and get set for the "1812." The musicians trooped off and clustered around the buffet table where the church ladies had set out plates of fudge bars and pots of coffee. Rachel saw Mother and Daddy standing together under a tree. She ran up and hugged Mother and then Daddy hugged both of them. "You were *so* incredible! I mean both of you!" cried Rachel.

Mother was shivering and her eyes were wet with tears. "I am a wreck," she said. "I'm wrung out like a dishrag. I tell you, I started that slow movement and I couldn't remember one note. I thought I was going to faint I was so scared. But the orchestra sounded good, *really* good!" A little boy tugged at Mother's dress.

"Excuse me, can I have your autograph?" he said.

Grandma and Grandpa appeared, and Grandpa looked old and frail and had a faraway look in his eyes. The music had moved him so much, he said. He dabbed at his eyes, and his lips quivered. Rachel put her arm around his waist.

259

"I can't tell you how much that meant to me," he whispered. "I can't say any more."

Grandma had more to say though. She reported that the mayor had fallen asleep in the Mendelssohn and was snoring and she had poked him twice and couldn't wake him. She said that bugs had landed in her hair and asked Mother to please get them out. She told Rachel that she looked so skinny onstage, as if a good wind would blow her away. "You need to gain about ten pounds," she said. "I don't know what these people feed you. What have you eaten today? Probably nothing. I have a friend whose granddaughter is anorexic. I hope that's not true of you, but I won't even ask you, because they say that anorexics don't tell the truth."

Someone tapped Rachel on the shoulder—it was Scott. "How about some ice cream?" he asked. He congratulated Mother and Daddy. And he and Rachel headed off to the ice-cream stand.

"Great music. We just love your music," people said to them as they made their way through the crowd.

Scott looked down at his starched white shirt, pressed black pants, and black dress shoes. "Gee, I wonder how they can tell we're in the orchestra?" he said.

Carol and Valerie were behind the counter, making cones, and when Carol saw Rachel, she ran out from behind the stand and threw her arms around her and screeched. "Rachel! It was fantastic! I loved it!"

Valerie looked up and smiled. "Me, too," she said. Rachel got a butter brickle and Scott a double mocha almond, and they walked back to the bandstand.

"Are you going to be in string ensemble next year?" said Scott.

"No," said Rachel. "I'm going to Interlochen." She was surprised to hear herself say it, but there it was. "If I'm accepted." she said.

"You will be," said Scott sadly. He put his arm around her shoulders. "I'll miss you," he said.

They wandered around the crowd—Mother was a big hit, Daddy was happy, and she was holding hands with a sweet boy. And Rachel thought she had never felt quite so happy.

The Veterans of Foreign Wars honor guard stood onstage where the piano had been, their rifles on their shoulders, and the chief of police stood by the podium, talking into a walkie-talkie to the volunteer firemen in the junior high parking lot across the street where the cannons were. "Ten minutes and we're on," he said, and garbled static came back. He called to Daddy, "Okay! It's a go!"

"Onstage!" called Mr. Robbins. "Onstage, everybody. Everyone onstage for the '1812.'"

Everyone lined up to go onstage. "I've got extra earplugs for whoever needs them," said Mr. Klonowski. He gave Rachel a pair. "Take 'em. Believe me, you'll be glad you did."

She sat down, but it was hard shoving the little yellow plugs in her ears. She got one in, but the other kept falling out. Then it was almost time to play.

"How can anyone hear with these in?" she asked Evelyn.

"What?" said Evelyn.

"How can we hear?" Rachel shouted.

"Doesn't matter! You don't want to!"

The crowd was noisy now, getting excited about the fireworks, and when Daddy took the stage, there was yelling and horn-honking and people were popping balloons. Daddy stood and grinned at the musicians, and then he waved his arms, the music started, and the crowd cheered. They were all standing, and many of them were facing the other way, toward the parking lot and the cannons.

Rachel wondered how loud the cannons would be. It had to be pretty bad if some people were wearing earplugs. Then they got to the fast part, like galloping horses, and Daddy kept looking at the chief, shaking his head *No, not yet, not yet*. You could tell the firemen were itching to set off the cannons, and Daddy kept holding them back, holding them back, and then he gave a big nod to the chief, who yelled into the walkie-talkie, and the honor guard raised their rifles, and *BOOOOM! BANG! BOOOOM!* It was so loud, Rachel rose six inches off her seat and her bow jumped off the strings and landed on the other side of the bridge.

With every boom, her insides shook. David was shouting and laughing at Mr. Klonowski, whose glasses had fallen off. Some of the violists were bent down, their hands over their ears. The trumpet players were purple from blowing so hard, and so were the trombones and tuba. Larry sat with his bassoon on his lap, shaking like a leaf. The crowd was cheering and yelling as the last cannon boomed and the honor guard fired a last barrage. Then the fireworks started. The sky flashed with streams of colored light and huge red and blue and green spidery patterns over the downtown. The crowd oohed with each burst. Nobody noticed the musicians leaving the stage and packing up their instruments, or Daddy taking Mother by the arm and leading her away, with Grandma and Grandpa in tow, toward their car, to go home. Rachel said good-bye to Scott. "See you in Menomonie next week," he said. He kissed her. "That was nice," she said. So he did it again. She slung her violin case over her shoulder by its strap and put her arms around him. A rocket went up in the sky and burst and the crowd yelled. She turned and ran to catch up with her family.